THE
MIRRORED
SHARD

ALSO BY CAITLIN KITTREDGE

The Iron Thorn
The Nightmare Garden

CAITLIN KITTREDGE

Delacorte Press

Text copyright © 2013 by Caitlin Kittredge
Jacket art copyright © 2013 by Eva Kolenko

All rights reserved. Published in the United States by Delacorte Press, an imprint of Random House Children's Books, a division of Random House, Inc., New York.

Delacorte Press is a registered trademark and the colophon is a trademark of Random House, Inc.

Visit us on the Web! randomhouse.com/teens

Educators and librarians, for a variety of teaching tools, visit us at RHTeachersLibrarians.com

Library of Congress Cataloging-in-Publication Data
Kittredge, Caitlin.
The mirrored shard / Caitlin Kittredge. — 1st ed.
p. cm. — (The iron codex ; bk. 3)
Summary: Aoife Grayson will do anything to make her way to the Deadlands and try to win back her love, Dean, who died helping her, even if that means killing Tremaine, who has vowed to keep her in the Thorn Lands, the faerie home of her mother Nerissa.
ISBN 978-0-385-73833-0 (hardback) — ISBN 978-0-385-90722-4 (glb) — ISBN 978-0-375-98570-6 (ebook) [1. Magic—Fiction. 2. Voyages and travels—Fiction. 3. Mothers and daughters—Fiction. 4. Death—Fiction. 5. Fantasy.] I. Title.
PZ7.K67163Mir 2013
[Fic]—dc23
2012020816

The text of this book is set in 11-point Berling.
Book design by Trish Parcell

Printed in the United States of America

10 9 8 7 6 5 4 3 2 1

First Edition

Random House Children's Books
supports the First Amendment and celebrates the right to read.

I have harnessed the shadows
that stride from world to world
to sow death and madness. . . .
—H. P. LOVECRAFT

The Empty Room

TIME MOVES DIFFERENTLY in the Thorn Land. The Fae, the pale, secretive natives of the place, live for hundreds, if not thousands, of years, and time to them means practically nothing.

I wish I could share the carelessness of the Fae. I really do. But I can't, because time is the one thing I don't have.

Since my mother and I had returned to Thorn—her willingly and me less so—all I could do was watch the sun rise and set, the shadows grow short and wither away at dawn before their teeth grew long again at dusk. Watch, and wait, and think. About what I'd left behind in the Iron Land, the place of men, the place I'd called home until a few weeks? months? before.

I'd left my brother, our human father, my friends and my entire life. I'd left behind the bad, too. The iron rule of the Proctors, who feared beings like me—changelings, half

Fae. If I'd stayed I would have been locked up for the rest of my life, if I was lucky.

But the bad was far outweighed by my greatest loss, something I felt like a hand pressing on my chest every single moment of every single interminable day.

Dean Harrison. The boy I loved. He was gone, dead and gone. Because of me. Because he'd loved me too, and tried to help me, and the people who helped me ended up like Dean, or worse. I bore that weight too, and I feared that before long it was going to crush me. I felt Dean's loss behind my eyes, squeezing out tears. In my throat, which silenced all but necessary conversation; in my stomach, which churned if I even thought about food. *What's the point?* a treacherous little voice would always whisper. *Dean is dead. Dead because of you.*

I'd come to the Thorn Land with my mother because she'd promised that things could be different here. Here, where magic lived alongside the grass and trees and Fae, she'd promised that I could get Dean back.

But then time had gone by, and my mother, my mad mother, seemed to forget. It only made the weight grow heavier, and now, as I sat across from her at a table laid with the best food the Winter Court had to offer, I felt something akin to a burning hot coal in my chest. I resented her for what I'd had to do to keep her from the Iron Land, where the iron infected her blood and made her insane. Eventually, if I returned to what I knew—my home in the Iron Land, my father, my friends—I'd travel the same road. Staying in Thorn was the only way to remain sane, but the choice to come here and be safe hadn't been mine, this time. I hated that my mother had acclimated so quickly to life in the Winter Court while I struggled. I hated that she was sitting there acting like nothing was wrong, and finally I'd reached my breaking point. I slammed my fork down.

My mother didn't react, except to raise one eyebrow. "Eat your supper, Aoife."

I stared at my plate, too furious to do anything except grit my teeth in frustration. The food in the Thorn Land was exotic, and even if I hadn't been sick with worry about the people I'd left behind, I doubted I could have stomached it. I was used to simple things.

My mother sliced off another piece of pheasant and popped it into her mouth. Once she'd chewed and swallowed, she pointed at me with her fork. "You're getting too skinny. You need to eat something."

"Mother," I said. The word still tasted foreign, even more so than the food. I'd called her Nerissa my entire life. We'd never been like other mothers and daughters, and I'd tried not to let that bother me, though when I thought about it, it cut me deep.

"Yes, Aoife?" she said, setting down her fork.

"How much longer are we going to do this?" I asked.

"What's 'this'?" she said, with the coy expression I'd grown to hate while she lived in the madhouses of Lovecraft, my home city. The expression that said she knew exactly what I meant but was going to make me say it out loud. I forced myself to stay calm, pressing the tabletop with the tips of my fingers. I no longer needed to do math in my head to keep the creeping thoughts, whispers and paranoia of iron madness at bay, but I did the calculations anyway so I could stay calm. I'd learned pretty quickly that yelling at my mother only made her close down. If I wanted answers, I'd have to be the good daughter tonight.

"Dean," I said bluntly. "You promised me that we'd help Dean, and every time I've brought it up since we came here you've refused to talk about it. You *promised* me, Mother. Why won't you do what you said?"

"I don't think I promised you anything," my mother said in a voice that was infuriatingly calm. "I told you there was a way you *might* be able to see him again. But it's a dangerous road, Aoife. Upon further thought, it's not something I want my daughter involved in. Contacting the dead is an activity best left to those with nothing at stake."

"It's not your choice," I whispered. The tears came, and I didn't even try to stop them. I put my hands over my face and sobbed, my shoulders heaving and my breath coming in hot, razor-laced gasps. I had nothing if I didn't have Dean. Nothing I wanted, anyway. Just an eternity in the cold embrace of Thorn, with nothing to look forward to except more eternity. The thought made me cry even harder.

"Oh, Aoife." My mother hurried around the table and wrapped her arms around my shoulders, rubbing my back through the thin cotton shift that passed for clothing among the Fae. "Don't cry, darling. It will be all right."

"No." I sniffled. "No, it won't." Nothing would be right again, until I'd found Dean, told him how sorry I was and tried to undo the fate that had befallen him. Until then, there would just be the inexorable weight, forever crushing me.

"I know I wasn't there for you," Nerissa whispered.

4

Having her so close was foreign, but I didn't fight it. I'd wanted my mother to hold me and tell me everything would be all right for so long I tried to take it whenever I could get it.

Nerissa pressed her chin into the top of my head. "I'm sorry. But I can't in good conscience let you see Dean again, Aoife. You have no idea what contacting the dead entails."

"Then tell me." I swiped at my eyes. My emotions came on like thunderstorms—rapid and drowning—and then they passed and I was merely numb again, as I had been ever since he'd died.

"I'm not afraid, Mother," I told Nerissa. Some of what I'd seen in both Iron and Thorn, the particulars of the gift given to me by my father's side of the family, to bend reality and pass between the two, had driven any residual fear of the unknown from me nearly a year ago.

"I know you're not," my mother whispered against my hair. She smelled like lilacs, sweet and summery. "But I am, Aoife. I'm so scared for you. You've seen a little, but you have no idea what's in the shadows out there."

"I don't care," I said stubbornly. "I want Dean. I *need* him." I needed him like air or water, like blood in my veins. His absence was slowly but surely killing me.

"It's not even foolproof," Nerissa said, dropping her hands when they failed to soothe me. "I heard—mind you, *heard*, as in heard a story—that when a soul is taken before its time, another soul, a living soul, can touch it and make it remember that it's not supposed to be dead. There's a story of a man whose love was taken away by the god of the underworld, and he went after her and led her away from death."

"What happened?" I said, swiping at my face to get rid of the last vestiges of tears. I'd die before I'd let any of the Fae see me crying.

"He looked back," my mother said, her eyes falling. Her face was incredibly sad, and I felt a little guilty for pushing her into this. "He looked back at Death, and he was trapped. Forever. So you see, Aoife, it's not as simple as contacting Dean's spirit. You'd have to visit the Deadlands, actually visit, risk your life and your soul. It's not worth it."

"It's Dean," I snapped, more harshly than I meant to. "Anything is worth it."

"Please," Nerissa said, her eyes welling with tears. "You're my only daughter, Aoife. I can't lose you again. . . ."

Before I could tell her that she'd already lost me long ago, when she'd been committed, the door opened soundlessly. I'd have known the spike of pain the presence outside brought anywhere. I'd been bitten by a shoggoth what seemed like an eternity ago, and sometimes the venom still reacted with creatures alien to my blood. Tremaine was about as alien as they came.

"Everything all right in here?" he purred. My mother left me and took her place on the other side of the table. I kept my head bowed so Tremaine wouldn't see my red face and eyes. I didn't want to give him the satisfaction of knowing how much I was hurting. Tremaine reveled in hurt, took pleasure from it like most people did from food or music or dancing. Watching others suffer was his preferred form of entertainment. He was a snake, and I despised him and would until one or both of us was dead and gone.

"Fine," my mother told him. She took a sip of wine.

Everyone drank wine in the Thorn Land, but its berry scent and cloying taste only increased my urge to vomit.

"Dear Aoife." Tremaine glided in and laid a hand on my shoulder. "Whatever is the matter?"

I slapped his hand off my shoulder. "Don't touch me," I said, my voice monotone. I might have to tolerate Tremaine's presence, as he was regent of the Winter Court, but I didn't have to tolerate his cold, pale fingers on me.

"Testy, are we?" Tremaine sighed and shared a look with my mother. "She is at that age. Her human blood is making her difficult."

"We're fine," my mother said. "Thank you for your attention, Tremaine."

My blood boiled, threatened to vault me out of my chair and force my fingers around Tremaine's throat, but I stayed where I was. I was afraid of Tremaine. The Fae scared me in a way the Proctors and even my own mind didn't. They were alien, even though half my blood was theirs. Unnatural, unknowable and tempestuous. Even Octavia, the Winter Queen and my mother's sister, scared the hell out of me.

Tremaine finally left and my mother let out a long sigh. "Tremaine always was a piece of work. You see why you must give up this ridiculous idea, Aoife?" She clasped her hands over mine. They were as warm as Tremaine's had been icy. "I know you miss Dean. I know you wish you didn't have to spend the rest of your life here, but that's just the way it is. To keep healthy and safe, we must live as Fae now, Aoife. I wish I could have been the mother who prepared you for all this, taught you how to sacrifice, but

I wasn't, so my job now is to make it up to you. And you must put aside your thoughts of the Iron Land and learn to accept this new life."

I looked at her, into her calm pale eyes. Mine were green and dark—my father's eyes. Human eyes. I felt another stone added to the weight, felt the desperation that had been growing since we arrived in Thorn boil over.

My mother could apologize and say whatever she liked, but she was wrong—the Thorn Land would never be my home.

We did what we always did in the evening: my mother sat by the fire sewing or reading aloud from a book in the Fae language, which sounded like liquid silver running over a rock to my ears, and I used Dean's pocketknife to carve wooden models of the machines I'd hoped to build, back when things were simple and I was an engineering student rather than a half-Fae anomaly.

There was no iron in Thorn, no mechanical devices except those approved by the queens, and no aether, the blue-white fire that powered everything from radios to lamps in the Iron Land. Whittling was as close as I could come to my chosen vocation. Just another reminder that this was my life now, boredom without end.

I tossed the wood aside and it clattered on the stone floor, far from the satisfying crash I'd hoped for.

My mother yawned and shut her book. "I think I'll retire," she said, and that was my signal to lay down my knife and announce that yes, I was tired too. We never did anything separately, were never apart, because she was afraid that a full-blooded Fae might try to harm me. She'd never stated it explicitly, but I saw the fear in her eyes whenever I so much as crossed the room to retrieve a book or a new block of wood.

Tonight, though, I had other plans. "Nerissa," I said. She flinched.

"I thought we'd at least gotten past using each other's first names as if we were at a tea party," she told me.

"I understand you're protecting me, but you need to do what you promised," I said. "You need to tell me what I have to do to see Dean again, or I'm going to leave."

Her book dropped to the carpet with a soft *thunk* and I saw the panic rise in her eyes like a flash flood. I felt horrible issuing such an ultimatum, like the worst kind of defiant child, but it had to be done.

I couldn't stay here. I'd always known that this wasn't permanent, safe as I might be. Living in Thorn might actually drive me madder than iron poisoning would.

"You mustn't . . . ," she started. "You can't."

"I can," I said. "You know what my Weird is, Mother. My gift. I don't even need a *hexenring* to leave Thorn." The Fae system of travel, enchanted rings that spirited the user from place to place, was arcane compared with the mechanical magic of the Gates, interdimensional devices designed by Tesla to travel all the lands one after the other as if they were beads on a necklace. But I didn't even need mechanics to do it—my gift was creating Gates, and I'd used the knowledge that I could leave Thorn anytime I wanted to keep myself patient and compliant.

But now my patience was at an end. I had to see Dean. And I had to know that my family—my real family, my father and brother and best friend, Cal—were all right.

"To speak that way will get you exactly the wrong kind of attention," Nerissa hissed.

"Tell me," I said, raising my voice, "or I'm going to disappear through a Gate right in front of Tremaine's bug-eyed face."

"All right!" my mother shouted, kicking the book at her feet. It flew like a dying bird, in a low arc, and hit the wall with a smack before wilting to the ground again. "Stone and sun, Aoife, you are a difficult child."

I raised my chin and tried to pretend that the words didn't sting coming from her. That I'd never wished for a mother who tried to be reasonable rather than one who got angry when I did, who was still largely lost in her own world. Wishing for things I could never have didn't work. I was still human enough to realize that.

"I'm not doing this to spite you," my mother said. "Believe it or not, I'm doing it because I care about you and I've hurt you enough. I won't contribute to any more disasters befalling you, Aoife. I simply won't."

I thought very carefully about how to phrase my next request. "Mother," I said, "I don't want you to be angry with me, but that's for me to decide. My entire life, I've had to decide everything for myself, whether I wanted to or not, and because of that I know what I can and can't do. I—"

But she cut me short. "You *can't* do this!" she shouted. "You think you're invincible with that dark blood the Graysons gave you, but this is beyond anything. You can't simply have this Dean boy alive again, Aoife—you'd have to visit the Deadlands, and no Gate goes there. Not even one you make yourself."

With that, she stalked over, snatched up her book and went to the door of her bedroom. "Now, that's the last I'll say on the matter," she snapped. "Go to sleep and stop whining like a little girl who didn't get a sweet."

Her door slammed, shutting off my reply, which was for the best. It was hot, and angry, and rude.

I didn't want the last thing I said to my mother to be in a fight, but it turned out that way.

At least she'd told me what I needed to know—to find Dean, I would have to visit the Deadlands. There was always a way to get somewhere, even if no Gate could reach it. But to find the way, I knew I was going to have to go home.

Sneaking around the Winter Court was actually much easier than sneaking around the estate of my father, Archibald Grayson, or around the Lovecraft Academy. Both had a more restrictive hold on me. The Winter Court was vast and sprawling, old beyond imagining, the original stone blocks of the foundation so worn down they were smooth as glass. I brushed the fingers of my free hand against them while clutching a survival pack with the other. Running away worked much better when you were prepared.

Each queen added something new to the court, but Queen Octavia seemed to be subtracting things, by decay and ruin. She left vast wings of the court to rot and built fanciful new structures atop already tottering towers. Just the week before, four workers had plunged to their deaths.

I found an empty room down the corridor from my mother's chambers. We were in the hall that, Tremaine had told me with a sneer, was normally reserved for nobility, ambassadors and great heroes of Fae, with the clear implication I was none of those things and never would be.

Never mind that if it weren't for me, Thorn would have been just as it was when I'd first met Tremaine: a dying land without a queen, due to a curse wrought by a particularly clever and vindictive human, Grey Draven. But Draven was the Fae's prisoner now, and the balance between the Lands had been restored. To the satisfaction of the Fae, anyway.

Handing Draven over and breaking the curse had bought me a little freedom to roam the Winter Court. No matter what my mother thought, there'd once been an Aoife who was meek and polite and would have never dreamed of defying her mother and running off. But she was long gone.

I liked the new Aoife. She was more like the me I'd always wanted to be, the me who did things and took charge and wasn't afraid. Or at least pretended she wasn't, though her hands shook against the dead bolt meant to lock herself inside.

"Going somewhere?"

I let out a scream, and my pack, stuffed with everything I'd brought from the Iron Land, tumbled to the dusty stone floor.

Queen Octavia glided into the sliver of moonlight streaming through the grime-caked windows. In broad daylight she could scare you speechless. At night, in the glow of the moon, she was a spectral entity, terrifying beyond measure.

Her pointed teeth flashed as she grinned. "Tell me, Aoife—are you a little human spy?"

I forced myself to look somewhere other than her face—at her brass-ribbed corset, worked with spikes that rode atop her breasts like guns at the prow of a battleship; at her thin, paper-white arms, which bore even paler scars in swirling patterns; at her skirt, which was more tatters woven with crow feathers than fabric; at the cat-skull pendant against her throat.

Anywhere but at her eyes. Fae have dead silver eyes that will drown you as surely as a black, bottomless pool.

"No," I whispered.

Octavia gestured. Outside, a colony of bats that lived in the hollow trunk of one of the great, ancient trees lining the courtyard took flight, black blood droplets for a moment against the canvas of the moon's face, and then winked out. "Is this place not to your liking? You want for nothing."

"I want to go home," I blurted, deciding that when the Queen of Winter catches you out, all you can do is be honest and not curl up in a ball on the floor and scream.

"Home? But this *is* your home, child. You are Fae."

"I'm a changeling," I said. "And you might tolerate it in my mother, but we both know I'm not welcome here."

"True," Octavia said. She reached out and brushed her silver-tipped nails across my face. They left tiny, jagged furrows that stung and sprouted pen lines of blood. I touched my cheek and my fingers came away red. "I confess, I do find you curious. I like curiosities. I have a wing full of

13

them. Two-headed hounds, a man with hair all over his body, a frog that sings in a human voice. But you, Aoife— you are the most curious of all." She narrowed her eyes. "You're like a closed box of cogs. I haven't yet figured out what makes you tick."

"I lost someone," I said. "I have to go to the Deadlands and see him."

"Why?" Octavia looked genuinely confused. "If he is dead, he is dead. His soul can be with you no longer."

I looked at my feet. I'd changed out of my Fae slippers and dress and into the clothes I'd been wearing when I'd arrived. They were musty and mud-covered but irrevocably human. I needed them, to remind me where I was going. "I have to see him again. To apologize, and to bring him back," I told Octavia. "It's my fault he's dead. It wasn't his time."

"Well," she drawled after a moment, stretching like the reptilian creature she was. "I can't have you running off. Even if you can rip holes in reality. That is by far the most curious of all my curiosities, and I think you'll remain right where you are. At least, if you want your mother to stay healthy."

Octavia gripped my arm before I could protest, and dragged me out of the room and through the corridors. The few Fae still awake stared as they stepped to the side. My stomach lurched as we passed through a half-rotted door, twice as high as me, and started down a set of steps carved to look like skeletons holding up the treads.

"Where are we going?" I ventured. Octavia smiled at me, her teeth more like blades than ever in the low light of this subterranean place.

"I'm practiced at witchery," she said. "I can make toads trip off your tongue and make you dance like a puppet, but I've found that nothing cements a lesson quite so well as a real-life example."

The room was dark and, from what I could tell, empty. Octavia yanked me to a stop in front of a small black cage. I wasn't sure what sort of metal it was—it couldn't be iron, but it appeared strong and the bars were woven to look like a thorn thicket. Probably constructed by Erlkin slaves, the goblin race the Fae caught and forced to work their mines and metal shops so they could avoid contact with anything poisonous.

"Have fun," Octavia hissed in my ear, then turned and stalked back to the staircase, her long blue and silver robe kicking up dust and the shells of dead beetles.

The door slammed and I heard a bolt click into place. I took a few deep breaths to calm myself, to stave off anger more than panic. I didn't know why she'd left me here, any more than I knew what was inside the cage, and I had no doubt that my confusion was part of Octavia's plan. Fae loved to leave you off balance. It was how they tricked you.

"You look like I feel." The voice was low and raspy, but I felt an instant spark of recognition. The cage was largely held in shadow. I stepped closer and squinted through the fist-sized holes in the mesh.

"Excuse me?"

"That expression. That hate. I'm glad to see you haven't lost that."

A hand flashed out and wrapped around mine, and I jerked involuntarily, the hot flush of shock pulsing through me. The grip was strong, and when I looked down I saw

15

that the flesh was the sort of pale that skin becomes when it sits too long in the dark and damp, veins standing out like road maps. The nails tipping each finger were shredded and bloody, and the knuckles crusted with dirt.

"I'm just glad to see you, Aoife," Grey Draven hissed. "Glad to know you're as miserable as I am."

"I . . ." I stopped trying to talk. I'd hoped to never see him again. Honestly, I'd thought the odds were good that Draven was dead, tortured for Octavia's amusement. I'd never expected us to be having a conversation, certainly. Draven stared at me with glee burning in his eyes.

"Don't look so alarmed. This is what happens when you don't behave like a good little pet. Nothing compared with what happens when the queen's in one of her moods. Care to see the scars?"

I jerked my hand free in disgust. Draven's fingers left red marks around my wrist. Even half-starved and caged, he was still strong. And even crazier than when I'd last seen him. I didn't see this ending well, for either of us.

"Leave me alone," I whispered. "Don't talk to me. We have nothing to say to each other."

Draven laughed. He sounded like a frog trying to talk. "I don't bear you any ill will, Aoife. You did exactly what I would have done. You protected yourself, and you got your revenge." He coughed, a deep, wet rattle that revealed sickness dug far into his lungs. The air was cold against my skin, and I could hear water dripping off the stones. "It's my own fault I let myself be outsmarted by a teenager."

"How long has Octavia kept you down here?" I rubbed my arms against the cold. If her plan was to lock me up with Draven as punishment, it was working. One might hope their mother would notice they were gone and raise a fuss, but only if one didn't have Nerissa for a parent. I doubted she'd notice until she got irritated with me for something and didn't have anyone to yell at.

"Always," Draven said. "Unless I'm trotted out at parties for her courtiers to view, or tortured by that pale-faced horror Tremaine for her amusement. Always in the dark." He coughed again, and I saw blood fleck his lips. "Always."

"I saved her life," I snarled, angrier than ever at Octavia. "I broke *your* curse, and she puts me down here with you like I'm no better than a prisoner."

"You stupid child," Draven said. "You *are* a prisoner. Even worse, you're a prisoner who doesn't know it. You think everything will be fine as long as you stay out of the queen's line of vision. But sooner or later you'll be in this cage with me. And then I'm not going to be so understanding about you putting me here."

"You're so generous," I muttered. I knew, though, deep down, that he was right. My time in Octavia's good graces was limited. I had to get out of here, and out of Thorn, before it expired entirely.

"I'm nothing of the sort," Draven said. "Maybe I'm just curious as to why you're still here, the girl who has the power to bend worlds together as if you were folding paper." He raised a finger when I opened my mouth to retort. "Either you don't have the nerve to make a run for it, or you're waiting for something. So which is it?"

"Why do you care?" I said. Draven grinned at me—that

same grin, tinged with insanity, that I'd had nightmares about since the first time I'd run afoul of him, back in Lovecraft.

"Because if you're waiting for something, there are only a few things. Your mother is happy as a crazy little clam here in the Thorn Land, and your human family has gone on without you just fine, so it must be . . . the dead kid? Dean?"

I turned away from him, partly so he wouldn't see my tears and partly so I wouldn't reach through the mesh and wring his neck.

"You don't want to talk to me about Dean."

"Oh, but I do," Draven said. "I know that someone must have told you there are ways to visit the dead. My research, shall we say . . . outside . . . of the norms of the Proctor laws told me plenty. And I bet your dear old dad knows all about it."

I snorted. As if my father would ever discuss that sort of thing with me.

"Not Dad, then. Mother." Draven hit the bars as if he'd just solved a great mystery. "Your mother told you how to reach the Deadlands and now you're darting off to rescue Dean."

"Why do you care what I do or don't do?" I said wearily. Draven made me tired. Nothing was ever direct with him. There was always an angle, always a scheme.

"Ah," he said. "Mother didn't tell you, then. You're just running off half-cocked, as usual."

I gritted my teeth, hating that I was so transparent to someone like Draven. "I asked you why you care," I snarled.

"You hate me. Why do you care if I run off and get myself hurt?"

"Because, Aoife," he said, "you're my ticket out of here, and if you want to get to the Deadlands, I can help with that. But only once we're safely back on human soil."

I stared at him for a long time, and he huffed. "I know the way, Aoife. It's not very hard. All I want in return for the information is a ride out of here. Even someone as scatterbrained as you can realize that's a good deal."

"I hate you," I told him, turning my stare to a glare.

"Good," Draven said. "Then the feeling's mutual. But you don't want to stay under the yoke of the Fae, and neither do I."

"Even if I did trust you and take you with me—and I *don't* trust you," I said, "I've never used a Fae Gate. I can't just plop us back into the Iron Land. We could end up anywhere."

"Anywhere's better than that silver-eyed bitch's torture room," Draven said.

I considered for several heartbeats. My mother wasn't telling me anything, and she never would—she was even more stubborn than I was. If I did manage to make it home, my father would likely have the same reaction. He'd want to keep me out of danger. He'd want me to move on with my life, and carry my grief like a stone on my back. That was how my father coped with his sadness over my mother, so why, in his eyes, should I be any different?

Draven was untrustworthy, that much was apparent, but he was also a survivor. When he wanted something, he'd make any deal, with anyone.

I walked to the ring of keys hanging on a hook by the stone steps and came back to Draven. I held up the keys, yanking them back as he snatched for them through the bars. "Don't make me regret this," I said, "or I'll send you through a Gate to somewhere so black and cold you'll never crawl out."

"Done," Draven said as I unlocked his cell. He burst out with surprising speed for somebody the pale, sickly color he was. Then he grabbed my arm. "Let's go."

We were back up the steps before I managed to break free of his grasp. "Stop!" I hissed. "You can't just run out of here."

Draven looked at me, his lips compressed to a thin line. "Don't make me take you out of here as a hostage," he said. "Because if I have to hold a sharp object to your neck to get free, I will. The queen needs you. She doesn't want you dead."

"I *do* want to leave, all right?" I said. "But the halls are patrolled and the *hexenring* is out in the open. We'll never make it if we just bolt."

"That's the difference between you and me," Draven said. "I don't care if I make it or not. Anything is better than here."

He banged loudly on the door, and then looked at me. "Call to be let out," he said. "Call or I'll throw you down those stairs."

I knew he wouldn't hesitate to carry out his threat. Draven never made a threat he wasn't perfectly prepared to act on, and that scared me. He was as ruthless as Octavia. In a different world they probably would have been good friends.

"Let me out, please!" I shouted, not needing to fake the fear in my voice. "I'm sorry, Octavia. Please let me out."

Nothing happened, so Draven banged and I yelled for a good five minutes. At last a small voice penetrated the door. "Aoife?"

"Nerissa?" I said.

"Aoife, what on earth?" I heard her fumbling with the door and grumbling to herself. "How could you sneak out and go running around the court at night? Don't you know it's not safe? You don't have the sense of a kitten, Aoife, you know that?"

The door swung open, and I tried to get between my mother and Draven. Pure panic drove me. I didn't know what he'd do to her. He was desperate, and desperation makes people crazy.

He knocked me forward. I slammed into Nerissa, and we both tumbled to the ground. Draven's hands were instantly on my collar, lifting me off my feet. He was strong, and I was smaller than I'd been when we last met. I'd barely eaten since arriving in Thorn.

"Sorry, Mommy," he said as Nerissa blinked up at us, not understanding. "But I need to borrow your darling daughter. I promise I'll keep her in good health."

"Aoife!" Nerissa screamed, trying to catch my ankle as Draven dragged me down the corridor.

I looked back at her. "I'm sorry," I managed to say before we were around the corner and gone. The agonized look on her face was like a knife to the gut. She thought I'd betrayed her, not because Draven had caught me but because she knew if I'd gotten caught out of our rooms, I'd been planning to run away in the first place. I just hoped I lived long enough to tell her I was sorry, that it couldn't be any other way. And I hoped she'd be able to forgive me.

Draven and I made it to the *hexenring*, where a solitary Fae soldier stood watch, nodding to sleep.

The ring itself was made from nothing more than luminescent mushrooms that glowed softly against the blackened grass. A dead tree, branches reaching skeletal fingers to grasp the moon and cradle it, drooped over the mushrooms, and the guard leaned against it, humming under his breath.

"Stay here," Draven said, crouching low.

I tried to stop him, but he came up on the soldier before I could do anything, and wrapped an arm around his neck, cutting off his air supply. I heard the man gasp and struggle for a second, before a crack like a twig snapping echoed in the still night air.

The soldier dropped in a heap, and Draven stood, chest rising and falling rapidly.

"It's been a while since I got my hands dirty," he said. He pointed to the ring. "Your turn, Aoife. Show me what you can do."

I walked to the ring, careful not to crush any of the mushrooms. The part of me that was connected to the Gates, the pathways that linked one world to the next, came to life and lit up behind my eyes.

Draven stood with me and put his hand on my shoulder. His eyes clouded and he frowned, no doubt feeling the gut-wrenching pull of the magic that linked the Gates to the fabric of the universe.

"What is that?"

"Gates slow down time," I said. "You get used to it." I didn't tell him that if you lingered too long inside a *hexen-ring* you could lose years, decades even. I figured that was best kept to myself.

Draven's grip became a vise, grinding the bones of my shoulder, and I gasped in pain. "Get moving," he growled in my ear. "I never want to see this muddy hellhole again."

I opened up my mind, and there was no resistance before the Gate rushed in to fill it.

The Encroaching Sky

I CAN'T EXPLAIN WHAT it's like to travel by Gate. Not really. Imagine your entire body being stretched, loose and wobbly, and then snapping back and falling an infinite distance. You feel all this at once, and see everything there is to see, and then you hit the ground as if you were made of lead.

Using my Weird always took a heavy toll. There was intense pressure in my skull, and my nose usually bled at least a bit. Mostly, though, I felt the echoes of the Gate inside me, the vastness of it, and it made me curl on the ground and lie very still until I realized I was being pelted by a light rain. I fished in my pack for my slicker.

I raised my head, seeing low rolling hills bordered by stone walls, a small white farmhouse in the distance, and the cotton-wool sky overhead. I smelled earth and mud. It was spring in the Iron Land. I'd been gone for at least four months.

That thought spurred me more than anything. I had to find out where I was and devise a way of getting home. My accuracy with the Gates wasn't the best—I could generally hit close to a target, but sometimes I'd be radically off and have to try again and again before I stepped out where I meant to.

This time I'd gotten only one try. I prayed I wasn't somewhere halfway around the world from home.

Next to me, Draven rolled over and looked up at the sky. "Fresh air," he said. "I did miss that."

He got up and frowned at the mud on his tattered black uniform. Once, I'd been terrified of the figure Draven cut. He had worn his Proctor's uniform like it was his skin, and his boots had gleamed as bright as the wings of the clockwork ravens that swept in his wake.

Now his uniform was a mess, faded and shredded, and he wasn't wearing shoes. He'd lost weight, and his pants sagged in the seat.

"I brought you back here. Now tell me how to find Dean," I said. I couldn't stand just yet—I felt, in using the Gates, as though I'd left part of myself back there in that great nothingness. "Tell me how to get to the Deadlands."

"Don't waste any time, do you?" Draven smirked. I hated how he could stand there, dirty and bedraggled and alone, and still act like he'd gotten the best of me.

"Just tell me," I said. "And then we can walk in opposite directions and never have to see each other again."

Draven laughed, the dry bark of a crow. "You really think it will be that easy? You think I'll just tell you what you want to know?"

"Listen," I said. "I could have dumped you in the middle of the ocean or the cold of space, but I didn't. In spite of what you are, I brought you back here." I folded my arms and forced myself to appear brave. "So it seems like you owe me, Draven. There's nobody else here besides us. What do you have to lose?"

His face twitched, and I could see he'd been planning to run. I hoped I wouldn't have to chase him to get what he knew.

"You have any idea what they did to me in that place?" he ground out. "What they did because of *you*?"

I watched him while he watched me. His arms and what I could see of his torso through his ripped uniform were scarred and pale, the result of months of torment, spent in the dark. His hair hung greasy and lank, and his handsome face was covered with bruises and scabs.

My mother had once told me that Octavia allowed nothing in the court more beautiful than her. Disfiguring Draven had probably been some kind of game.

"About what you would do to me if you managed to throw me in one of your prisons," I said. "And I know you would, if the situation were reversed."

"That's fair," Draven agreed, but he still tensed to spring at me. "But I'm afraid my time among the Kindly Folk has left me just a bit less forgiving than I used to be."

"Look, Draven." I sighed. "I don't care about you. I just want to get Dean back. I'm not going to apologize for turning you over to Tremaine, because you would have done the same to me."

Draven took a step toward me, and I darted back.

"Don't," I said, my voice grinding like mismatched gears. Even skinny and broken, Draven still had the ability to scare me.

"I could leave you here, you know," he said. His hand darted out and grabbed my wrist. "Knock you on the head and leave you for the crows."

Rather than pull away, as every instinct in my body was screaming at me to do, I yanked Draven closer, matching the force of his grip. "And I could send you somewhere so awful, mud and crows would seem like paradise."

After a moment Draven started laughing, a genuine laugh, tinged with hysteria. "Aoife, you and I are so much more alike than you realize."

"The Deadlands," I snarled, not rising to the bait. "Tell me."

"It's very simple," he managed between peals of laughter. "I can't believe you haven't figured it out."

"Figure what out!" I gave him a shake, trying to quell his laughter, but it didn't work.

"To go to the Deadlands, you have to die," Draven said. "Stone and sun, it's so simple."

I let go of him, shoving him back with disgust, and he sprawled in the mud, laughing so hard he disturbed a flight of birds from the nearby field. "Run on, Aoife!" he shouted. "Run away to die!"

I should have guessed he didn't really know anything, that he'd be useless and only out for himself, but I just turned my back and walked away to the east, rather than act out my rage by sending him through another Gate.

It was more than Draven ever would have done for me.

*   *   *

There was a road next to the stone wall bordering the field we'd landed in, and I jumped the wall and followed it.

After a time, I came to a signpost and nearly wept in relief. The post announced NEW CANAAN, 5 MI. I was in Connecticut. I could sneak aboard a train or a steam jitney, lay low, and in less than twelve hours, I'd be home.

I managed to get on a jitney by pretending I was with a large family. The ride was uneventful. I'd expected the jitney to be crawling with Proctors, but not only were there no black-uniformed officers, even the notice from the Bureau of Proctors had been torn down, replaced with an ad for toothpaste.

I fell asleep soon after boarding, and didn't wake until it was time to sneak off with the family at Springfield.

The village of Arkham lies tucked up against the mountains like a sleeping cat curled in a hidden place, bordered on all sides by granite hills and primeval forests. I was able to hitch a ride within a few miles, and now I walked.

I confess that I didn't walk quickly. I didn't know what I was going to find when I got to my father's house. I hoped it would be empty, that my father and his fiancée, Valentina, would still be at her home on Cape Cod. Then I could figure out what I was going to do, and avail myself of Graystone's library to find out more about the Deadlands.

I felt guilty for not wanting to see my father, but I couldn't imagine facing him after what he was sure to see as me running off to live in Thorn with Nerissa. My father wasn't exactly the warm and fuzzy type who offered sage advice and comforting pats on the hand. He was more of a drill sergeant.

Still, he was my father. I loved him, and I didn't want him to be angry with me. I didn't want him to look at me differently because I'd gone with my Fae blood rather than the human Grayson blood, even if I had had a choice.

Although, it was the human blood that gave me my Weird. My human blood that made me into something considered an abomination by those good people who populated the Iron Land. I couldn't blame them entirely. The Proctors had lied to them for a long time, and people were afraid of what they didn't understand. I got that. I just wished I didn't have to live with the constant, twitchy fear that somebody would see under my skin, see the two kinds of blood in my veins. See that I wasn't like them, would never be like them.

Graystone, the Grayson family estate, sat on the top of the mountain overlooking Arkham. I could have cut through the fields around the village and avoided people, but I decided instead to walk up the broad cobble road. I didn't want to sneak into my own home like I was a thief.

Arkham Village was protected by gates, high iron gates like two skeletal hands, folded in prayer. They stood askew, and I watched a few scraps of newspaper flutter across the cobbles as I passed through.

Where was everyone?

A piece of yellow parchment blew up against my foot, and I picked it up, smoothing it out and reading the bold black type.

EVACUATION ZONE
Citizens of Arkham are hereby ordered to vacate
and move to the nearest designated safe zone.
DO NOT attempt to stay in your homes!
Arkham Valley has been declared UNSAFE.

I read the words twice, not understanding what had happened. Arkham was deserted—a few windows had been broken by vandals, but mostly it was silent. A white cat hopped up on a windowsill a few feet from me and meowed.

I scooped the cat up, and he immediately started purring and nestled against my chest. "Where is everyone?" I asked him.

"Gone."

I shrieked and whirled toward the voice, clutching the cat to me. He hissed and squirmed. My heart thudded so violently it felt like a kick in the ribs.

An old woman stood a short distance from me, leaning heavily on a cane. Her pink skirt and shapeless gray sweater were streaked with dirt and some rust-colored substance that I sincerely hoped was gutter water and not blood.

"You scared me," I said.

"All gone," she cackled. "Guv'mint came and rounded them up."

I looked back at the evacuation notice, and saw that the Bureau of Proctors symbol was missing. The woman made me jump again when she snatched the paper from my hand.

"Ain't no Proctors round here no more," she wheezed, stamping the paper under her bare foot. It was black, scabbed and caked with grime. Up close, she smelled sour

30

as a room long shut, and my stomach flipped. She bothered me in a way I couldn't quite define. The cat hissed again and his claws dug into my flesh.

"Who's there?" I said, taking a step back. I scanned for escape routes from the corner of my eye, but the street was narrow and only the door of a house across the street, hanging off its hinges and creaking back and forth in the slight breeze, offered a possible exit.

"Me," the old woman croaked. She pointed upward conspiratorially and leaned in. "Them."

Overhead, I saw rows and rows of crows arrayed on rooflines. They were silent, not even ruffling a feather, and all stared toward the east, as if waiting for something.

That, a thousand times more than the old woman, caused a chill to race through me.

"They're comin'," the old woman hissed. "From the sky and from the sea. From the places you can only dream about, little girl. They're comin', the old things, the dark things, and the powers that be don't like folk round here sayin' so. Rounded 'em up, took 'em to a hospital." She turned her head and spit, and I edged backward another step, toward the village gates. I'd seen enough mad people to know the dangerous ones, and this woman was about two clock ticks away from scratching my eyes out.

"Hospital!" she hissed. "Ain't no hospital! They want to stop us dreamin'!"

I paused in my microscopic retreat. "What?" It couldn't be—that had been just a dream, just something I'd hallucinated while attempting to get control of my Weird before I realized such a thing was impossible.

"We all dreamed," the woman mumbled. "All the folk

in Arkham, the same thing, night after night. The arrival, the things on the shore, crawling through our houses and through our heads." She shuddered, dirty hair the color of muddy snow flying away from her face. "And then the men came and took us off. Said it was for our safety. Never is. Never, never is."

"Do you know anything about the house on the hill?" I whispered. My father's home could have easily been looted, or torn through by Proctors, and if they found some of the things I knew were there, my father was in certain danger, not to mention Valentina, Conrad and my friends.

The woman's eyes fairly bugged out of her skull. The cat snarled at her, and I felt my heartbeat accelerate. "Oh, I *see* you now," she hissed at me, baring her teeth. "Shoulda known you was one of them, those that live behind those walls."

She made a move for me, and I didn't hesitate any longer. I ran, and her ragged nails only tangled themselves in my hair, ripping strands free and leaving a stinging patch on my scalp.

"Demon!" the woman howled. "Go back to hell, where ya came from!"

My breath rattled, and I broke for the gates, stumbling through a welter of glass and furniture in the street, smashed dishes and toys and all the other remnants of someone's life.

I didn't stop. That was the most important thing when you were running; I'd learned that long ago, as a child other children loved to torment. Run until your lungs burn and your legs give out. Don't stop, because if you can just run long enough, your tormentors will give up, get tired and find someone else to throw rocks and chant names at.

The gates let me out of the village proper and I cut through the gardens of a few outlying cottages until I found the back path, the steep rocky trail up the hill to Graystone.

Before, I'd had some idea of what I'd find when I got there—empty house, cold bed, possibly a stray raccoon or two that'd made themselves at home.

Now, I had no idea. If the government, Proctors or not, had come to Arkham and evacuated it, my home could have been burned to the ground. And if that old woman *wasn't* crazy, and people in Arkham were having the same dreams I'd been having before I'd had to go back to the Thorn Land, then everyone in this valley—in the Iron Land—was in much worse trouble than I could imagine.

I was chilled, by both the wind and my thoughts. Only the small purring form of the cat, tucked in my sweater, kept me warm as I climbed up and up, into the mist that obscured the valley below.

Homecoming

THE VIEW OF Graystone would never stop startling me. It was a vast place—carved from rough-hewn granite, massive blocks twice my height stacked atop one another to form the bulk of the main house, wings flying off the sides and back like those of a desiccated bird lying on the ground. Twin turrets sprouted from the ridgeline, the blank blue glass reflecting the empty stare of the clouds and mist.

The gate was ajar. That was bad. I strapped my bag across my chest—wouldn't do to lose it after I'd managed to bring it all the way from Thorn—and soothed the cat into silence. I crept forward one step after another. I wasn't the type to rush in, like Dean or Conrad. I took my time. I'd wanted to be an engineer, and being meticulous was part of my makeup.

It was also what had kept me alive thus far.

The one time I'd been impulsive, had flown by my instincts, didn't bear talking about. The fallout from that choice was all around me, in the absolute silence of the woods around Graystone, the ever-present fog that hadn't burned away even though it was close to midday, the strange dreams of the populace.

I couldn't clearly remember what had happened in that place on top of the world, just flashes and fragments, but I knew I'd unleashed something. I'd opened a door so long shut that it had been forgotten by everyone except me and a few beings so ancient they didn't even have names.

The door of Graystone bore a knocker the size of my head. It was the face of a wolf, grinning at me with bronze teeth and a black iron tongue.

I raised it and let it fall once, twice, three times.

The crows were even more prevalent here. They clustered in the oak trees leading up to the gates, on the rim of the turrets and on windowsills, while hundreds more swooped and dove overhead, cawing so loudly their cries echoed off the stone walls, rolling back on my ears like a wave.

Just as I was about to go around to the back gardens and see if I could get in through the kitchen or a window, the door opened. I heard the creak of clockwork, felt it inside my skull, the low, secret place where the Weird lived. It reacted with iron and machines as well as the Gates between worlds, sensing its likeness forged from metal rather than human flesh.

"Hello?" I called, sticking my head inside. The air was dank and musty, much as it had been the first time I'd come here, looking for my father.

That time, he'd disappeared. I'd been alone, beset by the Fae.

I prayed that this time it'd be different, that I could find what I needed and go get Dean without encountering any more trouble.

I took a few steps into the grand foyer, setting the cat down to scamper off into a dark corner. Graystone was a clockwork house, run by mechanical means, and that kept it safe from the incursion of predatory creatures.

I heard a clank from upstairs and tensed. I doubted any animal could have breached Graystone's defenses, but that didn't rule out a person.

"Hello?" I said again, loudly. My voice rattled the long, dagger-shaped crystals in the chandelier above. "Anyone there?" A little quieter. "Say something." The last came as a whisper. No other sound echoed, and I forced myself to keep looking around. If someone was in the house, I wasn't going to be a sitting duck.

I started down the back hall toward the kitchen, where I'd always felt most comfortable. Graystone's luxury was oppressive and smothering, everything incalculably old and valuable, more like the set of a lantern reel or a museum piece than a home.

The kitchen was made for living, was old and worn but homey, and unlike the rest of the drafty mansion, always warm.

As I crossed the threshold, I felt a breath on my neck, but I wasn't fast enough. I felt a metal barrel jammed against my skin and a rough hand clamped against my mouth.

"What's your business here?" a voice hissed in my ear.

I struggled, panic rising. The voice and the hand sounded and felt human, at least, but I had no idea whom they belonged to; plus, he or she was armed. Maybe a shock pistol, maybe something worse, but at this range there was no way I could twist the metal with my Weird to render it harmless.

I tried to shout *Let go of me!* but all that came out was labored breathing as I struggled with the hand across my mouth.

"Are you real?" the voice grated. "Am I seeing you or am I dreaming?"

I twisted violently, and managed to catch a glimpse of black hair, pale skin and a jacket the same gray as my old school uniform, too short at the wrists, exposing knobby bones.

"Conrad?" I managed.

He let go of me as abruptly as he'd sprung at me, but when he backed away the gun didn't go down. It was old as the hills, metal dull, the energy bulb trapping aether at the barrel cloudy and nearly dead. Still, I wasn't going to make any sudden moves. My brother had a temper and changeable moods, and we hadn't parted on the best of terms. I would just as soon not have given him a good reason to shoot me.

"Are you real?" he repeated. His voice was raspy, and in the low light I saw deep circles beneath his eyes and a patchy growth of stubble on his high cheekbones.

"I'm real," I said. It was the only response I could think of. Conrad tightened his grip on the pistol. Though he was skinnier and more hollow-eyed since the last time I'd seen him, his arm never wavered.

"Prove it."

I swallowed hard against my throbbing heart. I'd never seen Conrad like this, except once, and it scared me. That time, he'd cut my throat and left me for dead. This time wasn't looking much better. "I don't know what you want me to say, Conrad."

"I've seen you," he whispered. "For weeks, I've had dreams because of that hole in the sky. Voices in my head. If you're really my sister, then prove it." His eyes narrowed. "You have five seconds."

I raised my hands slowly, but there was no escape route now. All I could do was run, and then Conrad would shoot me in the back. I had no doubt he'd do it. We might be blood, but something had scared my brother, badly enough that the look in his eye was the same as it was the night iron poisoning had made him try to kill me.

We both had the conviction to follow through on our actions, and Conrad was scared. *I* was scared. What could I possibly say to calm him?

"Starlight," I breathed. That night was in my mind anyway, why not use it?

The pistol dipped, just the smallest fraction. Conrad's thin black eyebrows drew together. "What did you say?"

" 'Have you ever seen your blood under starlight, Aoife?' " I quoted at him. " 'When it's quite black?' "

Conrad let out a shuddering breath, and then his arm dropped. He made a pained expression, as if the pistol suddenly weighed a thousand pounds. "It's really you," he muttered. "You don't know how glad I am to know that."

"Conrad," I said, moving toward him again now that his eyes weren't terrifying me. "*What* is happening here?"

"You know, you could have picked a happy memory," he said. "One of those times I read you the horror comics Mom didn't want you reading, or when we snuck into a showing of *The Green Hornet* three days in a row. You didn't have to pick *that*."

"I wasn't exactly thinking about happy memories," I said. "Not while my own brother is pointing a gun at me." I tentatively walked toward him and wrapped my arms around his shoulders. Conrad was tall and thin like our father, solid under his too-small jacket, and I felt relief wash over me as I touched him and convinced myself he was real.

"It's been a crazy couple of weeks," he said. "Months. Time isn't doing the same things it used to. I don't know what the hell's going on out there, Aoife."

I had an idea, but I wasn't about to throw myself on my sword and admit responsibility just yet. Tell Conrad I was responsible for all of the wrong that was happening? All the dreams? I couldn't be sure, could I? No need to alarm everyone.

I wondered how long I'd be able to rationalize it that way.

"What are you doing here and not on Cape Cod? Where's Dad?" I asked instead. Conrad's face fell, and I knew that something was gravely wrong.

"He's upstairs," he said. "We had to come back here— the Cape, it's not safe. . . . Look, you need to see him to understand. I'm glad you're back, but you could've gotten here a lot sooner."

I felt a pang of guilt. Of course I hadn't had to linger in Thorn so long. I could have risked more to escape sooner.

The desire I'd felt from the moment I'd left to come to the only place I'd ever considered home, even if living in it would slowly poison me, didn't make up for my delay.

"How are you doing?" I asked Conrad as we mounted the grand staircase. "I mean with the iron poisoning?"

"It comes and goes," he said. "I think not having a Weird helps. I'm doing all right, Aoife, you don't have to worry about me." He cast a sideways glance at me. "Do I need to worry about you?"

I could feel the pull already, the scream of the iron against my Fae blood like metal on metal, sparking and turning to slag inside me. "Nothing to worry about," I lied.

Conrad's raised eyebrow told me he wasn't buying it. "Uh-huh," he said. We went all the way to the back of the house, to the master suite, where I'd never been. That was my father's room. Even when he'd been gone, I'd felt it would be an unforgivable incursion to go inside.

"I really am fine," I insisted. "I'm more worried about what's going on down there in Arkham. What's happened, Conrad? Where's Dad, and Valentina? Why did you leave Cape Cod?"

Conrad paused at the master suite's double doors, which were carved high above our heads with phases of the sun and moon in great orbits.

"Speaking of questions, where did you go, Aoife?" he said. "What happened to you? I tried my damndest to get it out of Cal, but his mouth was locked up tighter than a bank vault."

I felt as if hours passed while we stared at each other; he was waiting for an answer. "I was in the Thorn Land," I said at last, bracing for Conrad's inevitable explosion. "With our mother."

"What?" Conrad's already haggard face took on a new crop of shadows, making him appear hard and unyielding as granite. I felt the nervous fear rise again. I knew from his expression this couldn't go anywhere good.

"I had to," I said.

"I don't understand why you'd ever give that woman the time of day, never mind run away with her," Conrad said.

"It was that or lose Dean forever," I said softly. "I'm sorry, Conrad. Do you at least believe that?"

He heaved a sigh, pushing his hands through his dark hair until it stood straight up. "Yeah," he said. "I believe you're sorry. But that doesn't mean this is all okay with me, Aoife. You know how I feel about the full-blooded Fae."

"Will you please stop acting like I'm a traitor and tell me what the hell is going on in Arkham?" I demanded. Conrad usually just needed somebody to bite back, to knock some sense into him, and then he'd return to being my slightly pompous but generally tolerable older brother.

Conrad heaved a sigh, and before he could say anything else, the door swung open. The tall, blond figure waved his arms in irritation. "What's all this noise? I told you that Mr. Grayson needs it quiet. . . ." Cal trailed off as he took me in, his pale, watery eyes going wide. "Aoife!" he exclaimed, and enfolded me into a hug that was all bony edges and Cal's distinct, musty scent.

"Hey there, Cal," I mumbled into his sweater. He squeezed me tighter, and his strength reminded me that I wasn't dealing with a human boy. Cal was a shape-shifter, and had the prodigious physical abilities to go with it. I'd learned to live with the fact that his kind usually ate human flesh and lived below ground in nests. Cal was Cal, and whatever he was, he was my best friend in the world.

"I was so worried," he said, holding me at arm's length. He'd cut his hair, and his clothes fit for the first time in my memory. I was half sure the gray wool sweater and flannel slacks he was sporting had been my father's at one point in my dad's misspent youth.

"I'm all right," I assured him, and cast a look at Conrad. He could hear it twice, and maybe believed me this time.

"Come in, come in," Cal told me, and before Conrad could protest, dragged me into the master suite. "It's good you're here," he said softly. "I hope it'll make a difference."

The first thing I noticed was that all the curtains were drawn. Heavy things, velvet and oppressive, full of dust that tickled my nostrils and trickled down the back of my throat. Blackout curtains, left over from the last war, or maybe the one before that.

The second was that my father was lying in bed, in his pajamas, sheets pulled up to his chest. At his side sat my friend Bethina, her copper curls in disarray, wearing a plain green dress rather than the maid's uniform she'd worn when we first met. She held my father's hand lightly, stroking the back of it with her fingertips. I felt a slow-encroaching sense of dread, like a rising tide.

"What's going on here?"

Bethina looked up at me and blinked rapidly. "Oh, Miss Aoife. Thank goodness you're back."

"He's been like this for a few days now," Cal said quietly. "He's fine as far as we can tell. He's just . . . asleep."

"Don't know why, or how," Conrad said, shutting the door and standing in front of it like an ill-tempered guard. "We've tried everything to wake him up, but he won't react to anything. Until the nightmares come."

Bethina nodded, her eyes wide. "Then he gets to screaming something awful. Noises like I never heard a man make."

I turned on Conrad. "How could this happen?" My brother was the one acting like the leader of men. He could at least tell me how such a thing could be possible. My father wasn't the sort to be caught by surprise, either by magic or by malady. He was strong—the strongest person I knew.

"I don't know any more than you do," Conrad snapped. "One minute he was fine, the next Arkham was going crazy, and the next he was like this."

Bethina moved aside to make room for me, and I took my father's hand. It was dry and cool, the hand of a patient rather than that of the strong man I knew my father to be. I felt the urge to cry, or scream, bubbling in my throat. I couldn't be sure which it was.

"I think you better start from the beginning," I said to Conrad. "Tell me exactly what's happened since I've been gone."

He sat next to me on the edge of the bed, but my father didn't stir even as the mattress shifted under my brother's weight. Conrad smoothed the blankets, adjusted the pillows and spoke without looking at anyone.

"It happened right after you left," he said. "People started falling asleep and not waking up. Or they'd dream so vividly they'd think it was actually happening and they'd do things like walk into traffic or attack their loved ones."

"The Proctors tried to control it and set up more quarantines," Cal added, "but they've lost a lot of power. There's all sorts of investigations by the government into their conduct, and without Draven, individual offices have pretty much gone off and done what they liked."

"Riots in some places," said Bethina, "and others are on total lockdown. Arkham pretty much got cleaned out, folks taken off to quarantine, after a bad rash of dreamers swept through and tried to light the place on fire."

"Same thing happened on Cape Cod," Conrad said. "Proctors were everywhere. Valentina decided to split up from us and try to find help, sympathetic folks in the Brotherhood of Iron, and she made me responsible for getting Dad back here, where he'd be safe."

I squeezed my father's hand. This was worse than I ever could have imagined. I'd been warned there were consequences to what I'd done to try to reverse the Fae's deception and save my mother, but I'd never imagined that they would be so direct, so tangible. That they would hurt my father.

"How long has he been like this? And having the dreams?" I said.

"Nightmares, more like," Conrad confirmed. "He thrashes and screams—it got so bad last night we had to hold him down. It started right after you left. Valentina found him on the floor of his study, asleep. Nothing on

44

this earth could rouse him, and she tried everything, believe me."

"It's an epidemic," Bethina said quietly. "All over the country. People goin' to sleep and not wakin' up for love or money."

"I'm so sorry," I whispered to my father. I didn't know if my being there could have prevented this, but the plain truth was I hadn't been. Hadn't been thinking of anyone except myself and the thin hope that I could get Dean back and put things right via some vague notion fed to me by my mother. She was insane, and by believing her, I was probably just as crazy and desperate in my own way.

My father would be ashamed of me. In that moment, *I* was ashamed of me.

"Can we talk outside?" I said to Conrad, and he looked as if he'd rather do anything but. "Please?" I insisted. Conrad nodded, and I'd never been so relieved to leave a room as when we stepped from the oppressive shadows back into the weak sunlight of the mist-laden day.

We walked in silence the entire length of the lawn and sat on a stone bench by the reflecting pond, the bench covered with moss and pockmarks from decades, if not centuries, of weather. It mirrored the pond, choked with algae and lily pads, speckled with the crimson shards of fallen leaves floating on the surface.

"What was it like?" Conrad said abruptly. He didn't look at me, just at the water, which rippled as something—a turtle or one of the ancient koi that lurked below the pads—surfaced to snatch at a late-season insect.

"Thorn?" I said. "Boring, mostly. Fae are very stuffy, and very odd. I spent a lot of time with Mother."

"No," Conrad said quietly. "Being with her—our mother."

I thought about that. I'd seen flashes of the old Nerissa, the one who told us stories, took us on walks to search for flowers between cracks in Lovecraft's sidewalks, let us watch clouds in the park for hours on end rather than going home and tending to things like chores and homework, but mostly I'd seen the new Nerissa, no longer mad, but wholly Fae.

"It was disappointing," I said, and left it at that. I didn't tell Conrad about the parts that had been all right, the evenings when we'd sit quietly, just spending time together. Conrad felt abandoned and lost, and I didn't blame him.

"Then why did you go with her?"

I dug my fingers into the bench, nails carving crescents into the moss and lichen. "I had to, Conrad. She promised me a way to find Dean."

Conrad turned and stared at me. It was a stare of pure pity, as if he hadn't realized I was ill and I'd just told him I was terminal.

"Aoife," he said carefully. "Dean is dead."

"I don't want to talk about it," I snapped. "I just want to be home and not talk about Thorn anymore." I prayed that Conrad would drop the Dean business, and thankfully he did. Trying to explain I was still looking for a way to the Deadlands would just get him thinking my iron poisoning was back, that I was mad.

"It's been weird since you left," he said. "All around.

46

Things are happening—it's almost like an epidemic. Dreams. Madness. The president might have to sit for an impeachment hearing, and the Rationalists are having a fit. It's like when things were wild all over again."

Something clicked into place, what the old woman had shouted at me earlier. "Somebody called me a demon this morning," I said. "A demon from hell. Nobody talks like that. I mean, if they want to stay out of Rationalist jail."

"Ever since people started falling asleep and the Proctors got stripped of their authority, a lot of that's been happening," Conrad said. "I've heard rumors that all sorts of creatures are cropping up. People who don't know the truth blame the necrovirus, but it sounds to me like the barriers between Thorn and Iron and . . . other places are easier to get past." He shrugged. "I don't know. It could all just be mass hysteria. People thinking the world is ending."

"It's not ending," I said quietly. "But this isn't nothing." I looked Conrad in the eye. He had our mother's eyes, pale blue and cloudless, like a new sky after rain. I looked more like my father, both in coloring and features.

Conrad frowned. "Aoife, what are you not telling me?"

I looked up at the sky, at the mist that roiled above our heads like a sea, ancient and birthing primordial creatures onto a phantom shore.

What I'd seen in the Arctic, in the space where dreams were born, had been real. That much was clear to me now.

I told Conrad the truth then, there in the garden. About how I'd tried to reverse what I'd done because of Tremaine, step back through the loopholes of time and undo the damage I'd done to the Lovecraft Engine and the city.

How it hadn't worked, and how I'd snapped something fundamental in the gears of the worlds, Thorn and Iron and everything in between.

"I thought they weren't so bad," I said. "The Old Ones. I thought letting them go was just returning the universe to its natural state. They're not evil, Conrad. They're just . . . alive. A different sort of alive than us, but not malicious."

"But, if I believe you, they've done this." Conrad's face was pale and drawn, and he made a sweeping gesture. "It's them, all of this. All the dreamers and the strangeness. They're returning to the Iron Land, right? And their influence is driving the entire world insane. How is that not so bad, exactly?" His brow had that crease in it, the one that meant he blamed me, and I couldn't argue with him.

"I wouldn't have done it if I'd known," I mumbled, but even to my ears, it wasn't convincing.

"I can't . . ." Conrad rubbed his hands across his face, and I waited. I'd hoped he'd forgive me, or at least understand. I'd had to do something. What had happened when Tremaine tricked me had to be undone. "I can't," Conrad repeated. "I'm sorry, Aoife. I'm done."

"What do you mean?" I rose as he did, panicked, watching him back away from me. "Conrad, don't. . . ."

"You did this," he said. "It's because of you that our father is like this. You tried to make it better, and I get that, but you've made it worse."

"Conrad—" I started, but he raised his hand.

"Don't talk to me, Aoife," he said. "Don't try to make this right. I can't count you as part of my family. We can't ever repair this." He started back toward the house. "What's

48

done is done. I expect you to be out of Graystone by the morning."

I could have screamed at him, or run after him and demanded that he hear my side of things, but I just stood there and watched him go. Conrad was even more stubborn than I was.

And he was right. I'd thought that the Old Ones weren't the evil that the Rationalists preached or the saviors that the Star Sisters, their worshipper sect, insisted they'd be when they returned. When I'd been in the dreaming place, the center of all the worlds, I'd seen them and felt their touch in my mind. It still burned there, as if the mere contact had scarred the channels of my conscience with acid. But I hadn't felt malice, simply ancient intelligence. Yet to human beings, with their fragile makeup, who was to say the two weren't one and the same? The Old Ones' return could simply be too much for the fragile barriers between worlds, and it could signal a fracture that would make them all collapse, one after the other, like dominoes.

I hadn't known what I was doing, not really, or what I'd set in motion. I'd been trying to save my family, myself. Everything I knew. Trying to put the world back the way it was. What I hadn't understood was that it couldn't be that way any longer. I wasn't the Aoife Grayson who'd left Lovecraft all those months ago, and the world wasn't the world I'd abandoned for Thorn.

So I let Conrad go, and let the dull ache sit in my chest like a stone while I tried to think of what to do.

Dean was the only thing I could save, at this point. The Old Ones were vast beyond my imagination. There was no way I could send them back, even if I knew how to access the small nucleus of the dreaming world where I'd found them. Crow, king of dreams, who controlled that place, would not welcome me back. We hadn't parted on good terms, to say the least. He'd spent millennia keeping the Old Ones at bay from Iron and Thorn and all the living worlds, and in one fell swoop, a changeling who didn't know what she was truly doing had opened the floodgates, released these ancient, implacable things to do whatever it was they planned to do upon their return to the living parts of the universe.

So it had to be Dean. The Deadlands were my destination now. At least I wouldn't have to go back into the house to get my things. I doubted that, in the place where the dead went, I'd need clothes or food or anything except what was on my back.

I walked around the edge of the reflecting pond, into the ragged hedge maze that made up one whole side of Graystone's property. The thing hadn't been cared for in years, and there were large gaps in the hedgerow that you could pass through, rendering the maze useless.

At the center was a statue, one of the heretical bits and pieces that the Graysons had kept out of view of the Proctors when the Rationalists took control. It depicted a woman holding a fallen soldier, a cowl covering her face. I scrubbed at the oxidized copper plaque until I could read CUCHULAINN AND THE MORRIGAN. I had no idea who they were supposed to be—magicians, I guessed, or old gods renounced by the Rationalists.

The crows sat all over the statue, and they didn't move at

my approach. I was close enough to touch the largest one, and it stared at me with glassy black eyes, never blinking, never moving.

I retreated, discomfited by the birds, who'd been everywhere since I'd emerged from Thorn. Dean had always said they were the watchers, the eyes of the old gods and the magic that veined the world. Even my father's airship was named after a raven, the most famous raven of all, Munin. My father had told me the story of Odin, a god who sacrificed his eye for wisdom, and who possessed two birds, Hunin and Munin—Thought and Memory—that flew into the world each day and brought knowledge back to Odin in Asgard, where he sat on his throne.

It wasn't so different, I supposed, from Thorn and Iron, two places connected by the dotted lines of the universe, but at the same time wholly apart. One magic, one iron, one replete with the fantastic and one rooted firmly in the earth whereon it sat. There could be crossover, but there could never be harmony.

I turned my back on the crows, focusing on the Deadlands. My Weird let me cross those lines, fold that page so that I could brush one world against the next, travel from one to the next.

My mother had lured me into the Thorn Land by telling me she knew the way to the Deadlands, but now I was sure it was simple as crossing over to a place I'd never been before. I'd managed to build a Gate to Crow's dreamworld, and it stood to reason that if I could access that place, I could access the Deadlands.

I didn't need Nerissa, I thought, bitterness welling in

my stomach. She'd strung me along for months while my father and my friends wasted away here, in an Iron Land thrown into chaos.

Putting aside my anger at my mother and her manipulation, I focused on building the Gate, as I had with the place of dreams. Then, I'd had a focus, something to channel my Weird. This time I was flying blind.

I wasn't the first person to be able to do this—my much more famous predecessor, Nikola Tesla, had had the gift as well, had conceived of worlds beyond imagination, and was eventually responsible for breaking the bonds between them, creating the world as we knew it.

I didn't have anything so spectacular in mind. I just needed to make a path, a bridge I could skip across before it collapsed.

Using my Weird felt a bit like standing on railroad tracks as a train approached—a rumble you could sense in your core, a disturbance that fed through every bit of you. My head started to pound, as it usually did, and a trickle of blood worked its way from my nose.

Forming a Gate, the sort of thing that Tesla constructed out of technology and the Fae constructed with their uncanny powers, took a lot of effort. It usually left me spent and drained, racked by headaches for at least a day, but I couldn't afford that now.

I had to find Dean, and I let that desire pull me toward the gray spots between the bright beacons of Thorn and Iron and all the places in between that I could travel.

I could practically feel him, his warm chest against my cheek, smell his smell, hear his laugh. I was so close that the tears leaking from my eyes had nothing to do with the pain I experienced as the Gate opened in front of me.

Then, as quickly as I'd felt my Weird begin to respond to my desires, everything went wrong.

A scream ripped through the empty spaces that I saw when I opened myself to my Weird, and I felt a tug against the center of myself as if a jitney had slammed into me. Light exploded in front of my eyes and panic rose in my throat, along with a scream of my own. This had never happened before, and I didn't know what I could do except be buffeted by a wave of resistance as I glimpsed a sliver of a gray sky and a black, twisted tree in a field of brown grass. Then I saw nothing, simply black velvet cut through by pinpricks of light.

Stars. I saw stars. I realized that I was in the vastness between worlds, and they weren't stars but spots in the fabric of space and time, worlds and destinations that I could visit if my Weird could only reach them.

The cool grasp of the Deadlands, like opening a room long locked, breathed its last and slipped away. No matter how hard I tried, I couldn't connect again.

And in a sudden upsurge of fear, I realized that I couldn't go anywhere else, either. That I was trapped in between, my Weird refusing to return me where I'd been or to move me forward, to any of the points of light.

I did scream, then. I knew that my body was still on the ground at Graystone, but my consciousness was scattered across a thousand light-years, the image I carried with me only a memory of my physical body.

Had anyone with my gift ever been trapped here? Was

my fate to float forever, always in between? I started to panic. It was the worst fate I could conceive of.

Then I saw them as I thrashed in the void: great shadows that blotted out the world-lights, one by one, long and lean, square and massive, or with tentacles that reached for each point of light, closing it amidst their incalculable bulk. I stared as the Old Ones passed by me close enough to touch, if I'd had fingers. Their inexorable journey from the dreaming place toward the point of light that represented the Iron Land was fast and relentless, and I watched, breathless, as their shimmering bodies slid by me, buffeting my Weird with their vast power.

I felt their desire to return to the Iron Land, their focus on it, their hunger to touch the shores that they had not touched for a hundred thousand years—a long time even for such creatures as they. They were coming, and it was clear there was no stopping them. I knew—I'd released them from their prison, let them loose into the in-between and sent them toward the Iron Land.

Long time, one of them agreed, and I didn't hear the voice so much as feel the brush of mind on mind.

We remember, another agreed. *How you freed us.*

How you need us.

How we knew you even before your creation.

Your blood, our blood.

Your flesh, our flesh.

"STOP!" I screamed. Their voices were shredding me, tearing this non-body of mine apart, and I saw the lights begin to dim.

I was lost. I was never going to make it out of here. It

went beyond panic now, into deep, true terror. I would hear the Old Ones' voices echoing in my head for as long as I lived. No living thing was meant to encounter them this closely. Perhaps in the ancient times when they'd last come, a primitive brain too dense to decipher their voices might have withstood it, but now? Now I felt their voices on me like physical scars, the indelible touch of the Old Ones' minds.

We will not forget, the first one whispered. *We will show our favor.*

"Aoife!"

The voice cut through the cacophony of the cosmos, the background radiation, the rumble of the Old Ones' passage.

"Aoife!"

My Weird snapped against my mind like a rubber band, and all at once I knew how to reel myself back in again, how to return to the point where my flesh resided, as well as my soul.

Opening my eyes was like taking a hammer blow to the forehead, and I lurched into the fetal position, riding out the wave of agony as I writhed and screamed on the gravel.

Small, strong hands wrapped around my wrists, and arms pulled me against a silk dress that smelled both familiar and terrifying—the overwhelming aroma of the orchid perfume favored by Fae.

I blinked the pain tears from my eyes and waited for the face above me to come into focus.

Nerissa stroked her thin fingers over my hair, my cheeks, brushed the tears from my face as if I were five years old again. I couldn't fathom how she could even be here, and simply stared at her.

"You?"

"I'm here," she confirmed. "When I heard you'd run away I had to follow you."

"But the iron . . ." I made myself sit up and scoot away from her. She still looked like her new, improved self. Well-dressed, hair up, cheeks flushed with life. The tinge of madness in her eyes I'd come to know as normal wasn't there. Yet.

"I'll be all right for a few minutes, out here where there's no metal," my mother said. "I had to use the *hexenring* to find you and see what on the scorched earth you thought you were doing, running off like that."

"What I had to do," I told her. "I have to find Dean."

"Well, you're not going to find him with your little parlor trick," Nerissa said crisply. "The Deadlands are closed to the living, Fae, human or anything else. Your Weird won't get you there, and you're lucky you're not dead from trying."

I tried standing, and found it a treacherous endeavor. I staggered over to the statue and sat by the fallen hero's feet. My skull was echoing, and the gravity of what Conrad had said was starting to sink in, now that I'd failed. "So, what, you came to scold me? I thought you didn't want me going to the Deadlands, so why come?"

"Because you ran off with that piece of scum Grey Draven, Octavia is beside herself with rage and I told her I'd go make sure you weren't colluding against the Fae."

"I'm doing what I have to," I repeated. "You wouldn't help me."

She shook her head, reaching to stroke my cheek, but I pulled away. "I told you it wouldn't be this simple, Aoife," she said. "Playing roulette with Death never is."

"It's so much worse than that," I whispered, and felt hot tears of helplessness and panic start to flow. I couldn't hold them back. I sobbed, and I let Nerissa rub my back and whisper soothing words, because nobody else would, and in that moment I needed it.

I didn't tell her about the Old Ones. I let her think all my tears were for Dean. I couldn't handle having yet another person look at me as if I'd set fire to everything they held near and dear.

"Poor girl," Nerissa whispered. "Everything seems so big and impossible at your age. This boy—surely he can't be worth killing yourself or melting your brains over?"

"He's the *only* person I know worth it," I snapped, and watched the pain blossom in Nerissa's eyes. Belatedly, I realized what I'd said.

"I see," she murmured, before I could backpedal or try to apologize. "If you're really insistent, then I might know of another way. Even though I think it's a foolish thing. The dead should stay dead, if you ask me."

That sounded like the Nerissa I knew—never a mother to coddle or console, even before the madness really sank tooth and claw into her mind. It helped, in an odd way. A mother who wanted to comfort me and have a heart-to-heart? I'd have no idea what to do with that or how to react.

"I didn't ask you, but I have a feeling you'll tell me anyway," I said. I didn't care that I was being a mouthy brat—not the way I'd care if it were my father across from me. I didn't feel the connection to Nerissa I did to him. I guessed Conrad was right. Our mother had left us long before she'd been committed.

"You really are a difficult child," my mother sighed.

"I'm not a child," I told her. "By this point, I think I've earned the right to be treated like an adult."

"You're not," my mother said. "But I can see you aren't going to give up this ridiculous idea, so I'll tell you what I know: when I was in the madhouse another patient told me about a man in San Francisco."

Oh, this was perfect. "Mother," I said, slow and direct, "your one idea comes from another inmate in a mental institution."

"I didn't belong there," my mother snapped. "Neither did he. He was a Spiritualist, and the Proctors locked him up for heresy. He worked with a doctor who had made a machine that could reach the Deadlands. Horatio Crawford, that was his name. Dr. Horatio Crawford."

"And?" I prompted. One madman's tale of a magical device that could peel back the layers of space and time when even my Weird failed was suspect, to say the least.

"You'll probably scoff, since it's a Fae tale and not made of math and metal," my mother said. "But I thought there was a thread that bound souls to life, a measure of time that was only theirs, and when the thread got cut, well . . . Octavia always used to tell me that was what led to spirits and phenomena and such."

I didn't reply. I didn't want to anger her now that she was talking by suggesting that Fae ghost stories held about as much water as the kind my classmates and I used to tell.

The notion of the thread, though—if there was a connection between worlds via the Gates, why not a connection of the soul to the Land it had inhabited in life?

"If Crawford found a way to use his machine to tether the soul to life but allow it to be free of a body . . . well, that makes sense to me," Nerissa said. "Your father always said magic was just science nobody could quantify yet."

"That sounds like him," I said. I desperately wanted to hear more about her and Archie's life together, but now wasn't the time. Now, time was precious.

"Thank you for trusting me," I said, when she only stared up at the high windows of Graystone, which reflected the mountains beyond, gray and implacable as stone eyes.

"I just know you're too stubborn to give up," she said. "And I don't want you to get hurt, or have your spirit broken worse than it already is. I do care about you, Daughter." She pressed her hand over mine, and I tried not to start at her cold skin. The gesture was so foreign, all I could do was squeeze her fingers, because I didn't want her to think it was in vain.

"Go to San Francisco and find Horatio Crawford," my mother said, giving my hand a squeeze back. "If he's still alive, then perhaps the two of you will be clever enough to cheat Death."

She rose and smoothed her skirts. "I've been here too long. Goodbye, Aoife." After a moment of hesitation, she reached out and cupped my face with her thin, cool palm. "Be careful," she whispered, an unidentifiable expression flitting across her face. Then she stepped back and walked away, and the mist swallowed her up.

I stayed where I was. My mother had never been reliable,

but when it came to Dean, could I really be picky about where I got help?

There was nothing I could do for Dean or my father by sitting on a garden bench moping. I finally had a sliver of hope, and not to follow it just because of the source would be the worst kind of foolish.

I stood up and turned back toward the house. There was only one direction to go, and that was west, to San Francisco.

Winging Westward

IT WASN'T HARD to convince Cal to come with me. Cal was always up for an adventure, for bucking authority, whether it was the Proctors or Conrad. That was one of my favorite things about him.

I should have been terrified of Cal. Ghouls lived under old cities like Lovecraft—infested the sewers built before the Proctors took control—and would attack like a lightning strike made of muscle and teeth when they were hunting. But Cal had been my friend before I'd found out the truth about myself and the world, the necrovirus, all of it. And he'd kept right on being my friend after. Besides, as a changeling, I didn't have much room to talk. If the two of us told a normal human the truth, it'd be a toss-up whom they'd turn their shotgun on first.

He procured extra clothes for both of us, plus food, money and a map of California from my father's vast library. I waited outside my father's room while Cal asked Bethina to look after him until we got back. I didn't want to antagonize Conrad any more than I had to, but I also didn't trust that he wouldn't go running off and leave my father to his own devices. Bethina was tough and trustworthy, and I knew my father would be safe with her.

"Now what?" Cal asked when he came back and handed me my bag. The white cat watched us leave from one of the upstairs windows. I looked at the road ahead. I didn't want to be reminded that my father was back there, insensible to the world, and that it was probably my fault.

"Airship terminal," I said, "and hope we have enough to buy passage to San Francisco."

"Don't you think that'll be kind of dangerous?" Cal said. "Going back to Lovecraft? Even with no Proctors, they don't exactly welcome people like us."

"I'm not going to just waltz in," I said. "I'll let you buy the tickets and I'll stick to the shadows." Of course, if we needed immigration papers or Proctors were still watching the airfield, then everything would go wrong. Theoretically, one could travel between quarantined cities without papers, but if the Proctors en route were feeling mercurial, who was to say what could happen?

"Okay," Cal said, casting me a sidelong look. We came to the three-sided shelter that was the Arkham jitney stop, the path that would take us to the airship field outside Lovecraft. "I gotta say, this isn't the most genius of your plans, Aoife."

"It's a bad plan," I agreed, shifting the weight of my bulging bag. "But it's the only one I've got."

Logan Airfield was supposed to be a modern marvel, something all the good citizens of Lovecraft could lord over San Francisco and New Amsterdam. The first things I saw when the express jitney pulled up were the swooping gull wings of the main terminal's roof, and the first thing I heard was the trumpet of loudspeakers announcing departing and arriving flights.

We joined the stream of well-dressed travelers and their luggage. Nobody gave us more than a cursory glance, and I stayed beneath the great sign, lit from within, that scrolled through flights, destinations and times.

In the shadows, I was able to watch the ordinary people approaching the ticket desks, giving their luggage to porters, retrieving their tickets. They all seemed so carefree, even the men with briefcases and frowns and the woman trying to wrangle four small, screeching children. Even the Proctors, standing with their arms folded, bored, or talking in groups while travelers flowed around them, didn't seem particularly concerned.

Maybe they hadn't heard about what had happened in Arkham. Maybe they were all willfully ignoring their bad dreams.

Cal shot me a look from the miles-long line, and I shrugged in sympathy. Patience wasn't something either of us possessed in spades. The next flight to San Francisco was in forty minutes, and if we didn't make it we'd be stuck at the airfield until morning, under the watchful eye of the high windows and the gleaming steel walls engraved with scenes of great engineering feats from the past—the Eerie Canal, the Babbage Bridge, the Lovecraft Engine.

That last was no more. Thanks to me. I shrank against one of the steel pillars holding up the monitor showing the flight departures, certain that my face was like a beacon to everyone passing. In my effort to be inconspicuous, I caught sight of another figure across the terminal trying to do the same thing.

The two-story terminal was open to the girdered ceiling, where every other panel was frosted glass. The shadows cast a great grid pattern on the floor and made it easy to lean against a wall in darkness and not be seen. The man was standing between the women's loo and a bank of aethervoxes contained in wooden booths, available for public use.

He'd be unremarkable to anyone but me, because I recognized him. The last time I'd seen him, he'd been in the Arctic, wrapped in cold-weather gear but with the same suspicious face. The same calculating eyes, eyes that had looked at me as little more than a lab rat, another cog in the machine that they'd use to drive back both the invasion of the Fae and the incursion of the Proctors. I thought the Proctors had locked him up, but without Draven and the breaking of their ranks, who knew what had happened since I'd been in Thorn?

The doctor of the Brotherhood of Iron stared at the crowd, calculated and discarded each face in turn. He hadn't seen me yet, and that was my only saving grace.

Cal turned away from the ticket counter in triumph, waving two red Pan Am ticket booklets. I shook my head as imperceptibly as I could, but it was too late. The doctor followed Cal's gaze to me.

There was nothing else to do. I had to draw them away from Cal. To the Brotherhood, he'd be worse than a lab rat—just something to be studied, poked, prodded and tortured, until he was of no more use and was vivisected to further the Brotherhood's fight against the ghouls.

I broke and ran. The doctor followed me, in a surprising burst of speed for an old man. I saw another figure in a black trench coat break and run after Cal as he bolted in the opposite direction. Good. They were divided. There'd be other agents outside at the curb, as well as watching the entrance to the gates, but they couldn't know where we were going—they had to have followed us.

Followed me. From the moment I'd reentered the Iron Land. I didn't know how I could have been so stupid, but I couldn't dwell on it now.

The doctor was gaining ground as we raced through the terminal, and I saw him throw aside a well-dressed woman and her travel case. She fell with a scream, case breaking open and scattering clothes and toiletries across the marble floor.

I wasn't going to outrun him. Wasn't going to evade the Brotherhood. My father had told me I had to think on my feet, to stop analyzing everything if I wanted to survive against adversaries who knew my every move. Knew about my Weird, knew about the other Lands, knew that the Proctors were full of it.

I made my decision, and as I skidded around a corner, I let myself fall against the black-clad, brass-buttoned chest of a ticket agent. "Oh, help me," I gasped, putting on my most pitiful expression and praying that my red face and flying hair would shield me from recognition. "There's a man chasing me, he tried to grab me. . . ."

I shouldn't have worried. The agent barely looked at me before he blew his whistle for a security guard, who shoved me aside.

I didn't linger. I was around the corner and gone before the doctor could do more than give an outraged yell.

Making my way to the gate for San Francisco, I nearly shrieked when a short, pudgy boy with brown hair tapped me on the arm. "What?" I demanded.

"Calm down," the boy said. "It's me, Cal."

"Cal?" I stared. I knew Cal had to work to look human—shift his shape, as it were—but I hadn't known he could look like other people.

"I swear," he said. "I had to duck into the boys' room to do this, but I think I lost that Brotherhood mook. He sure was confused when I didn't come out again."

"We have to get out of here." Now that I'd escaped, my heart was throbbing with how narrow that escape had been. If I was captured again by the Brotherhood, I'd never see the light of day. And now it would only be a matter of time before they figured out Cal was a ghoul.

Next time, they'd be ready with the appropriate measures.

"Boarding's started," Cal pointed out, and we joined the queue. After what had just happened, I expected there to be a problem with our tickets, and I didn't really breathe until we'd sunk into our seats.

We were in the first-class cabin, all red leather seats and dark wood paneling between the iron ribs of the zeppelin.

"I told the ticket gal we were flying home to see our sick father," Cal said. "She bumped us up without me even asking." His smug grin was only a small placebo against being in the proximity of so much iron.

"How long is this flight?" I asked, fidgeting in my seat. I was already hearing the whispers, the scraping of fingernails across metal that signaled the onset of iron poisoning.

"We stop in Cleveland, St. Louis and Las Vegas," Cal said. "That is, assuming the Las Vegas quarantine holds. That's what the ticket gal told me. It'll be about seven hours until we get a break."

"Stones." I pressed my face into my hands. I could hold out. I could stay sane. I'd managed it for fifteen years before I'd known the truth, I could manage it until Cleveland. At least, that was what I told myself as passengers flowed around us and stewardesses passed up and down the aisles fetching drinks and cigarettes and stowing baggage.

"I'd be more worried about those Brotherhood cats," Cal said. "I mean, how are they even still around? I thought the Proctors had 'em all rounded up."

"Who knows if they stayed that way?" I said. "Besides, I wouldn't put it past Valentina's father to still have it in for me."

Harold Crosley, Valentina's repulsive, scheming father, deserved to be locked up. He wanted to replace the Proctors with something that bargained with the Fae, that used their power as ours, and I knew nothing could come of that except betrayal and death. An alliance between Thorn and Iron wasn't natural.

Out of all the things the Proctors had done, locking up Harold Crosley was the one bright spot. But it appeared either he was out, or the Brotherhood had chugged right along without him.

"We have to be careful," I told Cal. "They're never going to stop trying to use my Weird, as long as their members are free." They wouldn't hesitate to lock me up and use me until my brain was mush, to further their goals. My father had left the Brotherhood, broken with the only family he'd known to protect me from that, and I'd be damned if I was going to hand myself over without a fight.

The airship bumped and jostled as it rose from its tie-downs, and I breathed a little easier.

"We're going to be all right now," Cal said, and patted the back of my hand. I gave him an insincere smile in response, then stared out the window as the countryside fell away below us, wishing I shared his convictions.

I made it to Cleveland, and practically ran off the ship and to the terminal's outside area, where I gulped great breaths of fresh air. The iron caused a throbbing headache and black spots to appear behind my eyes.

If we could have crossed the country by jitney, it would have been slightly more bearable, but I didn't have the time. Even as I relished being free of iron poisoning for a few moments, I scanned the crowd for the Brotherhood, but nobody paid Cal and me any attention. He'd kept his new shape. I'd had a hard time not jumping every time I looked at the seat beside mine and saw a pudgy brunet rather than my familiar lanky, blond friend.

The bell sounded, and Cal breathed a sigh of relief when I sat back down next to him. "I was beginning to wonder if you'd ditched me."

"Never," I said. "I'm just not sure how much longer I can take this."

Iron poisoning was insidious—it started small, flickers out of the corner of your eyes, then grew to pain in your joints and skull that progressed until you could no longer tell what was real and what was the iron working on your Fae blood, and you'd do anything to make the pain stop.

Cal closed his hand over mine, surprising me. "You'll be all right, Aoife," he said. "You're the strongest person I know."

The flight to St. Louis was a little easier—the stewardesses fussed over Cal and served lunch, and the food helped settle my stomach. Once we took off for Las Vegas, I watched the plains ripple and change by the hour to mountains, spiky and so close I felt I could reach out and grab a handful of snow from their caps.

The mountains bled into desert, and I saw the carcass of an airship below, iron bones scattered across the landscape, the track of its crash cutting into the belly of the land, exposing bloodred dirt.

I saw another, and another. "Cal," I said, and pointed.

"It's the updrafts," he said sagely. "Warm air from the desert and cold from the mountains. Turbulence."

I didn't bother to ask how he knew—Cal had an answer for almost everything. I guessed it came from being a ghoul, stuck in the sewers with nothing to do except read human books and adventure stories and dream of life above.

The airship bounced, and I gripped the arms of my seat. A woman behind me gave a small cry.

"Ladies and gentlemen"—a smooth voice came out of the trumpet-shaped speaker above my head—"we've encountered a little rough air, so we're going to ask everyone to remain in their seats until further notice."

I heard the rivets in the hull strain as the airship gained altitude. We bounced again, as if a giant child had us on the end of a string that he tugged mercilessly.

"Jeez," Cal said, wincing. "I'm going to upchuck if this keeps happening."

I passed him the empty bowl from my ice cream sundae. "If you throw up on me, I'll kill you."

"I can't help it!" he moaned. "I get a nervous stomach when I eat human food."

The next jolt knocked bags from their perches and slammed my head against the back of my seat so hard I saw stars. I heard a whine from the back of the airship, and we lurched, losing a hundred feet in the blink of an eye.

"Okay," Cal said, and screams and shouts went up from the other passengers. "What on the scorched earth is going on?"

"That wasn't normal," I agreed, craning a glance out of the bubble-glass window next to our seat. A trail of smoke blossomed against the pale white-blue sky, sprung from a black dot that quickly resolved itself into another airship as it gained on us.

"I don't think this is a good sign," I said to Cal. He peered over my shoulder. We both saw the flash, and a second later the impact rocked our ship.

A stewardess clawed her way through our cabin to the cockpit, and I could hear the pilots shouting at one another as she opened the door.

The airship behind us drew closer. Half of its cabin had been blasted away, leaving the batteries and fans exposed to the open air. Noxious-looking smoke filled the rest of the skeletal cabin structure, and I could see tiny figures moving back and forth inside.

"Oh man," Cal said. "Oh man. What are we going to do, Aoife?"

"I have no idea," I said as our craft shuddered and I heard the whine of the fans die. "I just hope our pilot stops running before we get shot down."

The other airship drew alongside us, and I saw the figures inside clearly. They wore masks—that explained how they could stand the high altitude and the thick smoke. Long chains with hooks on the end bit into our hull, closing the distance between the skeletal ship and ours. One shattered the window next to our seats and clasped the sill, and I shrieked as glass spilled into my lap.

Cal put an arm around me as the other ship passed a flexible gangway between the crafts, but I shrugged him off.

"Pirates," he said, excitement bleeding into his voice. "I never thought I'd actually see pirates. . . ."

"This is not going to be an adventure," I said. Inside, I was panicking. I'd heard stories of pirates lighting airships on fire after they'd stripped them, leaving the passengers

71

to burn alive, or breaking into the cockpit and setting the planes to crash to earth.

Worse, I'd heard of passengers being press-ganged into service on the pirate craft, or sold overseas to slavers in countries beyond the reach of the Proctors.

That couldn't happen to me. I had to get to San Francisco.

I watched as the pirates made their way across the gangplank to our airship, moving slowly and heavily, even considering the equipment that weighed them down.

I grabbed Cal's arm. "We have to hide," I hissed. I couldn't be caught here, not when we were still so far from San Francisco.

"Where?" Cal demanded. "Where are we supposed to go?"

I cast my eye about and saw the door to a water closet at the back of the cabin. "This way," I said. A clang resounded through the first-class cabin as the hatch blew off its hinges, and people screamed.

I didn't have any money or jewelry for the pirates, which meant that all they had to take from me was myself. I couldn't be kidnapped now.

The water closet wasn't big enough for both of us, really, and the door wouldn't shut completely. I squeezed in close to Cal, sharing air and heartbeats.

We heard shouting in the cabin, but it was all passengers. None of the usual screams of robbery. I peered through the tiny crack left in the door.

The pirates moved soundlessly and with purpose, snatching jewels off necks, watches off chains and wallets from shaking fingers. I felt my stomach tighten. This was all wrong. They were mechanical. They might have been automatons for all the emotion they showed.

They wore canvas pants and jackets, rusty weapons strapped to their bodies. Gas masks with bulging glass eye sockets and flexible hoses covered their faces explained how they could have survived in their half-ruined ship.

The leader glared at everyone he passed, and I could sense the weight of his gaze even through his mask.

"Something's wrong," I whispered to Cal. They didn't move like men, didn't speak. It was as if they'd been conjured out of the air and the smoke that surrounded their battered ship.

Cal flared his nostrils and sniffed. "They don't smell like men," he murmured. "They smell like dead things." His face rippled, and I could tell that he was fighting to keep the ghoul inside him under control. I didn't want to be close to him if it came out, but I'd rather be pressed against Cal as a ghoul than deal with whatever was out there.

"What do we do?" Cal whispered.

I watched as the pirates advanced. "I'm supposed to know?" Why did I always have to be the one with the plan? Why did I always get stuck in these horrible situations?

I thought about what Conrad had said, that creatures were spilling into the Iron Land from everywhere else. Could this be a part of it, these strange, lumbering creatures chasing humans through the sky? Could the airmen out there have risen from the wrecks in the desert below, animated once again to take to the sky and pillage crafts full of the living?

Given what was happening in Arkham, I decided that was as likely as anything else. But reasons didn't really matter now—what mattered was getting us out of this.

"Here's the plan," I whispered. "We stay here, and we don't move, and we hope they just pass us by."

"That's a crappy plan," Cal whispered back.

I shoved my hand over his mouth as the pirate leader drew within feet of us, head swinging back and forth as if he was sniffing the air.

The feeling of my heart nearly throbbing out of my chest was joined by a sharp, lancing pain in my shoulder. The shoggoth bite venom gave off only the faintest sense for Cal when he was in human shape, but from the pirate, also in human shape, there was pain so intense that flashbulbs exploded in front of my eyes.

I was only half surprised when the pirate whirled abruptly and yanked the water closet door open. Cal had been right—it was a crappy plan.

The pirate stood over me, staring. Finally, he put out his hand.

"I don't . . ." Pain made my voice small and insubstantial. "I don't have anything for you."

The pirate yanked me up with one hand, and the stench of decay rolling off him added another dimension to the senses-bending agony I was experiencing. He smelled like spoiled meat, like flowers wilted and rotted inside a greenhouse, like diesel exhaust trapped inside a tiny space.

He growled, low, and I got the impression that was the only sound he *could* make, that some horrible catastrophe had ripped his voice from him.

I panicked. I kicked against him, struggled, shoved. I hit him in the sternum and felt a give under my hands that sent nausea roiling in my guts. Under the jacket, a stain spread, and it fell open to show a mass of green and black flesh with snapped ribs beneath.

It looked as if he'd been in an accident, perhaps the one that destroyed his airship, the steering yoke slamming into his chest and leaving a long dent that crawled with maggots.

I screamed, and lost any advantage I might have had, thrashing wildly. I wanted to fight, but seeing a dead man walking around had driven reason from me.

The other pirates moaned and turned toward us, while the passengers had gone into a blind panic, trying to flee anywhere they could, crying, falling over seats. One of the stewardesses fell and twisted her leg, and I heard bone snap.

My Weird, usually the thing I clung to, was useless. I couldn't send this creature anywhere, couldn't even break the dead man's iron grip.

This might be it, I realized. I wouldn't be taken, if what I knew of the animated dead from Cal's magazines and comics was true. I'd be tossed off the side of the ship for amusement—or worse, I'd be food.

I managed to wrench free of the pirate's grasp, but he still loomed over me, and the pain from my shoulder was so bad I could barely see straight. His origin was definitely the result of the encroachment of the Old Ones—creatures of their ilk always made my bite scar flame with pain.

He raised a rusty wrench twice the width of my forearm.

It was so stupid—I'd managed to escape Thorn, survive the Mists and Draven's madness, and I was going to die by wrench.

Something flashed above me, something gray, like a streak of smoke, and then Cal slammed into the pirate from the side, falling on him, all teeth and claws and ashen, veined skin.

He wasn't human any longer. The pirate went down as Cal tore at him, and I managed to scramble up and grab the wrench.

"Move!" I shouted at Cal, and raised the wrench over my head. I brought it down, again and again. The pirate's gas mask goggles cracked, the canvas leaked, and I kept smashing until there was nothing but a crimson smear on the thick carpet of the airship.

Other passengers got the idea and fell on the pirates, using coffee servers and heavy cases and walking sticks to beat on the walking corpses until one by one they fell, snapping and snarling and trying to bite the passengers. I shivered. Looked like I'd been right about the purpose of the raid—food, not jewels.

Fortunately, the chaos meant nobody noticed that Cal had changed, and he ducked back into the closet to reverse into his human shape. His clothes were shredded, but there was nothing we could do about that.

I thought everything was going to be fine until the stewardess with the broken leg pointed at us and started to scream.

"That's a demon!" she shrieked. "Something from the underground, from my nightmares! Keep it away from me!"

One by one, heads, once finely coiffed or sporting natty hats, now with bloody cuts in their scalps, turned in our direction. Now that the pirates were subdued, the bedraggled, bruised faces were all focused on us.

"Crap," I muttered. Cal just stared, until I grabbed him and jerked him with me. There was nowhere to go but across the gangway, unless we wanted an angry mob burning Cal alive, or simply tossing us both out a hatch. I thought about pointing out to the ungrateful cow that Cal had probably saved all our lives by giving us an opening to attack the pirates, but I figured she wouldn't take the truth about what he was well. Humans never did. I turned and ran, my feet clanging on the rusty gangway.

The void below was dizzying, blue sky and orange earth meeting each other in an endless loop above and below the sliver of metal that connected the two ships.

I caught a whiff of the smoke still billowing from the battery compartment, but kept running. Cal clung to me, and angry passengers gathered around the hatch watching us. All we needed was the pilot to show up with his shock pistol and we'd be done for.

I found the clamps to disengage the gangplank after we reached the other side, and let it fall away. We bobbed up immediately, our slight weight in comparison with the huge zeppelin's making us rise far and away. The entire crew had boarded our ship, leaving theirs conveniently empty for us.

Cal wrinkled his nose and coughed. "I don't think these fumes are doing us any favors," he wheezed.

I found extra gas masks hanging in the cargo area and pulled one on. The ship was so small you could walk front to back in ten steps. The abandoned pilothouse, a bubble with the glass screens cracked and half fallen away, sat above the main cabin.

"Put this on," I told Cal. I checked the gas mask. It was free of blood and skull fragments. The leak must have caused the pirates to crash, but even with no pilot, something had brought them back, made them take to the sky even though they'd been smashed to pieces on the desert floor below.

"Thanks," Cal said, his voice tinny and distorted through the filters of the mask. "Now what do we do?"

"We . . ." I looked up at the pilothouse. Blood had painted the console, but the ship was still flying. The balloon bladders were intact, and we had at least a little bit of battery power.

"We should fly," I told him.

"You think we can figure it out?" I could sense Cal's skepticism.

"I mean, we have to," I said. "There's nothing down there to survive on, and Las Vegas is still hundreds of miles away."

I looked out at the desert and the low rumple of mountains in the distance. "We have to," I repeated. "*I* have to, for Dean."

"What if there's nothing there?" Cal asked. "What if this Horatio Crawford is a fraud and there's no way to bring him back?"

"Then at least I will have tried," I told Cal. "And I won't have to wonder anymore if there was something I could have done and didn't. I won't have to go through life missing him more than I already do."

Cal thought for a moment, and I waited, feeling every bit of me vibrate with anxiety. This was the only way. The only way I could try to help Dean.

"Okay," he said at last. "Let's see if we can't get this heap to stay in the air for just a little longer."

5

To the Walled City

I THREW MY ARMS around Cal and hugged him, hard. He grunted but hugged me back. "You know whatever stupid idea you have, I'm on board for it," he muttered. "You're pretty much the only friend I've got besides Bethina."

We climbed to the pilothouse, and I set about trying to figure out the controls. Cal squinted through the cracked windscreen.

"So what were those things back there?"

I ran my fingers over the panel. Dried blood flaked off under my touch and drifted to the scorched deck.

"I don't know," I told Cal. "Have you ever seen anything like them?"

"Never," he said. "Not even down in the Lovecraft sewers."

They could have come from the Mists, but the things that lurked there were generally alive.

I turned on the aether feed experimentally, but it was

dead. We had no navigation systems, just my eyes. The fans clattered, causing more smoke to billow around us and deposit a layer of soot on our exposed skin.

The ship lurched forward when I opened the throttle, and I moved the yoke until the pitch and yaw arrows lined up. I locked the yoke in place and set the compass to true west. At least this way we wouldn't crash. I kept us lined up with the mountains, tracking the sun as it made its way behind them.

"Aoife?" Cal said. "You all right?"

I shook my head. I couldn't get the pirate's face out of my mind, the spray of red, the stench as I'd thrust my hand into his rib cage. I knew in my gut the pirate had been human once, before he'd crashed into the desert. Only to rise again as . . . what?

Looking skyward, I saw the blot of the Gate that would admit the Great Old Ones and move them into the same sphere as the living world, until they landed upon the earth. The blot was the size of a silver dollar now, larger than the sun by half and impossible to ignore.

You did this, it whispered to me. *You're the cause of all of this—the dead rising, the dreams that are driving people mad.*

Crow, the figure who lived in the place of dreams where only a Gateminder could visit, had told me their influence could herald a golden age . . . or the end.

Judging by what had happened on the airship, it was definitely the latter.

Cal squeezed my shoulder. "We'll be all right," he said. "I mean, how hard can it be to get to San Francisco? Not like it's easy to miss."

He thought I was worried about piloting, about finding our way to the West Coast, and I let him think that. Eventually, I'd have to admit to Cal, and to myself, the price I'd paid to get my mother back. The price I might have made the world pay. I didn't know what the Old Ones would do when they arrived, but their influence led me to think it couldn't be anything that would help the world.

The Iron Land was torn enough as it was—the country was in disarray since Draven's disappearance, people were openly defying the Proctors, and those were just the obvious changes.

I stared out the windscreen again, watching the desert pass beneath us and trying not to think about what would happen when we landed.

We flew over Las Vegas in the dark, a glittering handful of jewels flung on the carpet of the desert around it, past the black, mirrored expanse of Lake Mead and over the Hoover Dam, aether rising from the refineries it powered in blue, silver and purple streams that buffeted the airship. It made me feel as if I were inside a vast dome made of light.

I didn't sleep, just sat on the edge of the deck and watched the land glide beneath us while Cal kept an eye on the instruments. I let myself imagine just for a few hours that I'd left my troubles on the ground and when I landed I'd know exactly what to do—about the return of the Old Ones, about getting Dean back, about everything.

The illusion lasted until the airship's balloon bladders

started to lose pressure somewhere over eastern California as the sun was coming up. Relieved that it was at least light out, I started looking for a place to land. Flat land wasn't in short supply—the earth below was barren, and I followed a dirt highway that was little more than jitney tracks carved out of scarred beige dirt, the sunrise already pale and waning as the day started.

My landing wasn't going to win any awards, but I managed to deflate the balloon enough that we simply set down, without needing to tie the ship up and use a ladder to reach the ground. It was all I could have hoped for—I was lucky we hadn't broken to pieces. Reaching San Francisco in the ship had been a pipe dream.

Cal and I stumbled back to the earth, and he squinted up at the sun. "This is cracked. We need to find food and water. And shade." Ghouls were nocturnal creatures—even in human skin, they didn't do well in direct sunlight.

"I know," I said. The road was below us, down a slope covered in scrub and loose gravel. We just had to follow the jitney tracks. "Come on," I said. "We follow the road long enough, we're bound to find someone."

We'd lost everything—my pack, Cal's bags, all of our meager cash. Walking was our only option.

A sign, pockmarked with buckshot, announced that we were fifteen miles from Bakersfield. "We can make it that far," I told Cal. "And then we'll figure something out."

He sighed, but wrapped his shirt around his head to keep off the sun and trudged after me. That was what I liked about Cal: the situation might be dire and he might be hating every minute of it, but he'd stick by me until the journey was done, and he complained a heck of a lot less than my brother would have.

Thinking of Conrad made me think of being in Arkham, what had happened to my father and how it was likely my fault.

I just had to get Dean back, and then I could help Archie. My dad would have to wait. I could deal with only one crisis at a time.

It took us half a day to get to Bakersfield, and we were parched, sweaty and covered in soot and dust by the time we stumbled into a jitney way station.

A fan made lazy, ineffective turns overhead, and the tile walls and floor put me in mind of a doctor's office or a madhouse dayroom, a place where nobody could get too comfortable.

A lunch counter, studded with silver rivets across the front, sat to one side and a ticket window to the other. Since we didn't have any money, I headed for the counter.

The woman behind it regarded us suspiciously from under a severe bun. "Yeah?"

I sat down, and noticed that soot and dust shook off my clothes as I did. Her frown deepened. "I'm sorry," I said. "Could we please have some water?"

She pointed at a hand-lettered sign. "Five cents."

"Oh, come on," Cal said. "We got stranded and we just walked from the back of beyond." He gave her his best gee-whiz look. "We only need one glass. We can share."

The woman pointed again. "Water rationing's been going on for months now. Five cents."

"Forget it," I told Cal, glaring at the woman with at least as much force as the look she gave me. "Some people just aren't helpful."

I looked at the arrival and departure board above the ticket window, and then turned to leave. There was nothing for us here.

"Hey," the clerk said. She was younger but bore a startling resemblance to the witch behind the lunch counter, minus the severe bun and the canyon-sized frown lines.

"What?" I sighed. "We're leaving, all right?"

"No," she said. "You should clean up before you go. In the washroom." She pointed to a blue door in the far wall. "Plenty of water there," she said in a low, conspiratorial way. "Hasn't been filtered, so it tastes like dirt, but it won't do nothin' bad to you."

"Thank you," I said, and meant it.

Washing off and getting a drink sounded like heaven, but I let Cal go first, to spend a little time in a cool room without any windows. I was sure he needed it more than I did.

"You all have an accident?" the ticket girl asked.

"You might say that," I said. "We had a long walk, that's for sure."

"Sometimes folks come in'll give you a few cents for toting their luggage," she said. "Fare to Folsom is only fifty cents, and they have a wire office where you can have someone send you money."

"Thanks again," I said. If carting suitcases was what it took to get moving again, then so be it. I wasn't some snooty rich girl too good to work.

The ticket taker shrugged.

"Just hate to see folks in a bad situation," she said, and went back to counting receipts.

Cal came out, clean of dirt except for directly around his hairline, and I slipped into the washroom.

I stripped to my underwear, washed and then took a long drink. The ticket girl was right—the water was earthy and bitter but cold, and I gulped it down.

I was getting dressed again when I heard a commotion from outside, and Cal shouting. "Aoife, run!"

Fists landed on the washroom door. "Bureau of Proctors!" a male voice bellowed. "Open this door or we'll break it down."

I shut my eyes, leaning my head back against the tile wall. I felt so stupid—kindness of strangers was something that existed only in cheap romance novels and morality plays. In reality, strangers were willing to turn in their own mothers for a favor from the government, or a few dollars for an informant's fee.

"Miss, you hearing me?" the man bellowed. "Come out of there!"

"All right!" I shouted. "I'm coming. Don't shoot."

I opened the door and two Proctors with shock pistols stood outside, business ends pointed at me. I put up my hands.

Sure enough, the ticket girl was peeking over the shoulders of the four-man squad, two of whom had Cal restrained.

"You—" I started, but she silenced me with a look.

"Save it," she said. "This isn't like some fancy city. Out here, you do for yourself or nobody will."

"Dammit, Sadie," her mother snapped. "They weren't doing anything. Just being a nuisance."

"And if they're wanted, we might actually make rent this month," the girl snarled.

"I thought you said you wanted to help me," I told her, meeting her eyes. If I could instill some guilt, so much the better.

"I'm helping myself," she said with a serene smile. "I told you, I hate seeing people in bad situations, especially me."

"You're horrible," I told her as the Proctors handcuffed me. The bite of iron caused a flare of pain in my mind, but I tried to push it away.

"Hey!" Sadie shouted, ignoring me. "Is there a reward for them, or what?"

"Somebody will be in touch," the Proctor grunted, and dragged us out, Sadie squeaking indignation the whole way.

I didn't bother protesting my innocence. As far as I knew, I was still a wanted terrorist in the eyes of the Proctors, and I'd be on my way to a dark hole unless I thought of something fast.

Cal caught my eye as we were loaded into a jitney, one Proctor sitting across from us.

"If you've done nothing wrong, you have nothing to fear," the Proctor said. "If you're wanted, you'll be processed and sent to a central facility. Understand?"

"Better than you know," I muttered as the jitney lurched into motion.

We rattled and shook over the road until we reached a brick building, bleached nearly the same color as the desert around it by dust, wind and time.

Cal squinted as they hauled us out into the sun, but when he started to say something I shook my head. I didn't want to incriminate us any more than I had to.

Maybe everything would be all right. Maybe the panic in my guts wasn't a harbinger of what I knew was coming but a natural reaction to being grabbed by the Proctors.

Maybe, but I knew I was in denial. This was about as bad as things could get, short of us having plunged to our deaths in that nearly destroyed airship.

I couldn't let it paralyze me. I had to stay alert and figure out a new plan. Adapt. That was what my father had tried to teach me, and now that I couldn't rely on him anymore, I had to rely on myself.

The Proctors separated Cal and me, and I was thrown in a holding cell occupied by two other women, both clearly smugglers or thieves of some sort. They were dusty and tired-looking, and I tried to sit well clear and look only at the floor. Out of the corner of my eye, I watched the Proctors move beyond the cells.

These weren't the sharply dressed, brass-buttoned Proctors of Lovecraft. Their uniforms were patched and often had pieces missing. Nobody wore a cap or carried the protective goggles, masks and truncheons the street patrols back home used to break up riots. But they were still organized, unlike the ones in Lovecraft. Still clearly upholding the mission of the Bureau: hunt down and punish anyone they considered a heretic or a criminal. All things considered, my day could have been going a lot better.

An aethervox droned about contamination levels in the

Mojave Desert, and it caused an odd sensation in me to think that there were still people who believed every strange thing in this world was caused by the necrovirus, the Proctor's fable to explain what happened when humans touched other worlds, and when creatures from those worlds came into the land of Iron.

A placard on the far wall read GREY DRAVEN, BUREAU DIRECTOR, but someone had torn down Draven's portrait, leaving only a lighter spot on the brick where the photograph had hung.

Thinking about how furious Draven would be made me smile in spite of myself.

"You," a female Proctor said, gesturing at me. "Up."

She took me to a room lit by a single aether globe, patted me down, made me strip to my underwear and put on a scratchy gray uniform shirt and skirt and then dragged me into an interrogation room and sat me in a hard wooden chair eerily similar to the ones in the headmaster's office at Lovecraft Academy.

After a time, a Proctor wearing an unbuttoned black jacket and a gray undershirt came in, and regarded me wearily.

"I know who you are," he said, passing a piece of vellum across the desk, "so don't bother denying it."

My face stared back at me, a blowup of a class photo from the Academy. AOIFE GRAYSON. WANTED FOR TERRORISM, SEDITION, SABOTAGE AND ACTS OF TREASON.

It was an impressive list. I sighed and looked up at the Proctor, who appeared as if he wished he was doing anything else.

"So?" I said. "What now?"

"Now you'll be transported to San Francisco to stand trial," he said, and formally arrested me.

I was made to change again—this time into dark gray coveralls bearing a prisoner number, and along with Cal, boarded a jitney filled with other silent and similarly gray-suited convicts.

When the Proctor who'd searched me stopped at my seat, she grinned. "These others are mostly headed for San Quentin for detention," she said. "But not you, missy. You're going straight to Alcatraz."

She kept talking, droning off the rules of the transport, but I wasn't listening. I was too busy feeling frantic. I'd heard of Alcatraz, the island in the San Francisco Bay where the great Engine turned below the rock, powering the entire city. Where eerie blue lights were said to emanate from the compound built atop it, and where if you went as a prisoner, you never returned.

It was the greatest Proctor stronghold in the country, and I was barreling directly toward it.

6

The Island of Pelicans

It took us almost a full day to reach San Francisco, even as the jitney cruised along, overtaking all other vehicles we encountered. We were allowed off twice for rest-stop breaks, during which people jeered at us. A small, sticky-faced boy threw what remained of his sandwich at Cal, who bared his full ghoul smile and sent the brat screaming back to his mother.

I'd been a prisoner before, less than nothing in the eyes of all the people around me, and it was the same vile feeling I remembered from when Draven had locked me up in Lovecraft. I didn't even feel like a person anymore, but like something on display, and the closer we came to the city, the sicker to my stomach I got.

When at last we reached the outer wall, I craned my neck to look out the window. I was finally here, and I couldn't have been more helpless or less thrilled.

San Francisco was built atop a series of hills that plunged down into the deep, velvety water of the bay. I noticed a conical white tower atop the largest hill, fingers of aether drifting to and from it. Communications, I decided, and maybe power, a line running under the water directly to the engine.

Gentle fog ringed the hills like lace collars on refined women, and small beetle-backed streetcars ran on cables up and down the hills to charging stations glowing with green aether. They looked like lampreys in a stormy sea, their green lights drifting among the fog-capped hills.

The wall itself wasn't much to look at. Iron spikes, rusty from the sea air, studded the outside, and ghoul traps, spitting aether fire laced with sulfur, ringed the base.

The gate was manned by a set of Proctors at ground level and two gunners with hunting rifles high in the tower. Nothing was getting into the city unseen, that much was certain.

I heard the horn of an airship as it drifted overhead sending out cables to tie up at the aether-ringed white tower I'd spotted earlier, and I felt an almost unbearable sense of longing. That should have been me. Not this, shackled in a filthy jitney with iron biting harder into my wrists and my sanity with every passing second.

The Proctors handed over some paperwork to the guards, and, as one, all three turned to stare at me.

Get a good look, I thought. *Everybody stare at the big, bad, underweight teenage girl. A supervillain if there ever was one.*

Cal was shuffled off the jitney with the other prisoners, but when I rose to follow, the guard pushed me back.

"Oh no," she said. "Don't you remember? You're a special case, Miss Grayson. You're going right across the bay." She grinned. "To Alcatraz."

The journey to Alcatraz Island felt nearly as interminable as the jitney ride, though it was in fact much shorter. The jitney moved at a snail's pace through streets thronged with crowds, up and down hills so steep and sharp they jutted from the earth like razor blades.

Steam and smoke that smelled like a million different flavors coated my skin and tongue.

A bottle banged off the side of the jitney and exploded, scattering shards of glass across the roads, and the guard leaned out and let off a shot above the crowd's head with her shock pistol.

There were screams, and all at once we had a clear path through the crowd.

"Damn hooligans," the guard muttered. "You'd think this was the Wild West, not the biggest city in California."

I remembered what Dean had said about San Francisco, that, unlike Lovecraft, the wall kept people too close together, that there often wasn't enough food or enough aether or power, and that there were parts of the city where even the Proctors wouldn't set foot.

Lovecraft had old sewers infested with ghouls, but at least I didn't feel like I was closed in with a hundred thousand malcontents who could explode at any second.

We reached a pier, and I was transferred to a barge that stank of fish. More Proctors surrounded me in a tight ring, and all I could see was the rough water ahead and the glowing lamps strung across the Golden Gate Bridge.

The water grew rougher, and the Proctors seemed nervous, muttering and shifting the grips on their guns. Before us, I saw a great, glowing body slide to the surface and then duck back under. Not man-made aether, not running lights on a submersible, but something organic, a luminescence that kept pace with the boat until we reached the dock.

I'd seen a leviathan before, but it had been angry and starving, driven close to shore by the blast of the Lovecraft Engine. That leviathan had terrified me, but this one was different—it stared at us out of its many eyes studded all along its lean body, and then, with a keening cry, dipped back below the waves with a splash. I could tell we mattered less to it than the pull of the currents.

My shoulder had started to throb at its approach, the shoggoth venom recognizing its own kind.

"Will you look at that?" said my female guard. "Never seen one that close."

"It's that damn dot in the sky," said another. "Been calling every monster out of the shadows. Must have something to do with the necrovirus."

The woman snorted. I had to wonder how many of the Proctors even believed the lie.

The dock at Alcatraz wasn't much to look at—I'd expected it to be far more intimidating. It was a simple wood pier; the only thing making it remarkable was the steel cage enclosing the walkway to a small white-brick building, probably to keep anyone from making a desperate leap over the side into the freezing bay. Knowing the leviathan was down there was plenty of deterrent for me, and I was shoved into the brick building, where the Proctors searched me again and blasted me with a controlled stream of steam to knock any parasites off me. It was unbearably hot, and then incredibly cold as the steam left moisture beads all over my exposed skin, dampening my clothes. I shivered, my teeth chattering.

"What's going to happen to me?" I asked my guard.

She narrowed her eyes. "Use your imagination."

I watched the tall square structure in front of us as we crossed the courtyard. Bars on the windows, the clang of cell doors echoing from inside and the general chatter of a lot of people locked in too small a space.

If you weren't looking too closely, you'd have thought it was a normal prison. But I spotted wires running to a central hub on the roof and down to each bar. Electrified iron—to keep prisoners in or something else out, I couldn't tell.

I also saw a flash from the top floor, blue light that flickered rhythmically and then shut off, over and over again. Each time it happened, the wires on the windows would buzz. Something was draining enormous power, and I had the distinct feeling I was about to find out what it was.

The guard handed me off to another woman, who processed my paperwork and then shoved me into a cell. When the door closed, the darkness was absolute.

I sat down, feeling my way to a dry spot, and put my head on my knees.

This could not have gone worse. I had completely failed. Failed Dean, failed my mother and father both.

I let a few tears leak out of my eyes, because if I didn't, I was going to start screaming like many of the voices around me.

I wasn't lost yet, I thought. I still had my sanity, at least until the iron lacing this place started to poison me.

Before it did, though, I could find a way out. I might not have been strong, and I might not have had much in the way of the sort of skills Dean had traded in—subterfuge and picking locks and being unseen—but I could use my wits to get out of this mess.

I breathed in, but the stench just reminded me where I was and I started to sob again.

"Don't cry."

The voice was a whisper, but I shrieked, not expecting anyone to be with me in this dark hole.

"Hello?" I said.

"Don't cry, Aoife," the voice whispered again.

I swallowed hard. My scar wasn't throbbing, so I knew it wasn't a monster, but a disembodied voice was never *not* going to be unsettling.

"How do you know my name?"

"I know a lot of things," the voice said. "Been here a long while. Long before the Storm. Saw it all."

"Are you . . . ," I started to ask, but my question was answered when the same kind of unearthly glow the leviathan had manifested sprang to life in the corner of the cell.

A small girl, younger than me, sat there, dressed in the sort of clothes you only saw in old magazines: pinafore, bloomers, a giant floppy bow holding back meticulous barrel curls.

She would have looked pretty normal, if out of date,

except that she was almost entirely translucent, like one of the reels for an Edison lamp held against a light. She had the same oily, filmy quality, like she might flicker out of existence at any second.

"I'm dead," she said in confirmation. "I died right here, in this room."

"You don't seem too upset about that," I ventured. I stayed where I was, not sure if I even *could* move.

Ghost stories were popular among my old classmates at the Academy, but they'd always been just that—stories. Things to scare one another with that wouldn't get us locked up for heresy, like stories of the Fae, or magic, or anything that wasn't based in science would.

Ghosts, nobody could quantify. I'd certainly never expected to be sitting here talking to one.

Then again, I'd never expected to be locked up in the worst Proctor prison in the country, either.

"Of course I am," she said. "I was the daughter of a guard. I had diphtheria, and I was in a fever haze. I heard a voice calling me, calling me. . . . In the fever, I thought it was an angel sent to take me home. But then I was here, in front of this door. I went in and I collapsed. Prisoners found me, shut my eyes, watched over me until my father came. But it was too late. This place drags you down. It always has."

"How old were you?" I asked.

She sighed. "Just nine. But they always said I was bright for my age."

"You talk to everyone who gets thrown in here?" I asked. Normal conversation was the only way I could keep my mind from screaming, *There's a dead girl, right in front of you, talking, and you need to panic.*

"Oh no," she said, and gave a smile that was a black razor slash across her face—a strange oily substance dribbling from her mouth, her eyes, her nostrils. "Just you, Aoife Grayson. Just you."

Her voice wasn't a little girl's voice any longer. Had never been, I realized. She wasn't a sad little ghost trapped here, dead of diphtheria. She was a recording, left in this place by someone who knew I'd be here.

"Why me?" I said again, a whisper this time. I was terrified. I'd traveled by the Gates, hopping worlds, and I'd spent enough time around the Fae that their cold skin and silver smiles hardly bothered me.

This, though—this wasn't Fae or human, just pure malice talking to me, using my name.

"Because you're looking for something you cannot have," the ghost hissed. "You're traveling to a place none of the living should go. And if you come any closer to the cold flame of death, it will burn you, Aoife Grayson."

She flickered, and was so close to me we could have shared breath, if she'd had any. "Then you'll come and you'll stay," she growled at me in a voice that sounded like rusty nails raking across bones. "You'll stay in the Deadlands, just like all the rest who came before."

She grabbed me by the chin, and her mouth was full of teeth, black lava glass bursting from her little-girl mouth. She was going to tear out my throat, and there was nothing I could do. Nothing except let pure panic flood my brain.

The cell door opened with a clang, and I screamed as light flooded in, burning the ghost out of existence and causing my pupils to react painfully.

"Come on," a guard said, grabbing my arm. He was tall and rail-thin. I hadn't seen him before. I struggled, still sure the thing in the cell was going to burst from the shadows and sink its teeth into me.

"Be quiet," he snarled. "Come."

Once I realized I was being taken out of the cell, I practically ran. The guard clamped down on my arm.

"Stay calm," he said. "Act normal."

I twisted my head to look at him, and I saw the flicker as his features changed, just for a second.

"Cal?" I hissed.

"I said, act normal," he growled, and moved me to the side as two Proctors passed, holding flashlights and passkeys, doing cell checks.

"Where you taking the terrorist?" one asked, curiosity lighting his eyes. "They got her in the box already?"

"Top floor," Cal said authoritatively.

"What, already?" said the other. "They ain't even gonna ask her any questions?"

"Hey, I don't give the orders," Cal said, and I could smell the sweat seeping through his ill-fitting uniform. I decided I didn't want to know where he'd gotten it.

"I hear that," said the first, and they walked on.

Cal exhaled. "That was close. Conrad's waiting down at the dock. We have to be fast, before they realize anything's amiss."

"Conrad?" I blinked in shock. It took me a moment to realize the only way my brother could have known where we were going, or that we'd been caught and taken to Alcatraz, was if he'd been following us. And for him to follow us, Cal would have had to tell him our eventual destination.

"I cannot believe him," I said. "Or you. Of all the bone-headed, stupid risks to make Conrad take . . . He doesn't even have a Weird, Cal! He could be in real danger coming after us!"

"Shut up," Cal said. "You're a prisoner, remember? Act like you're afraid of me."

I lowered my eyes, realizing he was right. If I wanted out, I had to act obedient. And Conrad might not have been able to change his skin or create Gates, but the plain fact was, he was outside the prison and we weren't. I was going to give my brother the largest hug. Right after I slapped him for taking such a huge chance and putting himself in real danger.

Cal and I hustled down what seemed an endless maze of halls, taking sharp rights and lefts, while the entire time my heart was screaming that at any moment this was all going to end with a bullet or the zap of a shock pistol.

Cal and I came to a mesh-enclosed staircase, which led down, into darkness, or up, toward the pulsing blue light.

This close, I could discern another sound over the buzz-ing of electric current—screaming. It was so high and sus-tained I'd taken it to be background noise, but it was the droning cry of a creature in unbearable pain.

Cal's nostrils flared and he began to shake. I couldn't move, shackled as I was, so I nudged him with my elbow. "What's wrong?"

"I know that sound," he whispered. "I remember that sound. . . ."

Before I could stop him, he was up the stairs, leaving me to follow awkwardly.

I had some inkling of what had Cal so upset, but nothing could have prepared me for what we saw when we crested the stairs and came to a small room at the top of the cell blocks.

Six tables were arranged in a circle, the sort of tables I'd often seen in the madhouse while visiting Nerissa—hard enamel surfaces fitted with leather straps to keep the patients still. A wheel and spring on the underside allowed the tables to be tilted this way or that.

My stomach lurched as I looked at the ghouls strapped to the tables. They didn't look like Cal—they had the gray sagging skin, stringy hair and vaguely canine faces of depth-dwelling ghouls, ones that had rarely seen the light.

Attached to each of their heads was a metal apparatus, and blue light pulsed from a glowing globe suspended from the ceiling. Each time it did, symbols projected on a screen flashed before the ghouls' eyes, and they started screaming anew.

I knew we should move, but Cal stood stock-still, shaking. In Lovecraft, Proctors burned ghoul nests, and the stink of burning hair and flesh sometimes wafted on the wind as far as the Academy.

But this was different—this wasn't something I had to imagine and could forget if I needed to. The ghouls were alive, and they were in pain.

I hadn't had the best encounters with Cal's more blood-thirsty brothers, but his pack, and Cal himself, had never given me any reason to hate ghouls.

Cal snarled, and I could see his human face start to slip away. He could only "take the skin" when he wasn't under stress or in pain, and when he started to lose control, the real Cal came out.

Distracted as we both were, it was a wonder I saw the flash of white before a doctor wearing a long coat leaped from the shadows beyond the table and slashed at Cal with a scalpel. It caught the arm of his too-big Proctor uniform and he howled in pain, lashing out blindly.

The doctor danced out of the way. He was screaming something, but it was hard to hear over the constant cries of pain, the buzzing of the current and the hiss of aether powering the whole thing.

Even shackled, I knew I had to do something. Cal was too angry and panicked to defend himself, so I slammed into the doctor from the side, using all my weight. My scarred shoulder, where the muscles had never quite been the same, gave a scream of pain as loud as the keening ghouls'.

We both went over, but the doctor had his hands free and got on top of me. When he saw my face, he blinked. "You're—" he started, but I snapped my forehead up and into his nose. It was a desperate move, and my skull rang with pain. I felt elated, though, when the doctor yelped and fell back, dropping the scalpel.

Cal appeared at my shoulder. "Stay down," he snarled, in a voice I'd only heard him use once before, "unless you want worse than that."

I didn't want to look at him, but I forced myself to. This was my friend. He wouldn't hurt me.

I hoped.

Cal's jaw was long, and his teeth were longer, poking over his lips. The uniform had shredded at the pressure points where his spiny limbs had changed. His eyes were pure gold, pupilless and inhuman. I held out my hands to him, in what I hoped was a slow and nonthreatening gesture. *This is Cal*, I reminded myself. *If you don't panic, he won't panic.*

"Can you unlock these?" I asked. "I think the secret of our daring escape is out."

Cal fumbled for the keys, his long veiny fingers having a hard time grasping the tiny tool.

I took it from him, and our skin brushed. My shoulder throbbed, the scar reminding me that even if I trusted him with my life, Cal was still a monster in this moment.

As my shackles unlocked, the doctor sprang up again and made a beeline for me. I turned, gripping one side of the shackle and swinging the other at his head. It connected with his temple and he dropped, his body making a wet, heavy sound against the cement floor.

"He doesn't listen," I told Cal. He was already starting for the tables, though, and paid me no attention.

"We have to help them," he said. "We have to do something."

"All right," I agreed tentatively. "But if we free them, they're going to attack me." I pointed at the sharp rib bones and cracked lips of every ghoul. "They're starving."

I wanted to help them—truly I did—but I would be no good to anyone, Cal included, if I were in pieces.

Cal ignored me, though, and I held tight to the shackles.

Even though they'd eventually be poison to me, I wasn't about to leave myself defenseless.

He freed each ghoul gently and started to unhook the steel contraption on the closest one's head, but then stopped. He went even paler, and gripped his stomach.

"I can't," he said. "They're bolted in."

I shut my eyes, forcing myself to breathe normally, and then approached. The ghoul on the table moaned, translucent eyelids fluttering.

"No way out," he muttered to Cal. *"They tried to put pictures in my brain. Tried to make me into a killer. For the humans. Tried to make me take their orders. All of us. The pictures are in our brain."*

I looked at Cal, whose face slackened. A cloudy tear worked its way down his cheek.

"I'm so sorry this was done to you," he murmured. "I'll get you out of here."

"No," the ghoul croaked. *"Nothing to be done. You have to help us."*

"I am," Cal told him. "I am helping you. I'll get this off somehow and you can get out of here."

"NO," the ghoul gasped. *"You need to end it. We're not going anywhere. The pictures, they talk to us. Tell us to kill our own kind for the Proctors."* He looked up at Cal. *"You have to flip the kill switch. End it now."*

He pointed at a circuit panel with a master switch, one that I could tell would release enormous voltage if flipped.

Understanding dawned on Cal's face, and he started to shake his head, but the ghoul on the table snarled. *"You owe it to us,"* he said. *"We're brothers, under the skin. We don't want to live like this."*

104

I touched Cal on the other arm. "It would be the kindest thing," I whispered, and meant it. Whatever the Proctors had done to these ghouls, it was cruel and had destroyed their minds beyond repair. Trapped as they were in this infernal machine, death would be the kindest way out.

Cal nodded at the ghoul and then at me, and then walked toward the circuit board.

"I'm sorry," I told the ghoul. "So sorry about everything." Was this where I'd been headed, I wondered? This room, to be brainwashed into being whatever the Proctors wanted me to be? Or tortured? Or simply to stay in that cell until I starved?

Who knew? And who cared? I'd known the Proctors were evil, but I'd never had it driven home quite so thoroughly how sick and disgusting the entire system and the lie it supported were.

Maybe the Great Old Ones coming was the best thing that could happen. Clean slate, start over. Wipe the Proctors and their ideas from the face of the world.

The ghoul grabbed my arm with his clawed hand and I shrieked, startled, as he gasped out a few words at me.

"*You,*" the ghoul said. "*You, the destroyer. The one who walks. He knows you. His great eye sees everything. There is nothing you can hide, nothing you can do. Stay away,*" he rasped. "*Stay in the light, and keep away from his sign. Do not gaze upon it. Do not even speak his name.*"

"Who?" I demanded. "Who are you talking about?"

"*He who lives beyond,*" the ghoul whispered. "*The enemy of the one who walks. Never meet. Never let him gaze into your soul.*"

Cal threw the switch. All six of the ghouls gasped and

twitched, but they stopped after a time and, one by one, went still.

The ghoul's grip slackened, and his hand fell away from me, but I stayed where I was, frozen to the spot, until Cal grabbed me and I realized the ghouls' screaming had been replaced by the whoop of alarms.

"Time to go," Cal said. He was human again, his face set into the sort of grim expression I'd hoped never to see on my happy, optimistic best friend.

We ran down the stairs and all the way to the docks. The source of the alarm was clearly the ghouls' room, and Proctors shoved past us without taking much notice. I kept my face shielded, and Cal slung his Proctor jacket over me and gave me his hat, so we looked as if we'd been rousted out of our bunks rather than escaped from a cell.

The boat Conrad had stolen, a small Proctor launch, was bobbing at the dock, and he stared at us as we jumped aboard.

"You can never manage to make a quiet exit, can you, Aoife?" he said. "I'm just sitting here and suddenly the entire place lights up. Are we going to get shot at?"

"Not if you drive the boat," I said. "And by the way, I'm happy to see you, too."

Conrad turned the boat around and pushed us out into the bay. He gave me a quick smile that let me know he wasn't really mad, and I had the sneaking suspicion he might even be enjoying himself a little. I decided that he deserved to forget about what had happened to Archie for a little while, and I surely was glad to see him.

Conrad opened up the throttle and Alcatraz retreated,

becoming only points of light behind us, indistinguishable from the leviathans roaming the bay.

Cal was silent, and I was equally mum, wrapping my arms around myself to guard against the chill and spray.

Relieved as I was to escape, and happy as I was that we'd all made it back toward the city, I couldn't shake the ghoul's words from my mind, and the terror they instilled within me was positively unnatural.

That made two messages now about what awaited me in the Deadlands, should I manage the crossing. Nothing specific, but that just made it worse. The phrase played over and over, like a broken aethervox, as the boat bounced across the waves toward the light and steam and life of the city.

"He who lives beyond," the ghoul had whispered in my ear. *"Enemy of the one who walks."*

Chinatown

WE PULLED UP to a rotting pier surrounded by sea lions sleeping on the decrepit platforms and long, thin boats lashed together to make seagoing homes. In the distance, a junk drifted just offshore, and I could hear music floating across the water.

"Only unguarded pier in the city that I could find," Conrad said. "Earthquake put a gap in the wall, and the local tongs control access."

"How do you know that?" Cal said, hopping out and tying up the boat. He was destroyed, I could tell from his posture and his voice, but I knew Cal, and knew he wasn't about to let Conrad see it. He'd always looked up to my brother, seen him as the stronger one, even though personally I'd always thought Cal was—he had a resilience at the core that no human I'd met had ever possessed. He could weather any storm and keep going. Most days, I wished I had his strength.

"I've had a day to poke around," Conrad said. "It's amazing what a little cash and a clean-cut face can get you in this town. Everyone says Chinatown is a place to lie low and not be seen, so that's where I headed after I got Cal." He helped me onto the dock. "We better ditch this blackbird gear," he said, unbuttoning his Proctor jacket and shoving it into an oil drum at the end of the dock. "Proctors aren't exactly welcome here."

I looked at the wall ahead, shattered and cracked just as Conrad said. Beyond, I could see red light and smell thick smoke, sweet and savory at the same time. Steam drifted above the wall, the same crimson, as if we were walking into a giant cooking pot.

Dean had said Chinatown had been his favorite place in the city. I wasn't as quick on my feet or as street-smart as he'd been, but I could manage. It made me feel a little better that we'd ended up in his old haunt, his favorite spot, as if I could pick up a glimpse or a whisper of him, even though he was gone. But not for long. He was coming back.

At the wall, two Chinese men wearing suits and silk ties and hefting machine guns stopped us. "What's your business?" one said, glaring at us. He had a thin mustache that made him look even more suspicious. Aside from the gangster suit and antique weapon, he would have made a fantastic Proctor.

"We're just passing through," Conrad said.

"And bringing trouble with you." One of the men spit. "Piss off, *gwai lo*. We don't need your kind."

"We're not here to cause trouble," I said, leaving off the part about how Cal and I had just escaped from the Proctor prison. "We're in the city to get a friend of mine back."

The second said something in Chinese, and the first snapped at him. Then they stepped aside.

"Fine, crazy girl," said the first. "You want in so bad, go ahead."

I started to walk forward, keeping my eyes down, but he stopped me with a hand on my arm. I sucked in a breath, afraid I was going to have to fight him off. "Your friend," he said. "If he's inside the wall, in this part of town, he's probably dead."

I met his eyes. They were flat and black, eyes that had seen so much they were simply mirrors now, with nothing behind them. I knew my own held the same emptiness. "No *probably* about it," I said. "Now, do you want to take your hand off me?"

He moved aside, one eyebrow skating up, and I stepped around him. "Thank you."

"Don't thank me," he said. "You go in there, you ain't coming out again."

"All right," Conrad said when we'd passed through the broken wall, past a knot of vendors and carts hawking food and cheap jewelry and porters trying to get work guiding us to various hotels. "We need to stop and regroup. What's this crazy idea you were telling Cal about that involves going to the Deadlands?"

I turned to shout at Cal, and he spread his hands to placate me. "I had to let Conrad know how urgent this was," he said. "He didn't want to leave your father."

"We shouldn't be arguing in the street," Conrad said, and I saw the obvious interest on the faces of passersby. We stood out, three non-Chinese young people in a street full of Chinese residents just going about their business, and sooner or later the wrong person was going to notice us. That couldn't happen, not until I'd had a chance to scour the city for Nerissa's doctor and find out what he knew.

Cal pointed to a teahouse with signs in Chinese and English proclaiming it the Jade Monkey. "In there," he said. "It's quiet."

I didn't want to stop—I wanted to find this man my mother had told me about and get it over with. But I could tell from the set of Conrad's shoulders that he wasn't going anywhere, and I was going to have to convince him that this was what I needed to do.

I let him and Cal lead me across the street. The red light we'd seen came from hundreds of lanterns strung between the thin, encroaching buildings of Chinatown. Red silk glowed like living things floating in the steam that reached from the manhole covers and grates scattered haphazardly across the rutted street.

Shouts and cries and a dozen languages floated around my ears, but I felt safe in the throng. I was anonymous here. Nobody cared, and I relaxed for the first time since Cal and I had boarded the airship.

I could see why Dean had loved it here. This place was like him, alive and hotheaded and unpredictable.

The Jade Monkey had ornate wooden furniture, low cushions to sit on, and a censer belching sweet smoke toward the ceiling. Statues of dragons and foo dogs looked down at us from alcoves, their blank ceramic eyes catching the low light and seeming to spring to life.

A figure paused outside the glass but then moved on,

and I finally allowed myself to relax. The Proctors wouldn't come here. Nobody was going to recognize me, take up the cry of "destroyer" that I hated, whether it was pejorative or worshipful.

"Tea, please," Conrad said to the woman who approached. She was wearing a smart dress and had her hair done up.

"Maybe some food, too?" she said. "You look hungry."

I thought back to the girl at the jitney station in Bakersfield who had betrayed us. But I *was* hungry—starved, in fact—so I nodded.

"Mm-hmm," she said, as if it had been completely obvious we'd say yes. "Be right back."

"Now," Conrad said, turning to me, "explain why you ran off to follow some idea that's obviously suicide."

"Explain why you followed me when you're putting yourself in far more jeopardy," I countered. Conrad always acted like he knew best simply by virtue of being older, and it always got my back up.

"Because when my kid sister runs off, it's my job to bring her back."

"I'm doing this for Dean, Conrad," I said. "It's the only way. I have to make up for what I did. It's my fault he got shot, and Nerissa said . . ." I drifted off, not able to continue my train of thought. My mother's information was probably just a flight of fancy, but it was all I had.

Conrad rubbed his forehead and then spread his hands out on the table, a move that reminded me too much of our father. "Aoife, you have to know that it can't be real. To visit the Deadlands, you have to be dead." He moved

112

one hand subtly, to cover mine. "I don't want you to be dead."

I felt a stab in my gut then. Conrad could be a pain. He was vain and superior and had a bad temper, but he was my brother, and I'd never doubted for a second that he loved me.

I couldn't say that about anyone else.

I turned my hand to give Conrad's a squeeze. "I'll be careful," I promised.

"How can you be careful if you're dead?" Conrad demanded. "This is exactly the kind of thinking that led to this whole mess, that led to that hole in the sky and our father being in a coma."

"Hey," Cal said. "If it weren't for Aoife, you'd still be hiding in the Mists and I'd still be under the thumb of the Proctors. She saved us both from that."

Quickly as I'd come to feel guilty about doing all of this to Conrad, anger replaced it, like flame turns water to steam.

"No," I said to Cal. "Let him get it out. No secrets between us, Conrad." I fixed him with a glare. "If you've got a problem, lay it on the table."

Conrad's lip twitched, the nervous tic he got when things weren't going his way. "I never should have sent you that letter." He sighed. "I was scared, and I made a bad decision."

He might as well have pulled back his hand and slapped me, because that was what it felt like. The letter—the one that had touched off my leaving the Academy, finding out what my family could do, encountering Tremaine—had been so simple. *Find the witch's alphabet. Save yourself.* A desperate plea from Conrad to stave off the iron poisoning that had consumed him, to free him from the Mists.

"So I should have stayed in Lovecraft?" I whispered. "I should have gone mad, just like our mother?"

"No!" Conrad snapped. "No . . . I just meant . . . you weren't ready. You let Tremaine sway you and I couldn't help you, because if I'd left the Mists he'd have found me, too."

There it was. The unspoken ball of anger and resentment between us finally had a name. Conrad blamed me for falling for Tremaine's tricks. Even though I'd tried to fix it. Even though there was no way I could have known the Fae were liars.

"You've got some nerve," I told Conrad quietly. I felt like turning over the table, throwing my tea in his face and storming out, but I wasn't one to give in to my rages.

"Do I?" he said. "I love you, Aoife, but you caused a lot of this, and I take partial blame because you didn't know about anything involving our family, and you weren't ready to fend off the Fae. I might not have a Weird, but at least I was prepared for the truth."

"Not because of that," I said. "That's all true. I let Tremaine trick me." I stood, smoothing my hands over the rough uniform the Proctors had put me in on Alcatraz. "You've got nerve for pretending that if it had been you he was offering the bargain to, you wouldn't have done the exact same thing."

I started to leave, quietly and without a tantrum. I could scream once I was out in the street. Cal moved to stop me, but before he could, I was intercepted by the waitress, holding a bevy of plates piled with steaming meats and vegetables.

I seethed. Conrad was incapable of seeing that he would also have taken the Fae's bargain. And I seriously doubted he would have tried so hard to set his mistake right after the fact, all the way up to voluntarily going to the Brotherhood and using Tesla's gate to the realm of nightmares. Bargaining with the Old Ones. Any of what I'd endured.

It made me sad, in an odd way, to know we were so fundamentally different that we'd never again be a family the way we had been when we were kids.

But then, that was what happened when you grew up. You found out that people you trusted weren't who they said they were, and that big brothers you idolized were painfully human.

It was the worst feeling in the world, and I waved the plate away when the waitress offered it to me. "I lost my appetite."

"Aoife," Conrad started. "Don't get upset. Don't be like that just because you don't like the truth."

I pointed my finger at him and gave him my worst glare, one that I'd first seen framed by Grey Draven's angular face. "Don't start with me, Conrad."

"Listen," the waitress said. "I hate to interrupt, but there's two *gwai lo* across the street who've been staring a hole in this place since you came in. Anybody you know?"

I examined the figures who'd been staring in the teahouse window. Hats pulled low over their faces, long coats, completely nondescript.

The Brotherhood's goons.

"We have to go," I said to Cal and Conrad. "Right now."

"There's a back door," the waitress said. "I don't know who you ticked off, but I got no beef with you. I didn't see anything."

We started for the kitchen as a throng of vendors pushing steaming carts passed, obscuring us from the Brotherhood for a few seconds.

"One more thing," I said to the waitress. "I'm looking for a scientist. His name is Horatio Crawford. He does experiments with the dead. Have you heard of anyone like that anywhere in the city?"

Her eyes widened, and she took a step away from me. "I don't mess with that stuff," she said. "And I ain't heard of no scientists. You want the dead, you go to the Spiritualist séances, down on Boneyard Row. But I don't mess with that. Dealing with ghosts is bound to make you one yourself."

"Boneyard Row?" I said. "Any particular Spiritualist?"

"I never been, but I hear the best one is Madame Xiang," the waitress said. "Now get out of here before those goons decide to come in."

We wound our way through a cramped and boiling kitchen and popped out into an alley.

"Well, this is perfect," Conrad said. "No money, no plan and the Brotherhood a dozen yards behind us at all times."

"It'll be all right," Cal said. "We can hide." But he was fidgeting, and I knew he wasn't any more optimistic than Conrad.

I wasn't as down in the dumps. I *did* have a plan. "Come on," I said, winding my way between rain barrels and piles of debris.

"Where are we going?" Conrad demanded.

"To see Madame Xiang," I said. "You can come or not. I don't really care." I held his gaze until he dropped it to his shoes. I did care what happened to Conrad, of course—I wasn't heartless. But I couldn't remember the last time I'd been so angry at him, and when we walked, I made sure I was in front so I didn't have to look at him.

Finding Boneyard Row wasn't much of a trick—everyone we asked knew where it was, and pointed us through an encroaching series of row houses, wooden and brick, thrown down seemingly at random and creating narrow alleys and streets teeming with people, carts and the occasional single-vent jitney, its two wheels bouncing over the rutted pavement.

We had to move at the pace of the crowd, and we inched along until one of the brightly hung windows, resplendent with gilt paint, silk curtains and crookedly painted statues of Chinese animals, read MADAME XIANG: SPIRITUAL COMMUNICATIONS FROM BEYOND THE AETHER TO YOU.

The surrounding storefronts all told the same story, but the burly man with a Fu Manchu mustache and long braid manning the door practically dragged us inside.

"Up the stairs and to the left!" he boomed. "Madame is always happy to help those in need, *gwai lo* or not."

"Don't know why they call us that," Cal muttered as our combined weight made the stairs creak and snap.

"It means 'foreigner,'" Conrad said. "It's not very nice."

Madame Xiang's drawing room was done in the same

117

opulent style, walls hung with red silk embroidered with flowers and forest scenes, deer and tigers and the aftermath of their meeting.

A table covered in green velvet sat at the center, a single ornate chair at the head and four chairs arrayed around it.

"Hello?" Cal called, peering cautiously toward the beaded curtain at the far end of the room.

The whole place gave off the air of a carnival—arranged for a specific purpose, but not real. I'd heard stories about Spiritualists, of course, mostly from Proctor information. They were heretics. Not only did they believe in a soul, an afterlife and magic, but they claimed they could use magic to communicate with the dead.

Believing in ghosts, the Proctors would allow. Believing in magical powers that allowed a living person to commune with the dead essence of their loved ones—that would earn you a fast trip to a heretic prison.

Madame Xiang might be full of it, but hopefully she'd know where Nerissa's doctor was, or if he existed at all.

When she appeared, Cal gave an audible squeak. I felt like joining him, and only a lifetime of not showing my true reactions in self-preservation kept my face composed.

Madame Xiang wore a long blue-and-gold gown weighed down with so much embroidery it bowed her shoulders. Her eyebrows were dramatic, and a tiny crimson bud of a mouth bloomed from the vast wasteland of white pancake makeup on her face. Her hair was done in elaborate loops, and giant glittering hair sticks protruded from the crown, studded with a bloody handful of rubies that swung and caught the golden light of the oil lamps.

"Welcome, travelers," she intoned in a perfect British accent. "Do you seek the counsel of spirits this night?"

"We . . . ," I started, but she minced across the room, sat in the largest chair and stuck out feet roughly the size of my fist.

I'd read about foot binding in my history classes, but to see the result was gruesome. I tried not to stare.

"Sit!" Madame Xiang commanded, then rang a small silver bell that she pulled from her voluminous sleeve.

I felt now as if we'd not only walked into a carnival but also gotten on a ride with no end in sight.

A servant appeared. He was enormous—quite possibly the largest fully human man I'd ever seen. So tall he had to duck under the beaded archway, his suit strained at every scam and the tea tray he carried was comically small in his hands.

I didn't know where to look—at Madame's face, at her feet or at this mountain, who set down the tea and retreated.

"Thank you, Fang," Madame said, and smiled at us. "Please. I can discern through the aether that you are weary. Warm yourselves."

We all took a small handleless cup, more to be polite than anything.

The tea was bitter. It reminded me of medicine Nerissa used to force on me when I was feverish and coughing.

"We have a question for you," I said.

Madame waved me away. Her nails were painted gold and shone like eagle talons under the lamps. They looked like they could rip my flesh.

"They all come with questions, but the spirits already know the answers," she said. "Drink! All will be revealed in time."

"No, you don't understand," Conrad said. "We didn't come here for a reading. . . ." He trailed off, and blinked in confusion, looking at Cal and me as if we'd all woken up in a particularly gaudy bad dream.

Worry started deep in my mind and quickly blossomed into alarm. Conrad's words sounded as if they came to me down a long tunnel, and were drowned out by the booming of Madame's precise English syllables.

"Just relax, dear hearts," she said. "It's nothing fatal. Just a little nip to help you sleep."

Too late, I recognized the taste hiding under the bitter tea. Medicine, yes, but the kind Nerissa used to help herself sleep. Strong opiates that would tumble you down a tunnel of dreams as quickly as you could swallow it.

"You . . . ," I slurred, but the horrible room tilted sideways, and I felt the faint impact of my body hitting the dusty Persian carpet.

Madame approached and nudged me with one of her horror-feet. "Don't worry, my sweet," she intoned as black whirlpools consumed my vision. "It will all be over soon enough."

When I woke up, I saw a much less nightmarish version of Madame Xiang standing over me. Her hair was done in short, fashionable curls. My drug-addled mind realized she'd probably been wearing a wig before.

Her makeup, too, was chic and light, though I could see a white rim where she'd wiped off the pancake stuff.

"Awake?" she said, and smiled at me. "Good. Beginning to think I gave you too much."

I tried to stay calm and see if I was tied up. I wasn't, but as my vision cleared I saw that Fang stood in front of the only door, arms folded, staring at me impassively. I didn't see anyone else, and hoped that Conrad and Cal had fared better than I had with the drugged tea. I still felt as if I were seasick on the deck of a ship.

"You . . . ," I started, but then thought better of it. She was fully aware of what she'd done, and I didn't have the strength to be righteously angry. Mostly, I was just relieved that I wasn't back among the Proctors.

"I've got good news," Madame Xiang said, "and I've got bad news." She was still wearing the robe, but she moved normally, and I saw that the bound feet were prosthetic, an illusion furthered by the folds of her robe.

"Good news," she said. "You and your friends are young and strong. That means Fang won't just dump you in the bay, or leave you to wander out into the street in a haze and get rolled for your vital organs. There are degenerates out there, you know."

"And the bad news?" My mouth felt like cotton and my mind felt like someone had used it for batting practice. I wondered what could be coming if *that* was the good news. I didn't like the way Madame was looking at me, but there was nothing I could do. I was weak and dizzy, and I knew from when Nerissa used laudanum to help her sleep that it took hours to wear off.

121

"The bad news," Madame said, patting her curls, "is that none of you have any money. So I'm going to have to make back the time I took with you some other way."

She gave me a nudge and a sweet, motherly smile. "What were you thinking coming to the Boneyard with no money, dear? It's positively silly."

"I . . ." I licked my lips, trying to work some feeling back into my face. "I didn't want a reading. I want Crawford—the Death Doctor."

"That sad drunk?" said Madame. "Why on earth does a sweet girl like you want him?" She stood, removing the robe and revealing a smart narrow-skirted day dress, stockings and subtle gold jewelry. She stepped into black pumps and affixed a small white hat to her hair.

"I lost . . . someone," I said. I rolled my eyes around, but I didn't see Cal or Conrad. I heard a snore, though, and that made me feel a bit better. At least one of them was still alive.

"Oh?" Madame paused, taking her hat back off. "I was going to go meet with the leader of our tong to negotiate a price for the three of you, but now I'm interested. You're actually going to attempt the doctor's journey?"

"I have to go to the Deadlands," I muttered, squinting against the glare of the lights. They seemed to grow brighter with each passing second. "I have to get Dean." The filter that kept me from blurting things out and that connected sentences was broken, that was for sure.

"And who is Dean?" Madame said, sitting back down. Even Fang seemed interested.

"I love him," I said. "It's my fault he's dead."

Madame patted me. "I'm sure that's not true, dear. You're far too young to be causing misery."

"I'm the destroyer," I told her earnestly. I couldn't shut myself up. Damn these drugs. "I'm Aoife Grayson. I blew up the Engine and I made the world end."

"Goodness," said Madame. "I thought that selling you to the tongs would be a great fall, but you're already as low as you can go."

She said something to Fang, and he shrugged.

"Old Ones return," she sighed. "I might be getting soft in my old age, but I'll take you to the doctor, if you promise me one thing in exchange." Her playful smile was nowhere in evidence.

"Sure," I said, feeling incredibly expansive. Why didn't I do more favors for people I barely knew? I had no idea. The laudanum certainly didn't.

"If this actually works," Madame said, "you find my brother and you give him a message for me." She looked away. "He died on the crossing from Hong Kong. Jammed in steerage. He was always a delicate one."

"What should I tell him?"

"Tell him I'm sorry," Madame said. "But it was him or me."

She snapped her fingers at Fang. "Get them something to wake them up," she said, "and then bring the car around." She looked back at me, and I was aware enough now to feel a chill at her perfect but perfectly blank smile.

"Our young lady here has an appointment with the Death Doctor."

To Speak with Spirits

MADAME XIANG'S JITNEY was a long Packard that belched steam from under the hood like a dragon as Fang maneuvered it through the crowded streets.

"Do you do this a lot?" I asked Madame. Cal, Conrad and I were crammed in the back while she sat up front. "Drug and rob people?"

"Only the gullible ones," she said. "I am quite an accomplished medium. My husband and I help the tong often." She gestured as people leaped out of our way. "I think my abilities scare them quite a lot."

We rode another few feet in silence, and then Madame turned to me. "And what about you?" she said. "I hear the destroyer has some fearsome abilities of her own."

"That's just a story," I said curtly. I wasn't about to get into it with a robber medium who worked with a criminal gang. I didn't want this woman to know I had the ability to push aside the very fabric of space and time. I was sure the leader of her tong would love the chance to travel via Gate between the worlds.

As the Packard made its way inch by inch through the crowds, the streets went from rutted to mud to barely there, and the character of the Boneyard changed. Where before the streets had been crowded and smelly but vibrant, now people hunched under overhangs, or peered through windows, faces half-obscured by the night.

A rain started, battering the Packard's roof, and the tidal stench from the mud in the streets smothered all of my senses. Cal coughed and I felt bad for him. It had to be ten times as bad with a ghoul nose.

The houses got worse, too—broken windows, boarded-over doors, women in scant clothing beckoning from upstairs balconies while sharp-faced men guarded the doors and watched the Packard pass, licking their lips with a sort of hunger that made me nervous

At last, we came to a stop, in front of a narrow Victorian row house with a sign across the front announcing it was the Fu Long Junk Shop.

"This is it," Madame said. She lit a cigarette in a long jade holder and waited for Fang to get out and open an umbrella. "Stay close to me," she said. "This is the part of Chinatown the *gwai lo* don't come to. Nobody likes you here."

"Well, I'm not too fond of the smell, so I suppose we're even," Conrad muttered.

Madame regarded him with a raised eyebrow. "You've got a sharp tongue, boyo," she said. "It'd be a shame if someone were to slice it out."

In spite of the nerves I felt prickling all over my skin, into my mind, down to the deepest spots where my Weird lived, I smiled a little. I couldn't help but like Madame. She might have been a charlatan and a gangster, but she clearly didn't give a whit what anyone thought. I'd always wished I could be that straightforward, and let go of the residual fear of saying the wrong thing and inviting scrutiny from teachers or Proctors or whoever was listening.

I climbed out of the car after her and we crossed the street, mud squelching in my boots, and mounted the steps of the shop. Madame rang the bell, jabbing at the enamel button with one of her perfect nails.

After what seemed like hours, as the people in the shadows stared holes in our backs and I waited for one of them to try and follow it up with a knife, I heard clockwork grinding. The door opened, just a crack.

Madame stepped aside and gestured. "I don't go any farther. A sign of respect—we don't cross each other's territories."

She looked up and down the street, and back to where Fang stood glaring beside the Packard. "In my part of town, the tongs keep order, but around here it's lawless. Triad country, bad men from Hong Kong and other places. And Doctor Death is the worst of them." She regarded me, smoke catching raindrops and turning them silver around her head. "You sure you still want this, dear?"

I nodded, looking at the storefront as Conrad and Cal joined me. Cal gave my shoulder a squeeze. "I'm sure," I said.

"Whoever this Dean is, I hope he's worth it," Madame

said, and tripped back to the dry, warm cover of the Packard.

"He is," I said, as I stepped over the threshold. I didn't know much for sure, but I knew that.

Inside the shop, junk was piled to the ceiling, and shadows seemed to move and curl on their own.

I thought of Fae creatures like the strix owl that could shadow a person in darkness, appearing and disappearing at will. I thought of the clockwork ravens employed by the Proctors, with their glowing eyes that saw and transmitted everything they flew over back to their masters.

Neither thought helped me take a step forward.

Cal came to my shoulder and inhaled deeply. "Nobody in here," he said.

I cast around, and saw a green light emanating from the back room. "This way," I whispered. I didn't know why I was being so quiet, but it seemed appropriate.

The shadows followed us, and I did my best to tell myself they weren't really moving, weren't really alive. Still, my heart skittered in my chest.

The green light was spilling out around the edges of a crooked door and its wavy glass window.

I raised a hand and knocked softly. "Hello?"

"Go away." The voice that came from within, rather than a baritone or a spectral growl, didn't sound all that much different from my brother's.

"Excuse me," I said, "but we need to speak with you, Doctor."

I heard a sigh from inside, a long inhale and exhale. An odd, sweet smell tickled my nostrils. It was cloying, almost sticky, and Cal coughed again.

"I said go away," the voice said again. "The doctor is out. He can't help you."

"I lost someone," I said softly. "You're the only one who can help me. I know it's a terrible imposition, but I really do need to speak with you."

Deciding I had nothing to lose, I put my hand on the knob and twisted. Instantly, I heard a sound like a hundred rats rushing through the piles of junk, the patter and chitter of tiny feet and teeth.

"I said," the voice snarled, and now it sounded more like the mad scientist I'd imagined, *"go away!"*

Conrad let out a yelp, and at the same moment I felt cold rushing up my legs and arms, all over my bare skin.

The shadows flowed over me, into my mouth and nose, cutting off my air and my voice.

It hadn't been my imagination. They were alive, these things that looked like patches of darkness. Two-dimensional and velvety, they hissed in my ear, chattered in voices too high to understand, and screamed as they wound skeletal fingers through my hair.

We all fell, and I knocked my head against one of the junk piles. The shadows laughed as they consumed the three of us, and just before my air ran out I heard the voice of one in my ear.

He who waits, he who watches, strips your skin, strings your teeth . . .

Another voice exploded in my ears, giving a loud command in a language I didn't know, and the shadows gave a disappointed cry before they skittered back into the mountains of junk.

Hands sat me up, checked my bloody head, and shined a light in my eyes. I flinched and swatted at it.

"Well, you're alive," said the voice. It was young but rough, as if the owner had seen more in a short time than he had voice to tell. "But on the other hand, you're here. What do you think you're doing, silly girl?"

"I need the doctor," I groaned. "I lost someone. . . ." My head was ringing, and my vision swam, but I picked out the face staring at me. I thought he was a vision for a moment, or a Fae, so perfect were his features.

Then he frowned, and the illusion broke. He was human. Delicate-featured and stunningly handsome, but human. The sort of face you expected to see glowing out at you from a lantern reel, not helping you up from a dirty floor in a bad part of town.

"Dr. Crawford's not seeing anyone," he said. He went over to a switch and aether hissed, illuminating two globes in a six-globe lamp overhead.

"He has to," I said desperately. "I need him more than you can possibly know."

The boy, who despite his authoritative tone didn't look any older or wiser than me, hesitated as Cal and Conrad got up and brushed themselves off. "Look," he said. "I'm sorry about all this—"

"After those things attacked us, the least you can do is let me talk to him," I pleaded. I held his eyes, black and glowing as the rest of him. *"Please."*

"Dammit," he sighed. "All right, all right. I'm a sucker for a girl with a sad story."

He went to the door and rapped hard. "Doc, it's Chang. Your stupid ass almost let these nice people get devoured, so we're coming in."

"I'm in a bad way!" the doctor shouted. "Leave me alone!"

"And whose fault is that?" Chang snapped, pulling out a ring of keys and unlocking the door. "Go in," he said to me. "But he won't be able to help you. He can't even help himself."

The three of us filed in, and I almost choked. The cloying smoke was worse in here, and I could feel it land on my skin and hair, sticking to every bit of me.

At one point the room had been a warren of back offices, half walls of polished wood dividing it into four sections. Postboxes took up one wall, and green glass lamp globes hung from the ceiling like delicate sea creatures.

Two of the cubes were piled with the sort of junk that my father kept in his workshop, which was reassuring. The doctor and my father dabbled in the same sort of worlds after all, and dealt with the same sort of creatures.

One cube held an office awash in papers, crumpled, crushed, ink-stained and scattered everywhere.

The last held a lamp, a table, a cot and a man in a suit several sizes too large for him. He lay on the cot, his arm over his eyes. Empty brown bottles crowded the bedside table, and a long, carved pipe lay at his side like a loyal pet.

The smell got worse the closer I came to him, and I crouched because there was nowhere for me to sit.

"Doctor?"

"Well, I'm not President McCarthy," he grumbled. He looked me over, and his bloodshot eyes and sunken cheeks reminded me of some of the patients at my mother's last madhouse. Worn down, hopeless, just trying to escape into their own minds. It was a look I'd hoped never to see again.

"I need your help," I said.

"Oh no," said the doctor. "I've never heard that before. Not once, in all the time I've been conducting séances."

He picked up a bottle and I caught the same bitter tang that had infused the tea Madame served us. The doctor took a swig of straight laudanum and didn't even flinch before flopping back on the bed.

"Well, I can't do it anymore. My Spiritualist hoodoo battery's dead. Find someone else to commune with Great-Aunt Martha."

He started to roll over, but I stopped him. "That's not what I want," I said desperately. "I know what you practice isn't hoodoo. I need your science. I need to get to the Deadlands and bring my friend back. He's not supposed to be dead. It wasn't his time."

The doctor looked at my hand, and then at me. Then he laughed, his bitter, acidic breath stinging my eyes. "The Deadlands?" he barked. "You think you're going to just pick up your skirts and waltz in there?"

I bristled. How dare he make light of this, of what I'd lost? "Something like that," I ground out.

"Then, girlie, you're even dumber than you look," he told me. "Now go away and let me sleep." He jerked his jacket out of my grasp and rolled over. A moment later, a deep snore emanated from him.

I stood, my hands shaking. I fought the urge to grab one of the bottles and smash it across his skull. That wouldn't help anyone, especially me.

Instead, I just left, kicking over a stack of papers as I went. They slid and slithered into the darkness that swallowed up the rest of the room.

Conrad and Cal waited for me, Conrad impatient and Cal worried. "Did he—" Cal started, but I shoved past him, through the junk and the dust, and out the door.

I collapsed on the stoop, letting the rain disguise my tears.

This was it. This was my only chance to save Dean, and it was a dead end. I should have known, given that it was information that came from my mother. Nobody else, not even my father, who I usually regarded as the smartest person I knew, could help me now.

I stayed there until I was thoroughly cold and soaked, and probably would have sat there even longer, watching the bums pick through the trash and the evening women call to one another from balconies, but the door opened and Chang came out.

He spread out an oilskin coat carefully before sitting next to me. "Told your friends you probably needed space," he said. When I didn't respond, he cleared his throat. "I'm sorry," he continued. "But I did tell you."

"You did," I agreed. I swiped at my cheeks and sniffed hard. No need to let complete strangers know I was a blubbering mess. "So is he always this friendly or did he really take a liking to me?"

Chang chuckled and stared out at the rain. "He had an

accident about a year ago. Bad one. It knocked something loose in his mind and he's been getting worse ever since. I try to care for him when I can. I used to be his lab assistant. Hired me right out of the university. I thought he was crazy, but there aren't many laboratories willing to hire, you know"—he made quotes with his fingers—"'one of those Chinamen.'"

"Is he a fraud, then?" I asked.

"No," Chang said. "And that might be the craziest part of all. He talks to the dead. He's not a medium, and he's not a fake. He uses his machines to open a window to the Deadlands. I've never seen anything like it."

That heartened me a bit. "I hope you know," I told Chang, "that I wouldn't be here if I wasn't desperate."

"People never come here until they are," he told me. "Mediums and Spiritualism are one thing, but really touching the dead? You'd have to be half mad with grief, but I guess death can make fools of us all."

He stood and opened the door back into the shop. "Come on," he said. "You can't stay out here, and you can't get out of Chinatown until morning. It's not safe for anyone in this place."

"There's no point in my coming inside unless you'll help me," I said, folding my hands into the damp creases of my coat, which did little to warm them. "If you won't, I have to be on to the next thing." I pointed at the sky, obscured by fog. I could still sense the echo of the Old Ones' Gate, ringing against my Weird like an ever-struck bell. "I'm running out of time. You work with shadowy practices—you must know that."

Chang considered, also looking at the sky. "I'll make you a deal," he said at last. "You tell me how you know about *that*"—he pointed at the sky—"and I'll listen to what you have to say about this friend of yours."

Hope sprouted in my chest, just a small shoot. The sensation was one I'd almost forgotten. "Thank you," I rushed. "I'll try my best, but I don't know how much I can—"

"Oh, I think you can tell me plenty, Aoife Grayson," said Chang. He gestured me inside.

My heart jumped. He knew who I was—which wasn't hard, I reminded myself. Before Draven had been taken to the Thorn Land, he'd plastered my picture as a wanted fugitive across every spot he could find.

But Chang's serene smile bespoke some deeper interest. I hoped it wasn't in harming me, but I didn't have a choice right now. I needed him, and he had his price.

I hoped it wasn't something I couldn't pay.

We went back inside, and Chang showed us a small sleeping area on the second floor, which Cal and Conrad seemed grateful for. I was far too jittery to sleep after all that had happened.

Chang sat me on one end of a ratty sofa and made tea from a steam hob, offering me a cup. I sniffed it suspiciously.

"I'm not Lei Xiang," he said. "I don't drug people and rob them. Clearly, or I wouldn't be living here."

I drank then. The tea was bitter but good, and it did warm me up. Chang offered me a blanket. "This might help."

I shivered against my will, feeling as if my skin were colder than the air. "I thought California was supposed to be warm."

"Not here," Chang said. "The fog makes sure of that." He sipped his tea and smiled at me. "You don't seem like the usual sort of person who comes to our doorstep, Aoife. Even knowing who you are." He sipped his tea again. "You said you lost someone."

"His name was Dean," I said quietly. Steam drifted from our cups, turning Chang's face into something even more beautiful and unearthly. He really was incredibly good-looking. If it wasn't for his friendly demeanor and the silence of my shoggoth scar, I'd say he could be Fae or some other creature that used its beauty as predatory camouflage.

"This Dean must be very special if you're willing to risk direct contact with the Deadlands," said Chang. "It's a strange place that does things to your mind. Reality has no role there."

"It's my fault he's dead," I said. Saying it out loud hadn't gotten any easier, and I felt the weight of the moment all over again. Cradling Dean in the snow. Feeling his blood turn cold against my hands and cheek. I took a long swallow of too-hot tea and let the pain burn out the memory. "It wasn't his time."

"Time doesn't have much sway in the Deadlands either," Chang said. "It really is eternal."

"Someone told me that everyone has a thread, a measure of time," I said softly. "That if yours is cut short, it's possible to get that time back." Too bad Crow, the creature who oversaw people's dreams, hadn't told me exactly how you were supposed to do that.

"Sounds like magic to me." Chang shrugged. "But I wouldn't know about that. I just know how the machine works. And I know that a lot of people die before their time, especially around here." He sipped his tea. "I'm sorry for you. That's never an easy fact to live with." He refilled my teacup. "How did Dean die?"

"He was shot," I said.

Chang lifted one eyebrow. "Not by you, I hope. Trying to contact a murder victim, even one that was an accident, is dangerous. And if you were the murderer . . ."

"No!" I cried. The very idea that I would hurt Dean horrified me, but then I realized that I hurt everyone I tried to keep safe. No matter how hard I tried to protect them, they all fell prey to the dangers of being my friend. Not to mention the thousands of people in Lovecraft who'd been hurt when I blew up the engine.

"Okay, okay. Calm down," Chang said. "I just had to ask." He took our empty cups and put them in a washbasin already overflowing with plates and silverware.

"Ask me anything but that," I muttered, pulling my legs under me and curling into the smallest ball possible.

"All right," Chang said. He sat back down and offered me a thick wool blanket that smelled like dry rot and mothballs. I wrapped up in it, trying to ward off the chill that had nothing to do with my wet clothes. I knew what was coming.

"Tell me about the hole in the sky," Chang said. "And about everything that's crawled up out of the ground to look at it."

He regarded me with that penetrating black gaze, and I sighed and examined the pattern in the blanket. "The Great Old Ones have returned," I said. I didn't elaborate, and thankfully Chang didn't ask me to.

"Makes sense," he said. "The doctor did a lot of research on other places, other than the Deadlands. He talked about the Old Ones, in a space so far away the brain couldn't even wrap around the idea of it."

"And now they're coming," I said. "And everything that appeared from their last visit—the shoggoths and the leviathans and the other monsters—are paving the way."

Chang grimaced. "Even the ghosts are acting up. Boneyard's never been so busy."

I kept quiet at that. I didn't know how I'd ever explain to Chang how it had been me who released the Old Ones. But I did know if he found out, he'd never help me.

"I've heard they're not bad," I said. "Not evil, I mean. That even though they birthed things like the shoggoths, they also gave people technology and art and the knowledge of the Gates—that there are other worlds besides Iron out there among the stars."

"Maybe that was well and good when humans were still living in mud huts," Chang said. "But now it'll sow chaos, no matter what their intentions." He tapped his fingers against the arms of the chair. "They need to be stopped, or I fear the whole world will suffer."

"I . . ." I chewed on my lip, thinking of how to phrase my enticement. "If you help me get to the Deadlands, I might be able to do something about them."

Chang cocked his head, but he didn't regard me as if I were insane, so I pressed on. "I can . . . I can visit other lands, travel between them, but I can't go to the Dead-lands. Maybe there, there's some answer to keep the living world safe."

I agreed with Chang. The world wasn't the same as when the Old Ones had come before. They could do real dam-age, and beyond damage, they could finally destroy life as we knew it. What I'd done in Lovecraft would pale in com-parison. I wanted to prove Crow wrong—I wanted to prove that I could help the Iron Land, not just tear it down.

If I wanted to help Dean, I wanted to find a way to undo my bargain with the Old Ones nearly as much. If there was a choice, I knew what I *should* do—but maybe I wouldn't have to choose after all.

"The question is, can you help me cross over?" I said. "And after I cross, come back again?"

"I know how to work the séance machines," Chang said, "and I can do this, but you have to realize the cost. Even if we do contact this Dean, he might not have anything to say. Depending on how rough a soul has it when it crosses over . . . sometimes they're going to be nothing but shreds. They won't even remember what it was to be alive."

"I don't want to just contact Dean," I said. That caused Chang to go still, and his perfect face to fold into a frown.

"Then . . . why are you here?"

"Because I know the machine can do more," I told him. "I don't want to contact the Deadlands. I want to go there. I want to find Dean, and I want to undo this mistake. He was never supposed to die. It should be possible to bring him back. And if you want to stop the Old Ones, I *have* to actually cross over. Either way, I can't just commune with Dean's spirit." I fixed Chang with the stare I'd learned from my father, hard and unyielding. "Or am I wrong?"

He stared back at me, worrying the buttons on his suit vest and the chain on his watch, and narrowed his eyes. "How do you know so much about the doctor's work?"

"Let's just say I have a thing for machines," I said. "Does it work to cross over or does it not?"

"You can't," Chang said instantly. Too fast. I was a good liar, and because of that I could spot a bad one in a second. "It was purely an experiment. It never worked right—"

"But it did work," I insisted, standing. "At least once, correct?"

"Not really!" Chang cried. "The doctor . . . he . . ." He sighed and went to the window, pressing his forehead against the glass.

"I *begged* him to let me try. I didn't want him to risk his body, his genius . . . but he wouldn't hear of it. Dangerous, he said. He said he'd never send a boy to do a job he should be doing himself."

He turned to me and ran his hands through his hair, disturbing the carefully Brylcreemed strands. "Now he's that mess you see downstairs. He went from being sober and respectable and a great mind of science to a paranoid junkie. That's what touching the Deadlands does to you. Not to mention the actual process you must use to cross over."

I straightened my spine. If he was telling me all this, he was close to yielding, so I pressed my advantage. "I'm different," I said. "I told you, I can cross worlds. It won't affect me like it would a normal person, and besides, I'm not going there as an experiment. I'm going there to get the boy I love back, to save him from torment for all eternity. Either I'll find him and we'll return or I'll be stuck there, but I'm not concerned with after. I'm just concerned with doing it."

Chang exhaled. "I don't know who this Dean is, but now I kind of want to meet him."

He went to the stairs. "Follow me. I want to show you exactly what you're in for."

Elated, I followed. I was so close. I was going to get Dean back. Then I could decide what to do about the Brotherhood, the Old Ones, all of the disasters of the living Lands.

But first, Dean. Was it selfish? Maybe. But I couldn't live without him, with his death on my conscience. I'd be useless to the rest of the world if I didn't have him. I could function, get through the gray sameness of each day, but part of me would always be in the Deadlands, with him.

And I owed the rest of the world more than that. Not to mention I owed Dean. He wouldn't be dead if he hadn't tried to help me above and beyond anything I could have asked for.

Chang bypassed the doctor's cube and led me to a back porch closed in with tin walls and a tar-paper roof. Everything was covered with cloths and looked as if it hadn't been used in years.

Chang lit an oil lamp above the main mass of the device, the bulk nearly as tall as I was, and pulled the cloths off. "We use a Tesla coil to generate enough power, and the doctor's apparatus opens a small door on the same electromagnetic frequency as the Deadlands. It vibrates on the same frequency as spirits. That's how we communicate."

He pointed to an aethervox equipped with a wax record

that had been hooked into the apparatus. "This records their voices, and we play it back to get answers to the questions people ask."

I watched as he moved around, smoothing the dust off things with his sleeve. So far it all sounded possible, but it wasn't what I needed.

"The real trick is the other way," Chang said. "The doctor had a theory that you could make a living person's soul vibrate at the same rate, let it cross the door into the Deadlands temporarily and then change the vibration to call it back. Enable your consciousness to cross over."

"How do you do it?" I asked, staring at the machine. It seemed impossible, but I was desperate and willing to try anything. I'd made peace with that fact long before I'd made it to San Francisco.

"That's the part I need to tell you about," Chang said, his expression somber. "In order to cross over to the Deadlands, your soul has to be untethered from your conscious mind. And to untether it, you have to die."

I must have stared at him, my mouth open. That defeated the whole purpose, didn't it? If you crossed into the Deadlands dead, you stayed. That was how they worked. That was why they were impenetrable even to someone like me, who could cross any living barrier between the Lands.

Draven's taunting grin popped back into my mind. *To get to the Deadlands, you have to die.* He couldn't be right. If Grey Draven was right about something and I was wrong, I was going to scream.

"Not permanently die," Chang clarified, sensing my

disbelief. "Just for a minute or two. To touch the same frequency as the dead. Then the operator brings you back and keeps you breathing, but your soul is free, floating outside your body."

"And your body?" I said. This was sounding worse and more foolhardy by the second.

"As long as you're crossed over," Chang said, "your body is vulnerable, lying there in a coma. It's soulless. Anything could fill the vessel. The doctor had some ideas to combat that, but we never got to try them. He came back and he was . . . well, different. Whatever he saw over there destroyed him."

"And that's the only way?" I said. I was desperate, but I also fervently wished there was an alternative.

"That's it," Chang said. "And we never found a trustworthy method of causing death, either. The doctor had me smother and then resuscitate him. I won't do that again. I just won't."

I contemplated the apparatus, the horn of the aethervox, the power coil, all of it. This was the only way, I reminded myself. The only way I could begin to even contemplate trying to stop what I'd caused with the Old Ones. Dean's soul was in there, just beyond what I could see, tormented and alone and afraid.

"All right." I faced Chang. "If I find a way to die that doesn't render my body useless or ask you to kill me, you'll help?"

"Will you leave me alone until I do?" Chang said. "Honestly, I thought that whole speech would put you right off, but you just might be even crazier than the doctor."

"Crazy and I are old friends," I confirmed. "So will you do it?"

"Fine," Chang sighed. "But only if you find a better way to go under. Smothering is dangerous—you might not wake up again if the other person presses too hard. You need something that will stop your heart without hurting the rest of you."

I thought of Madame and her deft hand with laudanum.

"That part won't be a problem," I told Chang.

Beyond the Spirit Wall

I SLEPT FITFULLY, AND only slept at all because I was so exhausted my body decided it didn't trust me to keep my eyes open. I didn't dream, and that was something. Constant nightmares had been my companion ever since Dean died.

I missed him so much it was a physical ache. His hands, his smile, the feel of his gaze against my skin. I needed him, and there was no use pretending otherwise.

Dawn was just a thought around the edges of the sky when I got up and got dressed. Or rather, I started to get dressed, then looked at the jumpsuit I'd worn since Alcatraz and wrinkled my nose.

"Clothes in the wardrobe."

I jumped at the voice, then saw Chang standing in the doorway, holding a mug that smelled of coffee and regarding me. I pulled the blanket around myself.

"Sorry. I didn't see you there."

"I'm quiet," he said, and smiled at me. "They're not girl's clothes, but they smell better than what you showed up in."

"Thank you," I said, shutting the door on him while I got dressed. I thought about Chang while I put on trousers and a shirt and jacket with sleeves far too long for my arms.

Chang was charming, that much was sure, and handsome, but in the balance of things he had agreed to help me awfully easily, and I hadn't survived by falling for every handsome face that offered me assistance without questioning the motive behind it. I'd made that mistake with Tremaine. It wasn't happening again. When I was clothed, I went down to the main part of the shop.

"Why are you doing this?"

Chang was cooking eggs on a small burner on top of a potbellied woodstove in a corner, and he raised an eyebrow at me. "Doing what?"

"Helping me," I said. "Really, you gave in with hardly any fight." I looked around and saw all the sharp and heavy things I could use to defend myself. That and Cal being within screaming distance emboldened me. "Are you with them? The Brotherhood of Iron?"

"Brotherhood?" Chang looked genuinely confused, eyebrows drawn and mouth slack. "I don't know what you're talking about, Aoife."

"I know the Brotherhood can be persuasive when it wants something," I said. "I know they keep tabs on people like you and the doctor. And I know that getting me to willingly put myself in a coma, ripe for capturing, would be just the sort of thing they'd pull."

I picked up the knife sticking out of the cutting board at Chang's elbow and ran the blade against my thumb. "It's a simple question. Did they bribe or threaten you to get to me? I know they're in San Francisco. Tell me the truth."

Chang shook his head. "I don't know where you're getting this idea from, Aoife, but I'm just doing this because I can tell you're going to keep trying with or without me. And next time, you might not run into someone who's as nice as I am. You might run into someone who truly wants to hurt you and your friends. Someone this Brotherhood of yours *has* gotten to."

He put the eggs on a plate and sat down to eat. "Desperation makes people stupid. I've seen that with the doctor, and I'd really prefer to keep others from that path, if I can."

He gestured to a seat across from him. "Now can I have the knife back? I need it to cut my fruit."

I took my seat, warily. Chang sighed when I handed over the blade. I still had misgivings, but he was so calm and open, so unruffled by my accusation, I had a hard time believing my own paranoia. The Brotherhood was sneaky, but they couldn't be everywhere.

"You haven't had many people be kind to you, have you?" Chang asked.

"No," I said honestly. "Nobody, really, except Cal and Conrad. And Dean."

"That explains it, then," he said. "Why you want him back so badly. And I'm smart enough to know I can't stop you. So why don't you eat something, and I'll see about getting the lab back to specs."

A bell jangled from the back room where the doctor stayed, and Chang's pleasant expression vanished. "I'll be back," he sighed. "Just have to go and see what he needs."

As soon as Chang left, I got up and found a pad of receipts and a pen. I scribbled a note to Cal and Conrad so they wouldn't worry about me, and then found a heavy rain jacket hanging by the back door. I had an idea of where I was going, and knew I wouldn't get another chance before I had to tell Cal or Conrad where I was going and they tried to convince me otherwise.

They'd probably be able to talk me out of it—I knew even as I slipped out this was a bad idea, but I didn't have a better one.

The way back to Madame Xiang's wasn't hard to figure out—we'd only made a few turns when she'd brought us to the Boneyard. The streets were quieter in the early morning, but not by much. Drunks were stumbling out of bars and laborers were crowding into round-the-clock diners. The smells and sounds were still persistent.

A Proctor airship hummed overhead, toward the bay, but it didn't slow down or drop altitude. This place truly was closed off to the Proctors, and, I hoped, to the Brotherhood after we'd escaped them.

Fang from the night before opened Madame's door with his same lack of expressiveness. I stood my ground.

"I need to see Madame," I said.

"She's asleep," Fang grunted.

"It's important," I told him. "I'll owe her a favor."

Fang grinned. "I think you already owe her one, little girl. I doubt you want to owe her a second."

"Fang, for goodness sake, stop letting all the warm air out." Madame was wearing an impeccable silk robe printed with cherry blossoms, and her hair was wrapped in an orange scarf that set off her skin. If possible, she was even more gorgeous than before.

"Oh," she said. "You again. I thought I'd shooed all the strays away from my doorstep."

"I need something," I said. Madame smiled, taking a cigarette from a small mesh purse and waiting for Fang to come light it. When he did, I moved inside and shut the door, which made him grunt with irritation. I hoped he didn't take too much offense. I didn't want to be on the bad side of somebody that large.

"I thought you needed something last night," Madame said. "I was under the impression I'd already bargained with you."

"I know, and I'll still carry the message," I said. "But in order to do that I need something, and I think you're the only one who can help me."

Madame sighed and stubbed out her cigarette in a nearby bowl. "Fine. What now?"

"I need something that will stop my heart," I said. "Just for a few moments. I need to be dead, but I also need something that will let them bring me back."

"So basically, you're asking me to help you cheat," Madame said. "Tsk, tsk."

"Please," I said. "It's the only way this will work."

"I didn't say no," Madame said. "I rather like cheating."

She drew close to me, and I could smell cold cream and a hint of old perfume rolling off her. "But you're going to owe me a lot more than a little message to my brother. You do understand, yes? What it means to owe the tong a favor?"

"I've owed favors to people a lot worse than you," I told Madame, and met her eyes.

She laughed. "All right. Come with me."

I felt my body loosen, the tension I'd been holding inside running out of my skin and bones. "Thank you, Madame Xiang."

"Call me Lei," she said. "Close as we've become, it seems only fitting."

She led me through the curtain, into the back room, which was a parlor and a small kitchen crammed together. Lei didn't stop, though. She took me to a door that led to the first floor, a windowless room that couldn't be seen from the street.

"I'd much rather do this in a basement," she said, "but this place isn't stable. Rat-infested mud hole that this city is. You know when they started the Engine under Alcatraz, it cracked the whole city in two? That there's still wreckage under the streets they covered up and pretended wasn't there? There's a giant chasm in the basement. Under this whole section of the city, really. We use the tunnels for smuggling, when we have things we'd rather the Proctors not see."

She lit an oil lamp and perused the shelves. They seemed to close in all around us, full of bottles and jars, some containing specimens of things both recognizable and not, most containing brilliantly hued liquids in every color of the spectrum.

"The medium thing just makes ends meet," Lei said. "What my mother taught me is to be a poisoner. I can mix and match anything you'd like from these jars. Even death."

I watched her as she ran her hands over the bottles. I didn't think Lei would poison me in any way that I couldn't wake up from eventually, but I didn't trust her either, so I kept my eyes on her.

"You're certainly good at knocking people out," I said.

"That?" She laughed lightly. "That's just a little sleepy-time, some opium and a few herbs. I have one that will leave you with no memory at all. But I wouldn't use that one on stupid kids. That's reserved for real problems."

She handed me a small vial of white liquid. "Here. This will work, but when you start breathing again it's going to take a while for the toxins to make their way out of your system. You'll be unconscious and vulnerable."

She blew out the lamp and let me walk ahead of her up the stairs. Fang watched us when we returned to the parlor.

"Now go away and let me have my rest," Lei said. "And if you don't survive, I don't want your mates showing up here, blaming me."

"Don't worry," I said. Now that it was light, I could see the dot in the sky—a blot, growing ever closer. "If I don't survive, you'll have bigger things to worry about."

* * *

Conrad and Cal were on the stoop when I returned, and Conrad jumped to his feet. "You can't just go running off like that!" he shouted.

"I left a note," I said.

"Dammit, a note's not enough when we're in a strange city." Conrad sighed. "You always go off and leave me to worry. . . ."

"What are you so afraid I'm going to do?" I said, fingering the vial in my pocket. "Start another apocalypse?"

"Okay, that's not fair," Conrad said. "I don't blame you for what's happening. I'm here helping you, aren't I?"

I sighed and nodded. I knew that Conrad didn't really blame me. That he was just as scared and clueless as I was. There was no way I could explain that by doing this, I might help our father as well as myself, not without Conrad thinking I'd succumbed to iron poisoning and gone mad again. It was better that he was irritated with me.

"I'm on your side," Conrad grumbled. "Not that you seem to want me there most of the time."

"Listen," Cal said. "Nobody is against anybody. How about we all go inside? Chang said he'd gotten things mostly ready." He looked at me. "That is, if you're still sure you want to do this."

"Yes," I said, though I wasn't sure now. I was terrified, both of becoming like the doctor and of the possibility that I would reach the Deadlands and wouldn't be able to find Dean. Or that I would find him and he wouldn't recognize me, would just be one of the shredded souls Chang had spoken of. Or that we'd both get trapped, and I'd die for good, a soul without a body, stuck as Dean was on the other side.

"That's good, then." Cal always knew when I was lying, but he never called me on it. He never forced me to feel any weaker or more scared than I already did. That was why he was my best friend, and always would be.

Inside, I could hear a clicking and whirring from the back of the shop, where the doctor's machine resided. My Weird prickled in response, sensing its potential to reach between the worlds.

I ignored it. To try to manipulate machines would just result in a stabbing headache and a nosebleed. My true power was the Gates. It had been nice, to be able to fix things purely with my mind, but that wasn't who I was any longer.

I wasn't anyone I recognized. I shivered as I thought of the vial Lei had given me, the weight of it in my palm. Soon, I wouldn't even be alive. I tried to look brave, even though on the inside I was shaking with fear.

"All right, everything appears to be operational," Chang said when he saw me. I glanced over the cube wall and saw that the doctor's bed was empty.

"Where is he?" I said. Chang's mouth tightened.

"Upstairs, sleeping it off. If he knew we were holding another séance he'd raise a fuss, and we don't need that."

"No," I agreed.

Chang pointed to a chair hooked up to the apparatus and took a seat in another chair, on the opposite side. "Sit. The copper will conduct your body's natural electricity and put you in tune with the device."

I sat, and felt a prickle across my exposed skin. The Tesla coil hummed and arced, and Cal and Conrad kept their distance.

There was so much to say to both of them, more than I could possibly express. If this was truly the last time we would be together, there was no way I could tell them everything.

I resolved to act as if it wasn't, as if I'd wake up, and everything would be fine and we'd have all the time in the world.

"Ready as we'll ever be," Chang said. "I'm going to ensure everything is working correctly."

I took the vial from my pocket and placed it next to the aethervox assembly. Chang eyed it.

"And what is that?"

"Lei Xiang gave it to me. She said it'll stop my heart for a few minutes, so as long as someone is there to bring me back. . . ." I rubbed my arms, already feeling cold. "No permanent damage to the body."

"Good," Chang said. "That's good. Don't worry, I've had a lot of experience reviving people. And I'll make sure your body is looked after while your soul is floating."

"Conrad and Cal will, too," I said. "You can trust them, if the situation gets bad."

"As much as I trust anyone, then," Chang said with a tight smile. He turned on the aethervox, acting as if everything were normal, so I tried to take my cue from him. The record spun lazily, needle not dropped. "How it works is, you take the poison on my signal. I'll only have a few seconds to hook you into the reader, so I need to be precise."

I nodded. "All right."

Chang examined his instruments and adjusted a few dials on the panel in front of him. "Here we go . . . ," he murmured to no one except himself.

I felt a hum rise in the room as the invisible energy of the aether crackled. The coil began to arc faster, the hum overriding everything, even the shouts and sounds from the street.

"Get ready," Chang told me. "And do exactly as I say. I'll resuscitate you, and if it works, you'll be alive, but you won't wake up until I unhook you."

I reached out and gripped the vial. It was cool to the touch, and the liquid inside vibrated along with everything else in the room.

Chang dropped the needle onto the record. "It's starting," he said, and over the hum I heard the barest whisper, the sound of a human voice.

Oh, help me, it wailed. *I am lost. . . . I am so alone. . . .*

Another joined in, screaming incoherently, as if they were being tortured beyond all ability to endure. I shuddered, watching my breath frost as the temperature in the room plummeted at least twenty degrees.

"It's a side effect," Chang said. "Of opening a passage between this world and the Deadlands. It's cold there." He cut a glance at me, and I tried to ignore the voices, of which there were more and more—children laughing, women crying, an endless cacophony of pleas, pain and denial.

"We call them whispers," Chang said, his voice cutting through my growing horror. "Just snippets of soul that haven't quite made it to the Deadlands, trapped in some sort of space between here and there. The doctor and I were never able to quantify. Ignore them—they can't hurt you."

"Can't we do something?" I said. The screams raked across my ears like claws, until I would have done anything to make them stop.

"No," Chang said, turning a final dial. "They're lost to us. Nobody can reach them. Neither in the Deadlands nor any other world. They're little more than echoes, really."

The record spun faster, the needle cutting into the wax, saving the whispers' words for posterity.

Chang checked his levels and then nodded to me. "Go ahead," he said loudly, over the crying and wailing. "If you still want to."

I'd never wanted anything less, but I also didn't want to show my fear to Chang and the others. I unscrewed the vial quickly and tilted it to my lips. The glass rim was cold, like a snowflake landing on my tongue.

The poison itself tasted horrible, like something left buried in the ground for a long time, then dug up and fermented. It coated my tongue with a sick flavor and sent a feverish heat down my throat.

I gagged as I swallowed, and to my horror couldn't stop gagging. My airway closed off and the most horrible spasms shot through my stomach. I did panic then, trying to stand, and knocking Chang's control panel askew.

"Help me," he snapped at Cal, who ran to my side and pinned my arms down.

I was dying, there was no doubt about it. I could feel each piece of me shutting down and drifting away as the pain intensified, replacing all thoughts and feelings except panic.

But this was the way it had to be, for me and for Dean. For everything.

Chang laid me flat on the wooden plank near the machine and started hooking leads to me. I saw the long flash of an IV needle but didn't feel it pierce my skin. I couldn't feel anything now, could see nothing but the purple glow of the Tesla coil.

"She's convulsing!" Cal cried. I could barely distinguish his voice from the whispers, which had gotten so loud I thought they might split my skull. "Do something!"

"Nothing to do," Chang said. "She's got to die for this to work."

Something flickered in and out of my vision, and I saw a woman in the sort of garb Lei had worn when she was trying to scam us standing over me, reaching for me, her nails jagged and the tips of her fingers bloody. *Oh, help me*, she hissed. *I'm so alone, so afraid. . . . They buried me there, all alone. . . .*

I tried to scream, but it died in my throat as I became aware that the woman wasn't the only person in the room. The machine was surrounded by black and silver figures, all of them wavering as if they were underwater. The whispers had bodies, bodies a living person couldn't perceive.

The pitch of the machine's whine increased, and I felt my last breath slip out of me as if a piece of silk had drifted through my fingers.

The whispers turned to look at me, and the woman who'd spoken reached out to grab my hair.

A small boy, also wearing traditional Chinese garb,

stopped her. "No, Mama," he said, looking at me with the same blank, bleeding eyes as the girl on Alcatraz. "She's not staying here."

The whispers converged on me, grabbing at my clothes and hair, trying to touch my face, and I lashed out, trying to fight them.

The pain had stopped, and I could move, but I felt as if I were drugged, moving slow and dull, not nearly at my usual speed.

In the center of the machine, between the coils, I saw a small fissure of the same black and silver light the whispers seemed to be made out of, and I tried to shove my way through them toward it.

Don't leave us! the woman screamed. *Don't go away like the man!*

That made me stop struggling for a moment. "Man? What man?"

Mama, stop, said the boy. *The man didn't stay. She won't stay. She'll go on to the Deadlands and we'll still be here.*

The fissure widened and arched into the shape I recognized, the tiny tear in space-time that Gateminders could perceive when they traveled from place to place. Now that I was dead, I could perceive the one to the Deadlands as well.

I tried to move again, and the whispers relaxed their hold this time, but when I took the first step, something hit my chest as if I'd been struck with a bat.

Chang had started trying to bring me back. I moved again, trying to fight against the blows Chang was raining on my physical body as he tried to resuscitate me.

My fingers grazed the fissure in the fabric of this

in-between place, and I felt as if I had been sucked into a whirlpool. There was no free will involved in this at all—I touched it, and the Deadlands dragged me down.

There wasn't the usual tug of the Gates, the feeling of being spread across the universe, my mind and body a million glittering points of light. This felt like sinking, like I was drowning in the deepest of oceans, powerless to do anything other than watch as I drifted down through the silver-gray fog, into a place no human eye had ever touched.

I saw other faces, other shapes, in the fog. More of the whispers, who hissed and gnashed their teeth and tried to grab for me, and other, larger things.

One turned an eye on me, sightless and cloudy, and if I'd had breath I would have gasped.

It looked like the Old Ones looked to my eyes, great star-sized bodies that held universes of their own under their translucent skin, drifting tentacles that brushed through galaxies, eyes like suns that burned you to the core.

But this one was small, and broken, and floated before me as if it, too, had drowned and was dead.

You came, it whispered to me. *You shouldn't have.*

"I had no choice," I said. I wasn't sure if I was talking or we were speaking in some other, more primal way that transcended voice and language.

That's what the other said, the Old One told me. *The one who came before.*

"The doctor," I said. "I know who he is."

Not the sad soul who fears death. The other, said the Old One. *The one touched by our gift, before you. He came here, for the same answers you seek.*

158

The thing had to be talking about Tesla. But it couldn't be. Tesla had built the Gates, but he'd never spoken of that part of his life to anyone except the Brotherhood.

"You're lying," I told the Old One, as we drifted through the silver. The cold increased. Below us, I saw a black whorl, toward which everything in this in-between place was slowly drawn. A whisper wavered at the edge, and then broke apart into a thousand blots of darkness and disappeared.

I am old beyond knowing. I cannot lie. I speak only what is true, the Old One said.

"I'm not here for you," I tried to explain. I was done acting as the tool of beings older and more powerful than myself. All that mattered was Dean.

But you are *here for us*, it said. *You are our agent, our herald in the Iron Land, whether you like it or not. You, Destroyer, and your vast gift are the harbinger of the wind that will sweep the world clean, just as the one before you was. And you have no choice in the matter, just as he had none. You will pave the way for our return, or you will perish. It is a simple truth, even for one as primitive as you.*

"Leave me alone!" I screamed. It couldn't be true. I'd made the bargain with the Old Ones out of desperation, not because I was fated to. Nothing in my life was predetermined. Everything that had brought me here had been my doing, my choice.

At least, that was what I had to believe if I didn't want to go insane for good.

Beware, said the figure. *You go to the realm of the one who waits. He watches. He schemes. He knows that you are coming.*

Before I could reply, I touched the edge of the black floor of this place, and it enveloped me.

When I opened my eyes, I was on solid ground, and I knew for sure from the cold and my lack of breathing that I was dead.

10

Deadlands

I LAY ON A road, paved in crushed white shells that poked into me every which way. I got up and brushed myself off. My skin was gray and I felt no heartbeat in my chest, nor air drawn into and out of my lungs. My soul was here, covered in the white dust. My physical body, I hoped, was still suspended somewhere in Chinatown, between life and death, and relying on Conrad, Cal and Chang to bring me back before I became permanently attached to the Deadlands and my body withered away, devoid of everything that made me Aoife Grayson.

I turned in a slow circle, examining the landscape. The road wound through black sand, a switchback snake as far as I could see. Red clay mountains rose to the east; their plateaus and spires looked as if real mountains had melted, peaks and valleys turned to slurry. In the other direction, I saw the faint outline of a distant city wreathed in noxious green-yellow smoke. I could hear the faint whine of air-raid sirens.

Some sort of bird with leathery wings and stained white feathers flew low over me and landed with a squawk on a lumpy object at the edge of the road.

I flinched when I realized that the object it perched on was a body, bloated with decay and covered with drab brown rags. A little farther away, I saw a wheeled caravan, the type pulled by horses, burned out and on its side. Picked-over bones scattered across the sand told me what had happened to the rest of the passengers.

Looking between the city and the mountains again, I picked the city and started walking. There would be someone there, I hoped, who could tell me what I was looking for.

The heat was oppressive—I had never thought about the Deadlands in terms of being a real place, a physical place with gravity and geography and atmosphere. I'd pictured a vast nothingness where the dead, if they still existed in some form, collected like pennies dropped into a bucket.

But it felt as real as any place I'd ever walked as a live person. The heat, the grit on my face, the sounds and certainly the smells, all real. Unpleasantly real.

I tried to tell myself that I seemed as if I belonged here, that no one could harm me. There was nobody here to do it, anyway.

As I walked, the shells crunching under my feet, I saw the air waver on the horizon, where a purple-cast sun burned. There was a dot in the sky here, too—the pernicious influence of the Old Ones had extended even into the land of the dead.

I was distracted by the movement, which had grown larger and faster, a wave of advancing chaos across the black sand.

I stopped walking and watched, mesmerized, as the horizon ceased to be a line and became a lacy black pattern against the pale violet sky.

A buzzing reached my ears, overriding the air-raid sirens and the wailing of the wind across the vast sands, and too late I realized that whatever was coming at me was sentient, alive and hungry.

The sand moved as if it were the skin of a living thing, lifted and formed into a swirling mass that appeared to be made of mouths and teeth.

I screamed, I think, as the first stinging bits of the thing touched my exposed skin, and then turned to run. It was all too clear now what had chewed those bodies on the road to pieces.

It was a curious sensation, to run but not breathe. I didn't get winded, but my limbs got heavier and heavier, and I started to feel detached from my body as I sprinted, as if I were floating just outside, watching the black tide encroach on me.

As I passed the overturned caravan, something darted out and grabbed me by the arm, whipping me around and slamming me to the ground.

Hands jerked me inside the wreckage of the caravan, and I thrashed reflexively to get free. "Quiet!" someone hissed in my ear. "They hunt by sound. I need you to be quiet."

I stilled myself. If I had had a beating heart it would have been thundering in my ribs. I'd gotten used to danger, enough so that when somebody who could get me out of it told me what I needed to do, I didn't panic. I'd have to thank my father for that, if I ever saw him again.

And apologize, because I was rapidly realizing that this entire expedition had been a terrible, terrible mistake.

The black cloud passed over the caravan with a scream, and the hands relaxed their grip on my arms. "Sorry," the voice said. "But I'm not about to get eaten on account of some Walker too stupid to know about the screaming sand."

I crawled out of the caravan and slumped in the dirt, grit digging into my palms. "Sorry. I'm new here."

The figure, who turned out to be a man not much older than me, snorted. "Yeah, I figured that out on my own."

"Well, you don't have to be a prat about it," I told him. "It's not my fault I didn't know about those things."

"Thing," said the man. "The sand is alive, a parasitic hive mind that tracks its prey by noise." He pushed his dark hair out of his eyes. It was as unruly as my own and covered with a thin layer of dust.

"All right," I said. "Thanks for the information. I'll try to stay quiet on the road, but I've got to be going."

I stood, and the man regarded me with such intensity that I folded my arms across my middle, self-conscious under his gaze. "You're not just a Walker, are you?" he said at last.

I sighed. "I don't even know what that is."

"Souls who escape the Catacombs," said the man. "They

wander, lost, unable to ever find rest. But you're not wandering. You have a purpose."

"I'm looking for someone," I said. I filed away the information about the Catacombs. If Dean was here, that was as good a place as any to start.

"Aren't we all," the man muttered. "I've been waiting for my brother for decades, but unlike me, he's got the good sense to keep on living."

"Well, good luck with that," I said, unwilling to be sidetracked by another soul who just wanted to keep my attention and freedom for themselves. "I really do have to be going."

"I'm sorry," the man said, standing and following me back to the road. "But I have the strangest feeling that I've seen you somewhere before."

"I don't think so," I told him, taking a step away to keep my distance. "I don't know you."

Yet there *was* something familiar about him as well, even though I didn't want to admit it. Something about the way the man carried himself, his direct stare, his mossy green eyes . . .

It clicked, like a gear slotting into its mate. "You're Ian," I said, my voice coming out so soft with shock that the wind nearly carried it away. "You're Ian Grayson. My uncle."

The man's face slackened, and he took a step away from me. "Archie's child?" He blinked and swiped a hand over his face. "I mean, I suppose it's not so outlandish that he'd have a child, but . . ." He reached for me, but I still didn't trust him that much, so I took another step back. "It's unbelievable. You look *just* like him."

165

Ian was staring at me as if I were his brother in a wig. "I'm sorry," I said. "But I really do need to be going."

"You can't go by yourself!" Ian exclaimed. "This place is an eternal hell. Nothing good can survive here."

I turned back to him and fixed him with my own gimlet stare. "You don't know me. Ian. What makes you think *I'm* any good?"

Before he could reply, I started walking again—straight to the polluted city and whatever lay within.

I looked back after a few minutes and saw that Ian was following me, his lanky stride the same as my father's. Both could close a gap quickly, and sure enough he caught up.

"How are you even here . . ." His mouth crimped. "I don't know your name."

"Aoife," I said. "My name is Aoife Grayson."

"I see. You're Archie's oldest?"

"Youngest," I corrected him. He wasn't trying to keep me from walking, so I decided to let him tag along. "I have a brother."

"Amazing." He shook his head. "Never thought Archie'd do it. Get married, I mean. He always had girls around him, but he was so damn devil-may-care he scared them off just as quickly. And he was never interested beyond a few dates anyway."

He looked me over, this time with a critical eye. "Your mother must be a knockout."

"Oh yes," I said, trying and failing to keep the bitter tinge out of my voice. "She's very pretty. And very crazy."

166

"I didn't mean to offend you. . . ." He sighed and gave me a sideways smile. "See, your uncle Ian never had a way with words. I was never the impressive one."

"You didn't have a Weird," I said. "I know. I read my father's journal."

Ian flinched. "You're blunt like him too."

I thought about spilling my guts to Ian, telling him that I'd never really known my father before a few months ago, about my time in the care of the city, about everything, but I didn't. I just walked. I didn't know Ian, and that meant I had no reason to trust him. The fact that we'd just stumbled upon each other made me even more resolute to keep things close to my vest. After all I'd seen, coincidence was not something I'd ever trust again.

"Yes," I said at last. "I suppose I am."

We walked for a time, keeping our eyes on the horizon for more signs of the screaming sand. "I've gotten pretty good at avoiding it," Ian told me, "but sometimes it catches you. Not to mention the Walkers. Some of them are feral, just rabid scraps of the people they used to be, and they want to feed on you."

"Like zombies?" I said, thinking of Cal's magazines, stories of creatures raised from the dead by magic or science.

"What's a zombie?" said Ian.

I thought about how long ago he'd died, and sighed. "Never mind."

"You don't belong here," Ian said in a rush. "Your soul may be solid as the rest of us, but your body, wherever it is, is still breathing. I can tell just by being near you, and if I can tell, then others can as well. However you got here, whatever happened, you have to leave." He stopped and pushed his hair out of his eyes, a repetitive, reflexive gesture as it was long and covered his eyes. "It's not safe for you here."

I kept walking. "I'm aware of that. And I'm not leaving until I get what I came for."

Ian had to run to keep up with me. "What's that, then? What could possibly be here for a living soul?"

"His name is Dean," I said. Even saying his name brought a prickle of tears, but I fought them.

Ian's brow drew down. "You can't bring the dead back, Aoife. They're here to stay."

"He was never supposed to die," I said. "It's my fault. I have to bring him back."

"I hate to tell you this," said Ian, "but whether he was meant to die or not, dead is dead. There's no help for it once a soul crosses the barrier from life to the Deadlands. It's not physical, like space and time, but it's a barrier all the same. I tend to think it's still physics, just laws we don't understand."

Any other time, I would have been thrilled to meet someone who could tell me more about the Gates, confirm or deny speculation, and just generally discuss science, but I waved him off. "No. My mother said that if someone dies before it's their time, they can be brought back. And she'd know."

Ian raised one eyebrow. "Your mother sounds like a smart lady, but it's still bunk. There's no way you can free a soul from this place. Dead is dead, Aoife. Once you cross, unless you're using a trick like whatever brought you here, then you're here for good. I'm sorry."

"Bargained, then," I snapped. "Everyone has their price."

A clouded look passed across Ian's face, and his eyes grew dark, gauging the road we'd been walking. "You don't want to go that way," he said, pointing ahead to the smog-shrouded city.

I stopped walking and folded my arms over my chest. "And why is that?"

He shifted uncomfortably from foot to foot. "It's dangerous there. In the city."

I softened. If he was anything like my father, he wouldn't respond well to being pushed around. "Look, Ian. You seem to know your way around this place, and I could really use your help."

He started to cut in and I held up a finger. "Let me finish. I'm going to find Dean with or without you, and do everything in my power to bring him back to the world of the living. So you can help me, or you can get out of my way." I dropped my hand and started walking again. After a few steps I stopped and turned back. "But I'd really prefer that you help me."

My uncle hesitated for so long that I thought he was going to refuse, and I was going to be on my own. The thought didn't scare me overmuch, but it would make what I had to do that much harder.

At last, though, he sighed and followed me as I started walking again, reluctant to waste any more time. "I suppose I won't change your mind? Not even when I tell you what's in that city?"

"Doubtful," I said. "What is it?"

"This place"—Ian gestured at the sands and the

road—"the Ossuary Trail, it's a neutral zone, where no-body except the most desperate go because it's so dangerous." He grimaced. "Like me, for instance. But in the city—the city is safe, because it's controlled. Controlled by things that have *never* been part of the living Lands, things that take human souls and twist them past the point of recognition to keep the lights on and the gears turning. To be in the city is to suffer eternal torment, and the souls who escape can never stay in one place for more than a few clock-ticks in living time. They call us Walkers—the damndest of the damned, except for our freedom. Those souls in the city—it's not a city, Aoife. It's a tomb." He shrugged. "Some prefer a tomb and the chance they'll be turned into kindling to what's out here, though. Which should tell you exactly how bad it can get in the wild parts of the Deadlands."

"No, I understand," I said. I'd seen the same effect in Lovecraft—people staying put in their comfortable lives and risking a Proctor burning rather than chance what lay beyond the walls. "So most of the souls stay in the Catacombs?" I said, thinking back to my conversation with Nerissa.

"The prison of the dead," Ian agreed. "If Dean is here, chances are he ended up there, on his own or by force. Those who run the Catacombs aren't picky about what you did in life, just what your soul is worth to them, and in return they offer a little protection. Not really worth it, but the souls they trap just want to exist. You stray from the city, you run the risk of . . . well . . . disintegrating. Forgetting who you are."

"I understand that part, too," I whispered. That couldn't have happened to Dean. He had to be safe, to remember me.

I had to be in time.

"It's hell," Ian said softly. "This existence of mine isn't much, but I escaped the Catacombs and I swore I'd never go back."

"I'm sorry to make you do it for me," I said, and I was being honest. "But if Dean is there, I've got to find him, and I think we've proved I don't stand much of a chance without someone who knows his way around."

Ian sighed. "Why not?" he said. "We Graysons have to stick together."

The air grew thicker as we approached the city, and though my chest didn't rise and fall as it did when I was alive, I could smell it. It was a toxic smell, one of acrid smoke and charred meat but also of rot, the kind of rot that takes centuries to build, the cloying odor of a forest floor, the musk of turned earth, and the rotten tang of flesh regurgitated by insects.

The closer we got to the city, the worse the stench became. Ian slowed to a plod, and I looked over my shoulder. I could tell by the set of his shoulders and his rigid expression that he was afraid.

I had to keep him talking, get his mind off where we were going. And my mind, while I was at it. I wanted to wake up, to snap my soul back to the living world, open my eyes and see the cobwebbed ceiling of Chang's shop, but if

I did, I knew I'd never forgive myself for failing Dean when he needed me the most. My soul-self could exist here a little longer. It was a small price to pay.

"How did you escape that place to begin with?" I asked Ian, pointing to the city. He flinched and shoved his hands into his pockets.

"In the Catacombs, there are guards—watchers who were never human, never part of anything living. They can be bribed, and I knew things that they wanted to know, things about the other prisoners. I was an informant," he said, as if dragging out the word physically hurt. "I got them to trust me, to think of me as amusing and harmless. Now I can't stay in the same place for more than an instant. The Deadlands are infinite. Physics here doesn't work the same as in a living Land. You could wander forever, compelled to drift, or cross your footsteps a hundred times in one day, but you better never slow down, because everything in this place is hungry for the energy your soul can provide."

I felt a strong stab of pity for Ian straight through my chest. Whatever he'd done in life, he didn't deserve this.

"I'm sorry I'm making you go back," I said softly.

Ian shrugged. "Don't feel bad on my account. Most Walkers forget their own names over time. They forget everything about who they were. I don't want that to happen. At least now I feel useful."

"Thank you," I said, but he said nothing in reply, so we walked silently as the sun went down and rose again, the sky changing every hour or so from rose to ink and back again.

I must have watched the sun rise a dozen times while Ian and I walked. He was right—physics didn't have the hold here it did in the living world. Finally Ian and I started talking again.

"You said someone in the city would know where Dean was," I began. "What are they going to want in return?"

Ian gave a thin smile. "You really are Archie's daughter, aren't you? Always looking for the angles."

"I didn't learn that from my father," I told him. "I learned that because he wasn't around."

"Ouch," Ian muttered. "Sorry."

"Just tell me how bad this is going to be," I said. I wanted to know what price would be culled from me, either in blood or in promises or in sanity. All of those were negotiable with the sort of creatures I'd met lurking in the shadows between worlds.

"There's a soul in there, one of the oldest I've met who still has her faculties," said Ian. "A Spiritualist when she was alive. She can find things, people. As for what she wants"—he scratched his temple—"it depends. Sometimes she does it because she thinks it'll be funny, other times she'll slice out part of your memories and take them. It's how she's stayed sane for so long."

I looked toward the city, listening to the endless wail of the sirens, the screaming of a place full of mindless pain. "Well, it's not like I expected this to be easy."

Ian didn't say anything, and I had run out of questions, so we walked on in silence, until we reached the city walls.

We joined a clot of gray-tinged spirits moving along the road, which forked into the distance until it shimmered out of existence at the horizon.

"Souls," Ian murmured in my ear. "The new dead. Just walk with them."

"Won't they realize we're not like them?" I whispered.

Ian shook his head.

"They don't notice much of anything. Some of them don't even realize they're dead yet."

The figures were in various states of decay and decomposition. I looked at Ian, who appeared as he must have in life, suit and tie and all. "How come they're in such bad shape?"

"Your soul manifests your true face when you die," Ian said. "Good or bad. If you're rotten to the core in life, your soul rots in death. Some of them hang on long enough to learn how to alter themselves so you can't see all the things they did in life."

Here and there, I picked out faces that were relatively normal-looking, but there were so many who were little more than skeletons with bits of flesh and cloth hanging from their bones that I focused on my feet, moving over the white ribbon of road. It crunched under my shoes.

"This isn't sand, is it?" I realized.

"No," Ian confirmed. "Ossuary Road is the bones of the things that lived in the Deadlands before men. The first creatures in the living world, the first to die. Eventually, even death grinds you down."

The white dust all over my feet and legs took on a new

weight. Who knew what came before the Fae, before men? "The Old Ones, you mean?" I said. "Things like that? I thought they were eternal."

" 'That is not dead which can eternal lie, yet with strange aeons even death may die,' " Ian said. "I don't know, Aoife. We had as little to do with the Great Old Ones in my day as we possibly could."

We had nearly reached the gates of the city and I looked up at the archway, carved with an open, lidless eye.

"Welcome home," Ian muttered. "Can't believe I'm walking back into this place."

Two black-clad figures stood by the gate like Proctors, making it seem almost like home. Their faces were shadowed with cowls, however, and I couldn't attest with certainty that they even had features to hide. Their robes reached the ground, and the only extremities I could see were hands, which held long, clicking devices that spun like oversized pocket watches.

"What are they?" I murmured, careful not to make eye contact. I knew how not to draw attention to myself, and I didn't *want* the attention of those things under any circumstances. Over time, since I'd left Lovecraft, I'd grown used to fear and uncertainty as background noise to everything I did, so when the hard, cold kind of primal fear cut straight to my gut, I didn't ignore it.

"Guards," Ian said. "Jailers. Protectors. Different things to different people." He steered me past a group of souls in Crimson Guard uniforms, their faces burned beyond recognition above their high collars.

"Those devices don't look friendly," I said, nodding to

the contraptions in the guards' hands. As the needles on the faces of the things spun, one of the black figures stepped forward and snatched a soldier out of line. I gasped as the figure got close enough to me to twinge the shoggoth venom that still lived in the bite on my shoulder, and Ian grabbed my arm, keeping me upright and moving.

"They're meant to pick out things from the outlands that try to creep into the city and steal souls," he said. "The decayed, the screaming sands, things like that."

The figures surrounded the soldier, more of them melting in from the shadows as if they'd dripped like inkblots from a pen, and the soldier began to scream. The appearance of a human soul sloughed away, and underneath was a skeletal thing with long legs that bent the wrong way and arms that scraped the ground. Its hands ended in long, bladed things that lived where fingers should on a person, and its jaw was elongated like a cricket's, underslung and full of teeth.

I braced myself to see carnage fly in every direction at the thing's exposure, but the four figures simply pressed closer, and after a moment the skeletal creature screamed and slumped to the ground, nothing but a pile of bones.

"Decayed," Ian said, and shivered as we walked on. "Hate those things."

I was glad I couldn't breathe, because I would have been hyperventilating with nerves. The figures had made short work of the monster disguised as a soldier's soul, but knowing things like that could be creeping among us made it difficult to keep walking, never mind keep my cool.

"The guards didn't seem too bothered by it," I ventured. "The Decayed, I mean. If they protect the souls from creatures like that, they can't be entirely bad news."

"Oh, no," Ian said. "They don't protect a damn thing but themselves. The Faceless are the worst thing in this place, by far. They feed on the energies of the souls. That's why they keep the monsters out—so the souls are all theirs for the taking."

He turned us away from the flow of new souls, which headed toward a central square much like Banishment Square in Lovecraft, where more of the Faceless waited. I craned my neck and saw the Faceless packing the souls in, shoulder to shoulder.

"Get deep enough into the Catacombs and the Faceless disappear," Ian said. "The old souls outnumber them, and they can fight back. They tend to stay up top, where the pickings are easy, and suck down the last little bit of life in a soul for their master."

"Master? You mean someone controls those things?" I said, casting a wary glance over my shoulder. I wasn't sure I wanted to meet such an individual.

"Some*thing*, and yes, they wear his sign," said Ian. "The sign of the Yellow King. He controls the Deadlands. Nobody sees him, but they're so scared of the Faceless they obey whatever he says."

"Sounds like a charming fellow," I said as we made a dozen more turns through a rat's maze of alleys that took us deeper and deeper into filth and squalor.

"I wouldn't know," Ian said. "I've never met him and I'm never going to. It's hard enough to dodge the Faceless without antagonizing them."

"Has it always been like this?" I asked as the sky blinked out, replaced by rooftops and smoke. "Is this really all that's waiting after you die? Torture and things like the Yellow King?"

Ian wrinkled his nose against the stale air. The smell was incredibly awful—one part butcher's shop, one part burning slag and many parts human filth and misery.

"People talk, of course," Ian said. "They say it wasn't always like this, that it was a land like any other and if you had a good life, you'd have a good death. An afterlife. But the Yellow King is all anyone knows now." He shrugged. "It's not like I can pick up and leave."

The idea of this being the end of the line made me sick to my stomach, so I changed the subject. "How far are we going?"

"Deep down," Ian said. "The guts of this place. That's where she lives."

He twitched at every sound, as rats—or something—ran over our feet, and I tried to put aside my own doubts and fears and reassure him. I was better at that than reassuring myself.

"I do appreciate your coming with me," I said. "More than you know."

"I just don't want you to get hurt when you figure out this insane plan of yours won't work," Ian muttered. "I told you, Aoife—dead is dead. The Deadlands can change you, but you'll never escape them."

"And I think differently," I snapped. "I guess we'll just have to agree to disagree."

"Until you realize that your Dean is stuck here," Ian grumbled. "And you might be, too, living soul or no."

"You must have been the life of every party before you expired," I told him. "Just a joy to be around."

"Archie had the same smart mouth," Ian said. "Nice to see you take after him so much."

We walked in silence after that, a silence that was thicker and tenser than before.

After a time, we reached a tumbledown brick well house, rife with rats and stink. A soul dressed in garb several centuries out of fashion dozed in the mud, snoring, with a bottle spilling sticky green liquid across the cobbles. Roaches scattered from the puddle when we approached.

"Finch," Ian said, kicking the man's foot. "Wake up."

Finch grunted and sniffed, red-rimmed eyes slowly rolling from his considerable gut to Ian's face. "You!" he exclaimed. "Stone and sun, Ian . . . we all thought you'd buggered off for the screaming sands."

"I did," Ian said. "But I'm back and I need to speak with her."

Finch grinned, exposing just how bad dentistry had been at the time he'd died. "They all come back sooner or later," he said. "Once you've had her in your skull you can't stay away."

"Enough," Ian snarled, and I saw something flash across his face, which at first I thought was anger but soon realized was shame. Ian was ashamed to be here, ashamed of what was about to happen.

I resolved to keep a straight face, no matter what occurred, and not reveal any reaction. He was jumpy enough as it was.

"Anyway," Ian said, "I'm not here for myself. I'm here for her."

"Oho!" Finch staggered up, and I caught the stench of absinthe as his breath blasted in my face like a furnace. "A pretty little one, ain't she, Ian?"

"You'll want to take a step back," I told him. "I may be little, but I'm not nice."

Finch laughed, deep and full-bellied, and then kicked open the door to the well house. "Same as it ever was, Ian," he said. "Go down till you can't go no more, then follow the trail into my lady's chambers. She'll be so happy to see you."

"You're a sad, stupid drunk," Ian growled. "You've never been anything but, in life and in death, and now you get to spend eternity knowing exactly how sad and stupid you are."

"Maybe so," Finch said, still grinning. "But at least I get to stay up here, Ian. I'm not like you. I don't have to see her. I don't need anyone but meself."

I caught Ian by the arm as he started to lunge for the fat man. "Come on," I said. "The quicker we get this over with, the quicker I'll be gone and you can go back to whatever you were doing."

"Just trying to exist," Ian muttered as the well house door swung shut behind us and left us in darkness. Gray light filtered through the broken roof, and I could just make out a huge bucket, large enough to hold me, with rusted sides.

Attached to the well chain was a sort of cage, equipped with a lever to move the chain from inside. The well was dry, and I swore I could hear music from far below.

"I know the feeling," I told Ian as we climbed into the cage. It swung back and forth at an alarming rate, but appeared solid under our feet.

I could be hurt here, I knew that much. My soul was floating free, and if it was injured, I might not be able to come back to myself. I held on to the side of the cage as Ian engaged the lever.

"You couldn't possibly know what I'm going through," he told me. "What it's meant to try to not be snuffed out ever since I came here."

"Really?" I faced him as the chain unfurled and lowered us into the well. A red glow rose from below, giving Ian's features a hollow quality, as if he really were disintegrating like the souls we'd seen on the road. I tried not to look at him. It just made the bad feeling I'd had ever since I'd woken up on the road worse.

"You don't know me," I told Ian. "You don't know what my life has been like. I've spent most of it just like you—trying to exist, hoping someone much more powerful wouldn't snuff me out. The only difference is that I'm not afraid. I'm stronger than the people trying to keep me from existing."

"That's great," Ian said. "But in this place, the things looking to take you out aren't some men in jackboots and a few Fae who whisper sweet lies in your ear. In this place, there are horrors you can't imagine."

"I don't know," I said, still furious that he was writing me off as a silly child. I'd had enough of that back in Lovecraft. "My imagination is pretty vivid."

"Well, after this you're going to have enough fodder for a lifetime of nightmares," Ian said. "So get ready."

The Graveyard of Memories

WE REACHED THE bottom of the well after an interminable ride punctuated only by the creaking of the cage and
the rattling of the chain.

Finally, the cage came to rest on the small bones of rats
and other, larger creatures with more teeth.

I was just glad they were only bones, and not entire souls
waiting for us in the blood-tinged darkness.

The lights came from dozens of aether bulbs hung along
a tunnel that had been bored into the rock and bricked
over, crooked and jagged, the ground covered with piles of
masonry from cave-ins.

The red light made everything shift and shimmer before
my eyes. I could barely make out Ian in his dark suit as he
walked ahead of me down the tunnel.

I stepped over the broken bricks, and managed not to cry
out when something scampered across my foot. The tunnel widened, and Ian slowed to a stop.

"Just through there," he said. He sighed and looked at me. "You're about to see a part of me I'm not proud of, Aoife." He ran a hand over his face and looked pained. "If you make it back to Archie, don't tell him about this. I beg you."

"Of course not," I said, reaching out to touch the back of his hand. Was that it? Ian was so ashamed of whatever he'd done for this oracle spirit that he didn't want his brother knowing what his afterlife had become?

I tried to smile, to let him know I was on his side. "It's all right, Ian. I don't have time to go into detail, but I of all people know that sometimes you do what you think you have to."

Ian visibly relaxed. "Thank you," he said. "Thank you so much."

I looked ahead into the darkness. "So what do I need to know before I talk to her?"

"She wants what's most precious to you," Ian said. "And she'll bleed you dry little by little because it amuses her to see you suffer. But you need her, and she knows it, because she has powers beyond anyone I've ever met."

"All right," I said, taking a step forward. "Thank you, Ian."

I wasn't above lying to myself, telling the nervous, scared Aoife who just wanted to wake up that there was nothing to worry about, nothing to getting this oracle to tell me where Dean was and how to bring him back to the Iron Land with me.

That Aoife wasn't a very good liar, but at least she gave me a little bit of comfort as Ian and I walked ahead. I could believe her, for the few minutes this would take.

We were inside an empty cistern, a storage place for water in the old times of the city, which were long gone now. "What does a dead city need with water and sewers?" I asked Ian.

"It's what you see," he said. "All the souls see a different city. Some see a medieval keep, some see a sleek metropolis. You and I know what lives under the ground in the Iron Land, and we know to be wary of it. So you and I see a soot-ridden industrial wasteland, because that's what my afterlife is and yours will be too—nothing but monsters and smoke and iron, as far as the eye can see."

"Thanks again for cheering me up," I told him. "Were you always this grim or was it brought on by death?"

"My brother often said I could make a clown weep tears of despair," Ian said. "But Archie mostly liked to hear himself talk."

"Clowns deserve it," I said. "After all, they make everyone else weep tears of despair."

The center of the cistern was built up out of junk that had fallen into the sewers: furniture, old metal cargo boxes, even the front end of a jitney, its windows papered over with illustrations from books depicting scared children fleeing through a darkened wood.

The jitney door was covered with a silk curtain, through which even more red light shone.

"What now?" I whispered to Ian.

"Now you come in," a rich, velvety female voice intoned, and the curtain twitched aside of its own accord.

"Go," Ian told me when I looked back at him in question. "What's said inside is meant for you and you alone."

I girded myself and climbed the rickety steps into the

jitney. It had been cut in half by some explosive accident, and the back was built out of old doors, some with carved gargoyle faces, some made of metal bars, all covered in silken rags and clothes.

In front of them was a pile of filthy cushions, and on that pile sat a woman wearing a mourning dress, the full skirt, corset and bustle speaking to a distant, more refined time.

Her face was pale but much younger than I was expecting, and she peered at me from under a hat and veil trimmed in black raven feathers.

"You're a sight, aren't you?" she said. "In my day, a girl would never run about in trousers, with her hair unpinned."

"In your day, you were still alive," I retorted. "So I guess we're even."

Her face split in a wide grin, and she patted the cushion next to her. "Sit down, my dear. I rather like you. How did you find me?"

I sat, but not too close. "Ian helped me."

"Ian *Grayson*?" Her laugh sounded like the rough, hungry call of a ghoul. "Well, well. There's a name I never thought I'd hear again."

"He's my uncle," I said, deciding the direct approach was best, "and I don't think he likes you much."

"You're correct," she said. "But there was a time that he liked me very much indeed. When he was my eyes and ears aboveground, my enforcer, convincing souls to come and give up part of themselves so I could stay alive. We were in love, and then he ran. So many love stories end that way."

I looked her in the eye. She had the same deep black

voids as the spirits who'd attacked me in the Iron Land. "I know all about Ian," I said. "I'm not shocked, so why don't you and I discuss what I came here to do?"

Her smile vanished. "You know, suddenly I don't think I like you so much anymore."

"I don't like you either," I said. "There, now we agree on something. Can I ask my question and get your price?"

She bared her teeth for a moment, but I kept my expression stony. I wasn't going to play games with this woman. She wasn't any different from the petty students at the Academy or the manipulative care-parents I'd had to live with. As long as I didn't show weakness, she didn't have power.

"What's your name, girl?" she said at last.

"Aoife," I answered. I dared her with my gaze to make some comment one way or the other. "What do they call you?" I countered.

She brought back the grin, hungrier and less sincere. "My name is Ariadne," she said. "In my time, there were legends of a maiden who led a hero through a maze to safety. That's why my father named me so—a fair girl with courage and heart."

"Looks like he went wrong somewhere," I muttered under my breath.

"Now they call me Miss Spider," she said. "No longer the way out of the maze but the monster at the center of it."

I forced myself to keep sitting still, holding her gaze. "I've met a lot of monsters. I just want to ask my question and be on my way."

"Ah," Spider said, running a fingernail up my arm. Her

187

touch was like fire. "But what do you have to offer me in return?"

"Whatever your price," I said. "I'm willing to negotiate." I decided to just plunge ahead and let it all out in one breath. "I'm trying to find a soul trapped here in the Catacombs. His name is Dean Harrison. He wasn't supposed to die, and I need to find him."

Spider tapped her chin, as if she were doing sums in her head. "To find one of the new dead among the clamoring horde . . . if he's even still in one piece after the Faceless are done with him—"

"Don't say you can't do it," I interrupted. "I know you can. Ian said if anyone could, it was you."

"Ian always was a flatterer," she said. "And you're right, Aoife. I can do it. But I won't. You don't have anything that's worth leading someone into the Catacombs. You don't have anything that will make me go head-to-head with the Faceless." She flounced her skirts and looked away. "There's nothing I can do."

"That's crap," I said loudly, standing up. "You can do it. You just don't want to."

"I'm a businesswoman." Spider stretched out on the cushions, dislodging a cluster of roaches that skittered into the darkness. "And you're just a sad little scrap with nothing I want."

I had sworn I wouldn't reveal what I was to anyone except Ian, but if this was the only way to Dean, I had no choice. "I'm not dead," I told Spider.

Her black drowning-pool eyes grew by halves. "*What* did you say?" she demanded.

"I'm alive," I said. "Back in the Iron Land. I'm using a machine to detach my soul from my body and venture here. But I'm alive, so that has to be worth something."

Spider stared at me, and I knew I had her. The pure hunger in her eyes was unnerving, the expression of a desperately starving girl suddenly within reach of sustenance.

"I suppose," she said carefully, "that we might work something out."

"You want memories?" I said. "My soul? What?"

"You're eager." Spider regained some of her composure, managed to rein in the starved expression in her eyes. "What's this Dean boy to you?"

"Everything," I said honestly. "That's why I'm willing to do whatever it takes."

"Very well," Spider said. "Your best memory. Your happiest moment. You want happiness back, I want what you hold most dear."

I couldn't remember a time I'd been truly happy or content. The joke was on Spider with this one.

"Done," I said, and held out my hand. "Take it."

"In time," Spider said, rising from the pillows with surprising alacrity for a woman wearing such a heavy dress. "I always deliver on my promises before I take payment." She came close, so close I could smell the heavy scent of dirt and decay wrapped around her as tightly as her clothing. "But I always get paid, Aoife. Make no mistake, and don't try to cheat me."

"I'm honest," I said. "You give me what I want and you can pry whatever happy moments you like free from my brain."

Spider gave me a bright smile and a pat on the shoulder. "That's what I like to hear. Come now, let's go meet Ian and find your boy before the Faceless chew him up and spit him out."

Ian was pacing the dirt outside the jitney, and his face pulled tighter than a slamming door when he saw Spider. "Look at you," she cooed. "Poor Ian. Those months and years of being a Walker have been so unkind."

She crossed the space between them and touched his cheek, sparing me a look as I stood by uncomfortably. "He used to have such a handsome face."

Ian recoiled from her touch. "Don't start with me, Spider. What's between you and the girl has nothing to do with me."

"She's your blood," Spider drawled. "And you have nothing to do with her?"

"Don't listen," Ian told me. "Spider will twist your ear as long as you let her, and twist your head in the bargain."

"Oh, Ian," she laughed. It wasn't a pleasant laugh. It was the sound a person would make as something sharp jabbed into her flesh. "You always were such a sweet-talker."

Spider led us down another long tunnel, part of the sewers that were apparently a piece of what was inside my head. I wondered at what memory the Deadlands had drawn on, what kind of darkness inside me that it fed on. I wasn't sure I really wanted to know.

As we walked deeper, the muddy ground sloping beneath our feet, the sewers gave way to something older.

The walls were studded with alcoves that held skulls, and the eyes lit up with a faint green glow as we passed.

"Just remnants of souls," said Spider. "What's left when the Faceless are done with them."

I felt a plummeting sensation in my gut. "Dean's not . . ."

"Oh no, dear," Spider said. "He's far too new. And if he was taken before his time, he's got fight in him. They could use him for centuries before they drain him dry."

"Thank you for being so reassuring to the girl," Ian said from behind me.

"I consider it part of the service," Spider said dryly. She stopped at a fork in the tunnel and took the left-hand path.

I followed, listening to water drip and things skitter in the darkness beyond the glowing eyes of the skulls. Just as I was beginning to think Spider had betrayed us, she stopped at a figure standing in the shadows.

"Ian," she snapped, "be a dear and give a lady some light."

Ian sighed, but drew out his lighter and flicked the lid open. A flame blossomed and illuminated the figure of a girl. Her dress was lush and purple, the sort of thing worn to the type of party a girl like me could only read about in old storybooks. Her hair was immaculate, but dry and weak as a spiderweb, so thin and pale that Ian's light penetrated it, turning it molten gold.

The waist of her dress had been cut away, and resting where her guts should have been sat the face of a clock, all brass and gear and ticking urgency. The girl's clockwork eyes rolled open, and camera irises regarded us with the dispassionate glare of a machine.

Spider bent to examine the face of the clock. "Counters,"

she said. "The Faceless use them to keep track of all the souls in any given quadrant of the city. We think they were alive, once—the lost and the forgotten sorts."

"They look human," I said.

"A lot of things in this place *look* human," Spider told me with a wink. "But rest assured, this pretty face was never anything but a predator stalking the red-light district and making herself sick on human souls."

She jabbed at the clock, causing the gears to seize. "Isn't that right, dearie?"

The girl's jaw was clockwork, but it worked a bit, and even though her eyes weren't human, I saw something in them—pain, and sadness. The same sort of look I saw on caged animals, ones who knew they had no hope of escape.

"Tell her who you're looking for," Spider said.

"Dean Harrison," I told the counter. "I need to find Dean Harrison."

Something inside her skull whirred, the spiderweb hair vibrating slightly, and then her torso rotated, the clockwork ticking, counting something off. Souls? Seconds? Last breaths?

I didn't know, but she pointed down one of the many tunnels around us. "Number sixty-three," she said in an echoey voice piped through some sort of aethervox.

"And there you have it," Spider said. She looked over her shoulder as a cry echoed through the tunnel. "And we better get moving, if we don't want to become just another pet for the Faceless to amuse themselves with."

We hurried down the tunnel. This place was completely different from the skull-lined corridors. Those had been like something out of a bad dream or a horror story. This place was all iron, like a prison back in the living world, each door marked with a clumsily painted number.

I could hear sounds from behind some doors, and shadows danced beyond the bars of others, small windows set at face level. I saw fangs, twisted features, skulls without skin and shrieking vapors without form.

"This is odd," Spider said. For the first time, she didn't sound as if she were two breaths away from mocking me. "This place . . . this is for the worst souls, murderers and the kinds the king wishes to keep under close observation." She turned her eyes on me. "You didn't withhold the fact that your Dean is some kind of bad boy, did you?"

"Dean shouldn't be here," I said. I was starting to feel frantic. This was worse than I'd thought. If the king kept souls that he particularly wanted here, why was he keeping Dean? And what price was I going to have to pay to release him?

"And yet, he is here," Spider said, coming to a stop. Her long, tattered skirt whispered around her feet, across the stone floor. "Right here, in fact." She raised her hand to point at the ragged 63 painted above the door.

I flew across the space, all of my senses leaving me. I felt my body collide with the iron door, felt bruises blossom, but at the same time didn't really process any of it. My eyes searched the cell and found only darkness save the tiny cube of light projected from the window.

"Ian!" I shouted, desperate. "I need light!"

"All right, all right," he said, putting his hand on my shoulder. He squeezed, and I knew he was trying to calm me. I was trying to calm myself but was having no success.

The light penetrated each corner of the cell, until it

finally lit on Dean. I let out a sob of relief, and banged my fists against the iron. Only Ian grabbing my wrists got me to stop.

Dean looked up, his gray eyes silver in the dim light. "Aoife?" he said softly. "Aoife . . . are you dead?"

"It's a long story," I said. "Sort of, but not really. But that doesn't matter, Dean. I'm here to get you out."

"Not now, you're not," Spider said, looking over her shoulder. I heard a whisper close by, the sound of a soft foot over stone. "Faceless," she said. "We have to leave, now."

"No." I grabbed the bars, reaching for Dean. "I'm not leaving without him."

"You stupid girl, there's nothing we can do!" Spider snapped. "Unless you plan to seek an audience with the king himself and bargain for the boy's release, he's here to stay."

I turned on her, feeling the slow-burning fury in me turn volcanic. "You said you would help me."

"And I could, if he were a regular soul!" Spider shouted. "But he's not! For whatever reason, the king's taken an interest in him, and there's nothing I or you or anyone can do about that."

She grabbed for me, but I wrenched my hand free. "I'm not leaving."

"We must!" Ian hissed. "Or the Faceless will apprehend us." His face blanched. "I'm not going back, Aoife. I'm not staying here, not in this rancid city. Do you have any idea what they'll do to me?"

Dean blinked, as if he'd just been woken from a dream. "Aoife, I never thought I'd see you again. . . ."

"Don't worry," I told Dean. "I'm going to get you out of here."

"Forget her!" Spider shouted, dragging Ian farther down the tunnel. "She's done for!"

I heard them, but it was as if they were already far away. I was far too focused on Dean.

"I'm sorry, Aoife . . . ," Ian started, but the shadows of the Faceless had penetrated the tunnel, and he turned and ran.

I stayed where I was, waiting for the silent hooded figures to approach. They surrounded me, and it took a moment before I could speak.

"I know that your job is to exterminate me," I said. "It's what you must do. But before you do, I seek an audience with your king."

The Faceless tilted their heads, and I knew they were staring at me even though I couldn't see their eyes.

"Aoife, no . . . ," Dean said from his cell. "No, don't do this. You don't know what he's like, what you're getting yourself into. . . ."

"I do," I said. "I'm doing what I have to."

Looking back at the Faceless, I put on my bravest expression. At least, I hoped it was brave. Or merely foolhardy, instead of terrified. "I know you can talk," I told the closest Faceless. "I know you can understand me."

"And if we were to take you to the king," it hissed at me, its voice like steam scalding skin, "what would you have to offer?"

"That's between me and the king, don't you think?" I snapped. "I don't deal with minions."

The Faceless hissed as one, but then they parted and gestured for me.

"Aoife, no . . . ," Dean said again, but I held up my hand to stop his arguments.

"It's all right, Dean." If this was the way it had to be, I'd do what I had to. I'd talk to the king, and I'd find a way to give him whatever he demanded for Dean's release.

I walked to the center of the Faceless, and was surrounded by them as they led me to the mouth of the tunnel.

"You must think you're very brave," said the Faceless in the lead.

"No," I said. "Not brave. Just determined."

"Come, then," another said. "Come with us, and see the one who waits."

Across the Bleak Plain

THE FACELESS TRAVELED on foot and kept their circle tight around me, until I felt as if I'd smother.

As we left the city behind, I tried to move out of the tight knot of black robes, but the nearest Faceless hissed, sounding more like a serpent than a thing that was even remotely human, and I shrank back. "I'm sorry," I said.

As we walked, the sun grew lower in the sky, a violet sunset that cast all of the land in a strange purple glow. I sped up my stride to get closer to the figure in the lead.

"How far are we going?"

"Two day's walk from here lies the domain of the Yellow King," said the Faceless.

"I am human," I reminded him. "I need rest and food and water."

"We will stop when it reaches full dark," said the creature. "At the edge of the Moaning Marsh."

"I can't tell you how excited I am about that," I muttered under my breath, but I resigned myself to walking until the Faceless were good and ready to stop.

The land flattened out, the short grass and scrub giving way to dense thickets and underbrush, and the land at the edges of the road growing wetter. The smell of decay and the whine of insects permeated the air around us, and I slapped at every inch of bare skin. I still ended up covered in welts.

I envied the Faceless their cloaks, and their lack of faces.

Finally, when I was just about to collapse and refuse to go any farther, the group circling me veered off the path. I saw a rough camp set up, a fire pit and some battered lean-tos. The stink of the marsh was all around us, and I realized that I'd be lucky to get any sleep.

"Here," said the leader. He was a bit taller than the others, but that was the only way I could differentiate him. "We rest."

The robed figures left the road and re-formed their circle, hunkering down on the ground like crows coming to roost. Their cowls drooped over the voids underneath, and after a time I could hear nothing but a slight wind through the reeds of the nearby marsh.

The ever-present cold of the Deadlands soon found its way into my bones, and I made my way back over to their small group and nudged the leader of the Faceless. "I'm cold."

I got no reaction, and when I waved my hand in front of their cowls, nothing stirred. At least that left me free to go build a fire, if I could find anything to burn.

The marsh stretched as far as I could see, the dank smell of rotting plants rising up to meet my nose as I squelched through the mud, picking off the gray branches of drowned trees where I could find them. The wood was light and dry and would burn well.

I missed my father all the time, but I'd never missed him more than at that moment. He could light fire with a thought—it was his Weird. I had to resort to finding two rocks and striking them together until a spark finally caught the dried grass and twigs I'd stuffed into the center of a pile of sticks.

The Faceless paid no more attention to the fire than they had to me, and I drew close to it, holding my hands above the flames and trying to tuck my jacket around me.

I didn't think I could sleep with all the worries about Dean, meeting the king and getting us both out of here banging in my head, but I'd drifted off, head bowed low, before I realized it.

The sound that woke me was inhuman, even for this place. It rose from within the earth, low and then oscillating higher and higher until I thought my eardrums would burst. It retreated, increased, as if everything around me in the marsh was screaming.

I got up and pulled a branch from the fire, the flame at the end of it flickering before me as I walked toward the sound. The Faceless never stirred, the wind ruffling the edges of their robes. They paid no more mind to it than statues would.

The marsh mud sucked at my feet, but the ground seemed firm enough a few inches down. I saw a blue light ahead, bobbing and weaving through the drowned forest, and doused my flame to follow it.

I couldn't say why I was creeping around the Deadlands in the dark, just that the strange sounds and the blue light had captivated me. Dimly, I realized I was under the same sort of compulsion as when Lei had drugged me, but I couldn't stop moving.

There were more lights, more moaning, only now it resolved into voices, whispers too indistinct to make out what they were saying.

All around me, the blue lights blossomed, and I could see they were tiny bodies, faces, with black eyes and long black teeth dripping with marsh muck.

I wanted to scream, but I couldn't even do that.

What is she? one hissed. *She's not dead.*

She's marked, another whispered. *Marked for the one who waits.*

Not anymore, said the first. *Now she'll stay here with us, and we'll let the marsh swallow up her bones.*

All at once, just as I was starting to panic, a different kind of glow filled the marsh, and the bobbing blue shapes fled, screeching. The marsh gave one last, heaving groan and then everything settled again, except for the ever-present wind.

"You shouldn't be out here alone," a voice said. The syllables were clipped, from somewhere in Europe.

Reality crashed down around me like a thunderstorm, and I came back to myself. I found myself no longer standing in mud but in water up to my chest, feet sinking deeper into the muck with every passing second.

"Stay calm," the voice said. "They lure you into the water

and you drown without even realizing it. Before you can blink, you're one of them, trapped in the Moaning Marsh for eternity."

"You sure know a lot about this place," I managed. The water was freezing, and my teeth chattered so violently I could barely talk.

"I've spent many nights here watching the glow," the voice said. "Those things—I think they're dead creatures from the marsh. Certainly not human." The owner of the voice glided into view, managing to stay on top of the marsh even as I sank deeper.

"I try to help travelers when I can," said Tesla. "But you're not just a traveler, are you?"

I gaped, and stopped trying to stay afloat. Rancid water flowed over my lips and up my nose and I choked.

"Easy, easy," he said. "You've got to move toward the shore." Like the souls I'd encountered in the Iron Land, he possessed a slight silver glow, and when he glided closer to me, he illuminated solid ground about five yards away. "You can do it," Tesla said. "You just can't panic."

I tried to move slowly, to float rather than sink, and eventually I pulled myself into the relatively solid mud, shaking uncontrollably.

"There, now." He crouched beside me as I spat marsh water. I took the opportunity to look him in the eye, still hardly able to believe that out of all the souls roaming the Deadlands, I'd encountered him. "That wasn't so bad, was it?"

"You and I have very different ideas about 'not so bad,'" I told him.

Tesla cracked a thin smile. "And I meant what I said

201

before. I see a lot of Walkers, but you're not one of them. You're not just passing through; you're going somewhere."

"To see the king," I agreed. His expression told me everything I needed to know about that idea. I tried to put on a brave face nonetheless.

"Then you're going somewhere, but somewhere you'll never return from."

"I have"—I took a deep breath and decided to just come out with it—"I have so much I need to ask you, Mr. Tesla."

He helped me to my feet and gave a wan smile as he regarded my soaked frame. "Please. Call me Nikola."

Before I could tell him that I wasn't sure I could do that, not until I processed that I'd actually met a great man such as him, albeit after death, he started walking, leaving me to follow.

We reached some rocks on the far side of the marsh. A line of blue sunlight had started at the horizon. "The nights are short here," I said, and then wanted to bang my head against the same rocks for saying something so inane to Tesla himself.

"Nothing makes sense here," said Tesla. "You'll find that out if you stay much longer."

"I can't," I said. "I'm just here for one thing."

"No," Tesla said. "You may have come here initially for selfish reasons, but now that the Yellow King knows of your existence, you are here at his pleasure. He will never allow you to find what you seek."

I took in a shaky breath. I couldn't seem to get rid of the bone-deep cold the marsh had put in me. "I just want to get my friend back. And I found him, so if the king is out to stop me, he's slow."

"I'm not talking about Dean Harrison," Tesla said. "I'm talking about the real reason you're here, Aoife. The Old Ones."

I stopped walking at that, and folded my arms. "How do you know so much if you're just a spirit?"

Tesla shrugged. "I was an inventor in life, and in death I have found ways to harness the energies of this bleak place. They feed me information, fluctuations in the fields." He scraped a hand across his eyes. "Time was, I knew everything. Now it seems as if bits and pieces fall away as quickly as the bones that the souls grind on Ossuary Road.

"Stopping the Old Ones is something you will never accomplish," Tesla said. "Imagine my horror when I found, through my Gates, that they were the spark, the source of magic and wonder in the universe. Something so horrible giving life to such brilliance, all across the Land."

"I really just want Dean," I lied, but Tesla shook his head.

"The king, the Old Ones—they are all threads binding the universe," he said. "And I have not as yet figured out how the knot is tied, but I do know that if you pull one string, it will all unravel."

I stared at Tesla and tried to look stony. "I have to try."

"And once you steal from the king, and upset the plans of the Old Ones, what is *your* plan?" Tesla snapped. "You will be a marked woman."

"I'm a living soul," I said. "Somebody in the Iron Land is waiting for me."

"And they found a way to come here and return to the living?" Tesla shook his head. "You know, I'd read theories. I even tried to construct a prototype once, but it failed miserably. Whoever sent you over is a genius."

"He's a drunk," I said. "He doesn't even know we're using his device."

Tesla barked a laugh. "I know how that feels. How you create something and can't see that it could be used for evil." His face drew down. "Can't see what you've done until it's too late."

"You couldn't possibly know what the Gates would do," I told him, picking up on his discomfort. "You couldn't know what was beyond them."

"I had hopes," Tesla said. "To see worlds beyond my own. Everyone in the scientific community laughed at me, but there were a few men, men who were not of science but of the otherworld, who didn't think what I'd said was at all laughable."

He went to the edge of the rock and stood silhouetted against the rising sun. "The Fae had been using their *hexen-rings* to visit the Iron Land since time immemorial, taking our children, playing with humans as if we were pets. We just wanted a way to strike back. I wanted to help. I had no idea that us constructing our own Gate, sending the flow the other way, would fracture the barriers between all the worlds, allow things to come from anywhere and everywhere." He rubbed his forehead. "Yes, things like you and I and full-blooded Fae need to use a Gate, but I always knew that the endgame would be the barriers fraying, time and space crashing into each other, and the destruction of the universe. Only the Old Ones will survive, and that's the way they like it. They're probably laughing at us right now."

"They're doing a lot more than that," I said softly. I

thought I'd feel shame, but it felt almost good to finally tell someone the truth. "I almost destroyed the Iron Land, and I bargained with them to set things right. All I really got was my mother back, though. They didn't fix the destruction, and now they're returning to the Lands because of what I did."

Tesla shut his eyes. "You found my last Gate. The one to the dreamland, to that awful man in black."

"Crow's not awful," I said, thinking of the sad, pale man who lived alone in the land that controlled the dreams of all the others. "He tried to stop me. But I didn't listen. And I didn't listen to anyone else, so now I'm here trying to save my friend who died because I couldn't live with what I'd done."

I didn't have to breathe in the Deadlands, but it appeared that I could cry. Tears slipped down my cheeks, colder than my frozen skin.

"Listen to me," Tesla said. He came back to me and took me by the shoulders. "Why you came here isn't important. You were probably doomed from the moment you went under. The Old Ones are the most powerful things in the universe, yes, but the worst one is Nylarthotep."

Tesla was solid, if gray, as if he were a piece of lantern reel in the world of color. I looked down at his hands. "What happened to you? You're not like the other Walkers."

He gave a dry laugh. "I'm what happens after you've been a Walker for a few hundred years. Eventually I'll dry up and blow away. But not today."

"The Great Old Ones grew terrified of the power Nylarthotep commanded," he said, "so they dumped him here,

205

cut off from everything, with only the dead for company. Here he's the Yellow King."

I shifted my feet. If the Faceless knew I was gone, then all this trying to get them to lead me to the Yellow King would be for nothing. "I should get back to the camp."

"No!" For the first time, Tesla's face hardened, and he grabbed me by the wrist when I tried to walk away. I struggled, panicked, but for a dead man he was strong.

"I must have an audience with him," I said. "It's the only way to get Dean out of here."

"And I'm telling you that there's no hope of that," Tesla said. "That Fae nonsense about everyone having a thread of life and only when it's cut by fate do you descend into the Deadlands? That's bunk. You die, you're dead, and the spheres keep turning without you."

"No . . ." I shook my head and tried to struggle, but there was no undoing his grasp. "No, I heard if it wasn't your time . . ."

"You were marked the moment you came to the Deadlands," Tesla told me. "The Yellow King knows someone with your gifts is his only hope of getting free, of returning to the power he once commanded. The Old Ones might destroy us, or they might usher in a new age of science and prosperity, but if Nylarthotep is freed it will be the end of everything—for the Fae, for the Iron Land, for *everything*."

"You can't know that," I told him. I didn't want to believe anything he was saying, but I had a horrible, sinking feeling in my guts that it was true.

"I can," Tesla said. "Because when I died and came here, he tried to do the same thing with me."

A wan smile lit his face, and in the growing light I could see the hollow pain in his eyes, the look of permanent loss, of things he could never get back, only remember. My mother had had the same look, for as long as I'd known her.

"He took me from the Catacombs, when my soul had barely realized it was dead," Tesla continued, "and he asked me to open a Gate. I was dead, so I could no longer use any of my Weird, but he didn't believe there wasn't *something* I could do for him."

Tesla released me, but he didn't need to keep me close. I wasn't going anywhere now. I had to hear the end of his story.

"He tortured me for months—maybe years," Tesla said. "Time flows differently here, I'm sure you can feel. He tormented me, kept me as his special amusement. And you're walking into his trap. He'll string you along, promising to release your friend's soul back into the world, and then he'll cut you a deal—your friend's new life for his own freedom."

Tesla shut his eyes and sucked in a breath. "And you'll take it. Because if I had had the power, at the end of my time under him, I would have done anything he asked just to make it stop."

"I—" I started, but he cut me off.

"You'll sacrifice what's left of the Lands for your friend, because that's what he wants. Nothing but death and destruction. An age under the Yellow Sign, and even the Old Ones won't be able to stop him if he escapes."

I tried to stand, but my knees went weak. I'd been tunnel-visioned for so long, focusing only on Dean, that everyone telling me that what I wanted was impossible had flown in one ear and out the other.

"It can't be true," I whispered, but even to my ears my voice was thready and unconvincing. More important, *I* wasn't convinced anymore.

Where had I gotten the information from? My mother, who was unreliable under the best of circumstances and given to spinning outright fantasies at the worst.

And ever since I'd come here, Ian and Spider and everyone else had told me it was impossible.

"I'll just . . ." I swallowed hard. Letting Dean go felt as if I'd reached into my chest and torn out my own heart, as if I grasped it bloody and warm and still beating in my fist, squeezing the last of the life from it.

"Just wake up?" Tesla snorted. "No. Your body is alive but your soul is here, and now that Nylarthotep knows about you, only he can allow you to leave. And he won't do that unless you bargain with him."

"Then what am I supposed to do?" I screamed. A flight of birds lifted from the marsh at the sound, disappearing into the sky.

Tesla shook his head. "He only let me go because I was useless to him. I hope you're smarter than I am, Aoife. I really do."

He started to say more, but his head jerked up at a whisper of sound from behind us, and all at once I was surrounded by the Faceless. Tesla had vanished surely as a vapor.

What do you think you're doing? one of them hissed at me.

"I'm sorry," I said, putting the appropriate amount of

quaver in my voice. It wasn't hard. "I followed one of those blue lights . . . I . . ."

The leader of the Faceless grabbed me by the arm. "Stupid girl," he growled, dragging me back to the road.

"We reach the place today," he said. "No more time for you wandering off."

"I'm sorry," I said again, but they'd circled me already and didn't reply.

We walked, but I barely paid attention to my surroundings. My mind was full of what Tesla had told me, and boiled over when I added to the mix the fact that I was never going to get Dean back.

Had never been going to.

Had let myself be blinded by hope and grief.

Was this what had happened to Tesla, after he caused the Storm? Had he become so numb that he simply faded away?

And what waited for me with the Yellow King? According to Tesla, he was the worst thing in the universe. The root of all evil, really.

Waiting for me. Waiting for me to free him, which was something I was almost sure I couldn't do here, in the Deadlands.

As if losing Dean wasn't bad enough, a splitting pain ripped through my skull, stopping me in my tracks.

I moaned and lost my footing, going to ground on the gritty roadbed.

The Faceless surrounded me, whispering among themselves, but I couldn't focus on anything except the pain. It felt like when I'd first tried to make a Gate without any sort of apparatus to support my Weird. Like I was being torn in half and sent to opposite ends of the universe.

Cal and Conrad must be trying to wake me up, I realized through the pain and my own screaming. I writhed in the dust, stinging crystals coating my throat.

But it was as Tesla had said—nothing happened, and after a moment the pain ceased and I was left shaking and nauseated on the road.

"What happened?" one of the Faceless asked their leader.

"I don't understand humans," the leader said. "Get her up. Keep walking. The king is expecting us."

If I hadn't been sure that Nylarthotep was expecting me before, that this was all part of his plan, I was now.

I was going into the lair of the one all the spirits had warned me about, and there wasn't a damn thing I could do to protect myself.

The One Who Waits

As we walked, I detected a subtle change in the landscape around us. The Deadlands were varied and terrifying in every aspect, but now I sensed a shift in the very fabric of reality itself. My Weird made me sensitive to such things. The trees turned in odd directions, the branches curling into spirals. The ground appeared to shimmer and reappear, first as sand, then water, then back to sand.

I sensed the insidious influence of something, someone, on the landscape, on the very physics that made up this twisted mockery of reality that was the Deadlands.

Tesla had been right. Nylarthotep, if this was him, was powerful beyond anyone I had encountered.

I tried not to let that sink me into a panic as we walked on, the landscape shimmering more and more at the edges.

"So when do we get to the palace?" I asked, more to

distract myself than to make conversation. The Faceless wouldn't answer me anyway.

"There is no palace," the leader said, surprising me. "There is only the view of the Yellow King, or his absence."

"All right, then," I muttered. I thought the Fae had loved to be cryptic, to muck around with people's heads, but they had nothing on the Faceless. Tremaine could take lessons from them.

"If I'm to have an audience with him," I said loudly, "I am going to have to actually see him."

"You're awfully eager for a mortal," said the Faceless. "To look upon his visage is to endure madness and pain beyond anything you can imagine."

I stopped, stared into the black hole beneath the creature's cowl. "You have no idea what I can imagine. Or endure."

He wheezed something in a language made of whispers and wind. I think he might have been cursing my stubborn refusal to be scared.

"Come," he said. "We draw near."

We walked on until the road disappeared, shimmering into a thousand gently glowing lines that contained stars, supernovas, suns—shreds of the universe peeking through tears in reality.

I winced, and forced myself not to put my hands to my temples. Each of the tears felt like a Gate, and my Weird ached to explore them, control them, bend and shape them until they'd take me anywhere I wished to go.

"This is as far as we go," the Faceless said. "We are creatures of the dead, and what lies beyond . . ."

A slight wind came from the rifts, ruffling the capes of the Faceless. It almost appeared that they were scared themselves.

I knew I was.

"What lies beyond is not," I said. "I get it."

"I don't understand the living," the Faceless said. "Why you would voluntarily subject yourself to such a thing?"

"Because sometimes there are things more important than living," I said.

I stepped forward, away from the creatures, and knew I was no longer speaking solely about Dean. Tesla had shown me that my coming here was never really about Dean, and Chang before him had made it clear too. It was about my inexorable destiny, both as the bringer of destruction and the only one who could reconstruct reality. Because of my Weird, and my position as Gateminder, that would always be my destiny.

I had made a bad bargain once. I had bargained selfishly—the Old Ones' return for my mother. I'd been selfish here, too, but there was still time to fix it.

All I had to do was strike a good bargain with the worst creature in all the Lands, and I'd be home free.

"No pressure, Aoife," I muttered to myself as I took another step forward.

The rifts hummed all around me. There was no sound in space, but the sheer power of the cosmos, the background music of the stars and planets, sang to my Weird, urging me to merge with the universe, become stardust.

I ignored it as best I could.

Nylarthotep had to be somewhere beyond these tears

213

in reality. His power was distorting the Deadlands, but that didn't mean I wasn't still standing on solid ground. Controlling reality was a Fae trick—keep your enemy off-balance, keep control of their reactions. It hadn't worked when I'd been in the Thorn Land, and it wasn't going to work now.

As I moved between the star roads, I became aware of a faint sound, of black smoke and dust rising all around me.

"Is it her?"

Her.

Her.

The Gateminder.

The destroyer.

The one who walks between worlds.

I flinched. I hated that name, the name the rebel factions in Lovecraft had coined for me after I blew the Engine trying to make a bad deal with Tremaine.

"I want the king," I said, loud enough that my voice echoed back at me. "I want Nylarthotep."

She wants the king.

The king.

The watcher.

The planner.

The devourer of minds.

Well, that was encouraging.

"I know you're here!" I shouted. "Stop playing games with me."

Games, the smoke hissed at me.

Games and riddles and ciphers.

Secrets.

Lies.

I squinted into the dust, feeling it sting my eyes. A face came into focus here and there, frozen in an expression of torment. They were like the souls and spirits I'd encountered before, but these were torn and shredded, twisted. They were just as affected by the proximity of the rifts as my Weird was.

"What happened to you?" I asked the cloud of souls. "Why are you here?"

We came.

We crossed the barrier.

We saw.

And now we wait.

"Wait for what?" I said, trying to be patient. If souls decayed even in the Deadlands, it must be exponentially faster.

For the end.

The end of Fae and man.

The end of days.

The end of the stars and planets.

The end of all things.

"I want to see Nylarthotep," I said again. "And I want to see him now."

I sensed a shift, and the spirits drew back. I wondered if they were like me, humans with a Weird trapped by the Gates, or if they'd been tricked by Fae into walking through *hexenrings* only to end up here, or simply stumbled off the edge of the page, the way people did in the old stories, the ones people furtively passed around when the Proctors couldn't hear.

It was easy to forget there'd been a world without magic before the first Storm exploded into the human world. A world where these things were just stories for children, distilled from stories for adults, to keep the darkness beyond the campfires out there, where it belonged.

But there had been, and these people were relics of it.

"You're a rare case," a voice said. It was textured and cultured, a rich velvet curtain of a voice, far from the rasp or growl I'd expected. "Most men would give up their lives to avoid meeting me face to face."

"I'm not most," I told the voice. "And I'm not a man."

A laugh. Low, like a warm finger dragged across skin. "Then approach, girl who is not like most. Tell me why you seek the favor of the one who waits."

I took one step, then another. It wasn't like I could turn around. Reality was so distorted, I wouldn't be able to find my way back without opening a Gate, and I couldn't imagine that, in the Deadlands, a new Gate would lead anywhere good.

The distortion grew stronger as I approached, and the rifts fell away. My stomach lurched. I'd never gotten close to another being who could manipulate reality the way Tesla or I could. There was probably a good reason for that, because this was the worst I'd ever felt and still managed to stay conscious.

"Does it bother you?" Nylarthotep asked. He sat in a simple black chair with a high back, a robe similar to the ones the Faceless wore swirling to hide his figure. He wore a cowl emblazoned with the Yellow Sign. It wasn't embroidered or painted, though—Nylarthotep's robe was made of the universe, and the Yellow Sign was a slice of a sun, churning and flaming upon his brow.

I felt dizzy looking at him, and it wasn't just because the vortex of unreality had grabbed me with its iron grip and refused to let go. I'd never seen anything like Nylarthotep up close. He felt like the Old Ones.

Worse, though. The Old Ones were incredibly ancient, but they were neither good nor evil. They simply existed, in the way of planets and the universe, an existence that could no more be denied than sunlight could.

Nylarthotep pulsed with malignance. If you could describe evil and malice as a figure, as a feeling, it would be this. This nausea, this panic, my hindbrain screaming that I was close to something no human was ever meant to see.

"Of course you bother me," I said. "I've been dreading meeting you ever since I decided to come here, back in San Francisco."

"I do not know this place, San Francisco," Nylarthotep intoned. He shifted, and the stars in his robe canted and re-sorted themselves into new constellations. "I have no knowledge of the human world. When I was sent here, the Iron Land did not yet exist."

"I want you to release a soul from your grasp," I said. "Just one. Surely you can spare that." I figured getting down to business might stop him from staring at me from beneath his cowl. I could feel his eyes. They felt like a sunburn— inexorable and with the sting of permanent damage.

"That's interesting," Nylarthotep said. "But the answer is no. The Deadlands are my domain and the souls within are my property."

He stood, drawing to nearly seven feet tall. I got the sense that there was something inside Nylarthotep's physical form, something incredibly large, indescribably ancient and aching to be let free. What I was seeing was the watered-down version, and my Weird kicked and screamed at the proximity of the larger thing.

"Please," I said. "I'm here asking. Not demanding. All I want is Dean."

"Hmm?" Nylarthotep cocked his head. "Oh, that's right. I forget you give each other names. Odd. Like cockroaches naming each other."

I tried to keep calm. If my heart had a beat, it would have been thudding. "I know you rule the Deadlands. That's why I'm here. I just want you to give me Dean."

"Rule the Deadlands?" The laughter came again, louder this time. "Girl, I do not rule this place. When the ancients cast me out, they cast me into a void, a place where all the dead came to their own final rest, be it good or ill. There was no unity, no collecting point for souls. What you see around you? This is a manifestation of my will. Of my boredom, of my wrath. I saw the souls, some happy, and I saw that they were weak and could be controlled."

My mouth dropped open. It was worse than I had suspected. "You don't rule," I repeated, letting it sink in. "You . . . you *made* the Deadlands?"

"They sprang from my hand. And when the first soul became entangled, I was curious, so I allowed it to exist rather than snuffing it out. Then another, and another. No more happy deaths or simple endings. All souls continue to exist and act as fuel for my world, my land. And I do with them as I see fit."

I felt like I would faint. Before that, I'd vomit, and fall to the ground, because this revelation was the worst thing I'd ever heard.

"So there really was just a void before," I said, "where souls could do as they liked."

Nylarthotep nodded. "There was nothing of greatness. Until me."

"Then what harm would it do?" I said. My voice was shaking, but I managed to stay upright, and decided to count that as a victory. "You have all this, by the power of your own mind. What difference would one soul make?"

"Because it would not be my will," Nylarthotep said. "I do not grant requests. Everything that happens—the city, the Faceless, the monsters that live in the wilds beyond, even the Walkers—happens at my will. And when this place ceases to amuse me, I will crush it and make it anew, a sculptor at his clay. The void and the dead are mine to use, forever."

I had to think fast. I could tell he was almost ready to boot me down one of the rifts and dump me into some airless vacuum.

"A bargain, then," I said. I'd been expecting it.

Nylarthotep grinned. I saw a flash of white teeth shaped like a shark's under his cowl. "Now we're getting somewhere," he said. "Sit, little human, and tell me of your so-called bargain with the Yellow King."

I watched as another black throne materialized. The Yellow King beckoned me. "Don't look so shocked, little

219

human. There was a time I could create entire worlds with a flick of my wrist. I was worshipped by the primitives as a god."

"But you're not," I said. "You're just drifting through the universe like the rest of us." I didn't know what possessed me to back-talk something like Nylarthotep. Maybe I was tired of being treated as if I were small, to be wiped off the map as he saw fit.

Nylarthotep sat forward. Where he gripped the arms of his chair, I saw long, blood-encrusted claws. I didn't know what he'd been using them for, but I drew back as far as I could without seeming like a coward.

"I am not flotsam. I am eternal," he snarled, and I did flinch then, as if he'd raked me with those claws.

"All right," I said quietly. "I'm sorry. I was mistaken."

"Tell me the terms of this bargain or leave before I make you an amusement," Nylarthotep grumbled, slumping back.

I took a breath and said, "You can have something from me. And in return, you let Dean go. I know you said no soul would escape you, but those are my terms, take it or leave it."

"Really." He leaned forward and licked his lips. "Tough talk. I'm intrigued. Be more specific, dear."

"I have a Weird. I have the gift that you need." I couldn't believe I was about to do this again. "I could get you a way out of here."

Nylarthotep didn't laugh or mock me this time. He simply tilted his head and considered my words, and that scared me more than anything.

"No, you can't," he said. "Tesla couldn't, and neither can you."

I sighed. It was my only bargaining chip, but I didn't want to use it. If Nylarthotep thought I was useless, at least he wouldn't imprison and torture me.

"But you do have something I want," he said. "You are a living soul in the Deadlands, and I've never come across that before."

I raised my chin, already not liking where this was going. "I'm listening."

"I grow weary of this place," said Nylarthotep. "I grow weary of my own creations. Let me test you. Let me see exactly what the soul of a Gateminder can endure, and then if it pleases me, I'll let your insignificant little friend fly free."

This was a bad bargain. I knew it, he knew it. He also knew I didn't have a choice, and so did I. Though this way, at least I wouldn't run the risk of setting him free. Because something like Nylarthotep could never be free, not ever. That would truly be the end of the world, the culmination of the second Storm. What I'd started was bad enough, but to let something like this monster into the Iron Land would mean the end of everything, and this time I'd be well and truly to blame.

So I nodded, and said, "I'll do whatever it takes. I just want to go home."

I knew now I was beneath the Deadlands, where no one could find me, not Chang's machine, not even a Gate of my own creation.

"As do we all," Nylarthotep said. "Come with me."

He led me to the edge of the swirling space that he lived in, and it resolved itself into a long hallway, industrial as anything in the Iron Land, flickering bulbs caged with wire, and iron doors stretching as far as the eye could see.

I twitched reflexively, waiting for my Fae blood to react with the iron, but it wasn't real. Nothing stirred in my blood or in my mind. That was a relief. Dealing with a bout of iron poisoning and the associated hallucinations was the last thing I needed right now.

"What's behind these doors, only you can know," said Nylarthotep. "Did you know that I used to slip into minds while asleep? That I used to pick apart dreams and nightmares?" He snorted. "Of course, that was before they sent me here and that foul upstart crawled out of the mud and took over the dreams, made them a refuge rather than what they should be."

"And what's that?" I said. Screams echoed from behind some of the doors, and even worse sounds, scratching and hissing, from behind others.

"The most terrible thing in all the universe," the Yellow King said. "Because your own mind is the thing you should fear most. It is the originator of nightmares. Without the fear, things like me would not exist."

He gave me a small shove forward. His touch sent shivers down my spinal cord and running through my entire body, borne on my own nerves.

"Go on," he whispered in my ear. "This is what I found in your mind, Aoife. Let's see what kind of fear lives there."

I stepped into the hall. Not because I wanted to, but because I didn't have a choice. If I wanted to get out of here, and with Dean, this was what I had to do.

Knowing it was my only choice didn't make it any easier to face what was behind the doors. Nylarthotep had been right. I was terrified of what was inside my own mind. And now I was going to meet it face to face.

The Dark Corridor

I USED TO PLAY in the hallway of the Lovecraft apartment that Conrad and I shared with our mother. It was a terrible place. It smelled musty and the carpet was damp no matter the season or the time of day. Roaches scuttled to and fro, and the aether feed was bad, so bulbs were constantly exploding, raining glass as fine as paper down on me and my sad excuses for dolls, which I usually constructed out of paper or shirts stuffed with packing material I found in the bins behind the building.

Terrible though it was, I had happy memories of that hallway. I'd listen to my mother singing to herself, or wait for Conrad's footsteps as he came home from school. Usually he'd blow right past me without a word. We weren't close then like we would be after our mother was sent to the madhouse.

Our only neighbor who wasn't a drunk and stayed longer

than a week was an elderly woman, Mrs. Loemann, who'd fled the war. She'd lost her entire family, grandchildren through husband, to the camps, and she used to come out and talk to me in German. She didn't speak much English, and she made me hard, nutty-tasting cookies that I pretended to eat to be polite and secretly put out for the pigeons, but she was nice to me, and always patted me on the head with her knotty-fingered hand. She looked like a kind fairy-tale grandmother, like someone had carved her out of wood, put her on strings and moved her around.

She died just before we moved out, and nobody noticed until the hallway started to smell much worse than usual.

I always wondered what it would be like to be totally alone, knowing that everyone who was your blood was dead.

I had a much better idea now, as I stood in this hallway, the maze that the Yellow King had created.

At least it smelled better.

I resolved I wasn't going to stand frozen like a scared rabbit, and took a hard left, pushing open the first door that my hand met.

Reality flickered around me, and I felt the same sick lurch as when I stepped through a Gate. Whether I'd traveled in time or space I didn't know, but I'd definitely crossed some threshold.

This was different from when Crow had shown me my nightmares, made me face them and come through the other side. I'd crossed some other barrier this time, something that was real, as far from a dream as I was from the Iron Land right now.

Except I was in the Iron Land when I opened my eyes, in a snug cottage, all one room except for a staircase off to one side.

I tried to orient myself, and spun around as the door opened.

I was glad I was too shocked to make any sound, because the one that would have come out was a scream.

"Hey there, darlin'," Dean said, shrugging out of his coat and hanging it on a hook by the door. "Sorry I'm home so late."

"I . . ." I was sure I was staring at him like he'd sprouted a second head. This wasn't fear, this was just cruel. Whatever game Nylarthotep was playing was worse than anything I could have imagined.

"Princess," Dean said. He approached and put a hand on my cheek. "Are you okay?"

He was real. Real and warm and alive, looking at me with concern. I put my hand over his, reflexively.

"I am now," I said, squeezing it.

His warm silver-gray eyes, liquid like mercury, lit with relief. "Oh, good. Thought you might be sore at me, on account of my being late."

"No," I said softly. "No, I could never be mad at you, Dean."

He laughed. "Never? Well, I guess that makes me the luckiest guy in Lovecraft."

"I . . . what?" I peered out the window, through the sheer curtains. We were in Lovecraft, in Uptown, on one of the side streets of small neat houses that eventually gave way to the mansions of the wealthy residents. A street that had been thoroughly destroyed when the Lovecraft Engine blew.

This was wrong. This was all wrong. I'd expected screaming and nightmares, blood and all my worst fears laid bare before my eyes. Not this. Not happiness and everything I ever wanted.

"You sure nothing's up?" Dean said. "You're worrying me, princess."

"I'm fine," I said. "I . . . This is going to be an odd question, all right?"

Dean squeezed my hand. "What's on your mind, Aoife?"

"What year is this?" I said.

Concern flared on Dean's face, but he did an admirable job of hiding it. If I hadn't spent so many hours memorizing the planes of his cheeks, the square of his chin and the tiny lines around his eyes, I never would have seen it. "It's 1956, Aoife. Just like yesterday, and the day before that."

He touched me on the shoulder. "Is the cure your mother gave you not working? Is the iron affecting you again?"

I jerked, and Dean, thinking I was jerking away from him, stepped back. "I'm sorry. I didn't mean—"

"No!" I cried. I hadn't even realized I wasn't feeling the familiar prickle of iron poisoning. I was only part Fae, so the progression was slower, but when puberty hit, the iron built faster and faster, until on our sixteenth birthdays we changelings succumbed and went insane. Conrad had. I nearly had. But now . . .

"No," I said in a calmer fashion. Whatever game this was, I could adapt; I could learn the rules.

I would still win Dean's freedom. The real Dean, not whatever construct this was.

"My mother's cure is working just fine," I said. "I'm sorry, Dean. It was a joke, but I'm afraid it wasn't a very good one."

He didn't believe me, but Dean wasn't an alarmist like Cal. He could play along just as well as I could. "No, doll," he said. "That was the opposite of a good one. But hey—I brought home those cupcakes you like."

I smiled and looked at the sugar-spotted pink box tied up with twine. "Thank you," I said. "I'll just go wash up."

"Hey," Dean said as I headed to a narrow ladder for what I assumed was the attic of the cottage. "I like this, Aoife. Never thought your pop would go for us living in the city, but the money he put up for this place—it's the best thing that's ever happened to me." He looked so grave I almost ran back to him, comforted him. It caused a physical ache, from my head to my belly button, to stand still. "Love you, princess," he said, and came to me and kissed my forehead.

Drawing back, I ducked my head and retreated so he wouldn't see the tears forming in my eyes. This was worse than any torment. It felt so real.

But it's not real, I told myself. *This isn't you, and that isn't Dean.*

I found the washroom in the snug attic, off a pocket-sized bedroom painted light blue and full to the sloped ceiling with belongings that were mine and Dean's: my notebooks; some oversized furniture I recognized from my father's house; my clothes and Dean's leather jacket, draped over a bedpost.

228

I locked the door and leaned against it. I had to get my head on straight before I lost it completely.

First things first: it wasn't really Dean down there. The Dean I knew was dead, and that pained me just as greatly as it had the moment I'd knelt in the snow, feeling his last breath on my cheek.

Second: this wasn't Lovecraft. If it were, it would be in ruins and I'd be going mad from iron poisoning.

Third: I didn't know what Nylarthotep's endgame was. To make me realize what I'd given up? To break me because I was happy rather than terrified and alone?

Whatever it was, I had to ferret it out before this projection of Dean got suspicious and things turned ugly. I didn't know how far Nylarthotep would go to keep me here.

I could do that, couldn't I? Remember what it was like to have my old life? I could be normal for a few hours, long enough to satisfy the curiosity of the Yellow King.

A knock sounded at the door, nearly scaring me out of my skin. "Princess?" Dean called. "Your cupcake is gonna get stale. Come on out of there."

The doorknob rattled. I waited, gripping the basin edge with all my might. This was it. This was when the illusion shattered and the nightmares began.

Dean rattled the doorknob once more and then I heard his boots pacing around the bedroom. "You sure you're all right, Aoife?"

I forced my fingers to unlock from the copper basin and grip the doorknob. I threw the door open with some force and Dean jumped back. "Whoa. You're edgy today. Maybe sugar isn't what you need."

He'd gotten Dean almost right, I thought. Almost but not quite. The real Dean wasn't so close in, so patronizing. Not so much like all the boys I'd known in Lovecraft. He loved me and understood me. That had been what drew me to him.

"I think I know better than you what I need," I snapped. That was one of the rules of survival I'd learned after the apartment with the hallway: if you stayed angry, they couldn't touch you. It could be quiet anger, expressed in silent screams rather than defiance, but you had to keep the flame burning. Otherwise, you succumbed.

Dean held up his hands. "I don't know what's with you today. I'm going out for a smoke."

After he'd left I sat on the bed, but I got restless. I explored the house a bit. I didn't appear to be trapped—I could open windows, and I could smell the salted air of Lovecraft as it blew in from the sea. I even took a bite of the damnable cupcake covered in candied violets but found it cloyingly sweet.

I heard the back door open downstairs—Dean coming in, shaking off the chill—and knew I had to go now or never. The ground wasn't far, and there was a trellis full of dead roses next to the window.

I swung my leg over the sill. I felt thorns grasp at my pants and then at my skin, and the cool damp of blood against the winter air.

I dropped the last ten feet, feeling the impact all the way up to my molars, but I didn't let it stop me. I wasn't as familiar with Uptown as I was with Old Town, the district that held most of Lovecraft's madhouses, where I'd visited my mother, but I could find my way. If this dream mirror of the city matched the real one, I'd be gone in no time, out of the main city gates and on my way back to Arkham. Those memories were murkier, and I figured Nylarthotep would have a harder time keeping me trapped there.

My hope lasted until I turned down one blind alley, doubled back and promptly found another. I didn't think it was any sinister design, either—the tiny streets, lined with stone cottages so close they could have touched had they elbows, were simply a warren only residents could navigate.

I'd had no reason to come here before. This was a place for content people, for families, for couples living normal, predictable lives. That was never going to be me. Before I could try to find my way to one of the main roads, I heard footsteps and shouting. "Aoife!"

Dean was chasing me, shirttail flying, boots half unlaced. "Aoife!" he shouted again, catching me by the back of my shirt. "What in hell do you think you're doing?"

I wanted to fight, to lash out, but I forced myself to stay calm. "I'm sorry," I blurted, the only thing I could think of to say. "I just—"

"Where were you *going?*" Dean demanded.

"I don't know," I lied, looking at my feet. "I'm sorry."

Dean merely sighed, and wrapped his arms around me. "Come on, darlin'," he said. "Let's get out of the street before the police see us."

"Police?" I said. "Don't you mean Proctors?"

Dean laughed. "Sure don't. You know the Bureau was disbanded months ago. Nice to be able to walk around your own city without worrying somebody'll lock you in a dark hole, isn't it?"

"Sure," I agreed. I was getting better at pretending nothing shocked me.

"Dean?" a familiar voice called through the fog. I felt my eyebrows rise as Bethina appeared on the front steps of another neat cottage. She looked good, wearing a fashionable dress, her neat copper curls tamed.

"Everything's fine," he called back. "Nothing to worry about."

Bethina lifted her skirt and came running down the street, fluttering her hands around me but not actually touching. "I saw you fly by like a nightjar was on your tail. Are you sure you're all right, Aoife?"

Aoife. No Miss or any title attached. That was new.

"I'm fine," I said with a wide smile that felt insane but I hoped looked normal. "Just getting some air."

Bethina crinkled her nose. I could tell she wasn't the least bit convinced. "Well, maybe I'll have Cal stop by when he gets home from his classes at the university."

Cal going to a human university? I didn't even have to ask if he'd told Bethina the truth about what he was. This whole place was a lie, so why should I be surprised?

"You do that," I said. "I'll be going back inside now."

I practically dragged Dean away, back toward our cottage. *Our* cottage. So odd to think of it that way.

"I know Bethina can hover a little bit," he said. "But she means well. It's nice to have someone motherly around, I think. Especially after what happened with your mother."

I flinched but disguised it as a deep breath. "Of course," I said. "It's . . . wonderful."

That was the icing, the final touch on this little test of my mettle. It couldn't be too perfect. There had to be a tragedy to remind me how lucky I was.

I didn't ask after my mother. She could be wearing an apron and running a bake sale every weekend for all I cared. It wouldn't be real. None of this was real.

Though that was the hardest thing on earth to believe when Dean was so close. Close enough that I could smell him, feel his heat, the pressure of his arms as he wrapped them around me.

"I know we have good days and bad days," he said into my hair. "But I'm not giving up on you, Aoife. Not giving up on us. I'll never let you go."

I couldn't bear to be stiff in his arms. I let myself relax into his embrace, press my face into his neck and breathe in his scent of soap and tobacco. "I'll never let you go either," I choked out, feeling the tears build in the corners of my eyes. They spilled over, absorbed by the worn linen of Dean's shirt. "Never. Not in this life or any other."

"Love you," Dean whispered, and gently let me go.

I think it was the release that broke me. I couldn't simply run out again—I'd only get lost, and he'd catch me. I had to think. And would it be so bad to plan my way out of here in the comfort of the cottage?

"I think I need to lie down for a bit," I told Dean. "Get myself collected."

"Sure, princess," he said. "Go ahead. I'll put something together for supper."

I went upstairs and stretched out on the bed. I intended to pretend to nap, and figure a way out, but I ended up falling asleep.

Dean woke me, and we ate cold sandwiches for dinner while he talked about the job he'd gotten as a dockworker down at the shipyard. It beat steel work, which his father had done and which Dean had despised with every bone in his body.

I was noncommittal, just enjoying speaking to him, even if it was an illusion. I was doing this *for* Dean, wasn't I? The real one, trapped in the Deadlands. For Dean and every other soul across all the living Lands. Even Tremaine, even Grey Draven—much as I hated them, I didn't want to see them suffer at Nylarthotep's hand.

We went to sleep, and I woke up, and the next day proceeded much as the first.

As did the next.

And the next.

When nearly a month had passed, I had to admit to myself that it wasn't just a matter of finding a way out. Not that it was easy, by any means—Dean rarely left me unwatched, either by himself or Bethina, and the neighborhood, the few times I'd walked it, was definitely bewitched. Streets folded back on themselves, houses duplicated as if they were being copied with ink on printers' plates, and everyone watched me from their gardens and behind their curtains with narrowed, suspicious eyes.

But there was more to it. Life with Dean was everything I'd ever wanted. It was calm, normal, free of all the fear and uncertainty that had plagued me since the night I'd run away from the Academy to search for Conrad. Really, since I'd been old enough to realize our family wasn't usual, that people regarded us differently.

I kept coming up with little excuses—even if I could find my way out of the neighborhood, I had no idea what I had to do to convince Nylarthotep I'd passed his test.

I knew this world wasn't real. I still had all my memories. What more could he want from me? How could this be amusing, other than to watch me suffer, trapped in a perfect life I knew I could never really have?

That was it, I realized one bright morning. The plain, unadulterated suffering as everyone else in this little fantasy went about their business while I knew none of it was real and never would be.

It didn't change the fact that I saw no way out and was running out of brainpower to solve the puzzle.

Another month slipped by. And another.

When blossoms appeared on the trees, I finally realized that I wasn't getting out of here by passing some test or answering a riddle. This wasn't the Thorn Land. I wasn't playing a game of wits with Tremaine. I was amusement for an ancient evil, and I existed or perished at his whim.

That, I decided, feeling some of the old stubbornness left over from my living self creep into my thoughts, was going to change starting this moment, this second. I was nobody's mere amusement, and it was time the Yellow King saw that for himself.

"Dean," I said. He was sitting listening to the aethervox.

It was the first baseball game of the season, and the Red Sox were losing, though not as badly as usual.

"Yeah, darlin'?" he said, looking up.

"I'm going," I said.

His brows drew together. "Going where?"

"I don't know," I said. "I'll start with outside and take it from there."

He was up, and it was impossible to walk away all over again. Concern flooded his face, a flash flood that swept away all reason, and I knew in that moment it was now or never. This was a wonderful life. A beautiful life. A perfect life.

And none of it was real. Not Dean. Not even how I felt as I looked at him.

"Don't," he said.

"I'm sorry," I told him, and then bolted for the door.

I expected another run around Nylarthotep's maze, but instead I ran into blinding bright light.

I stopped short, the energy to run shocked out of me. I realized after a moment that I wasn't in a pure white void, but standing on an arctic ledge, snow stretching out behind me and glaciers rising to meet a shining pale sky.

In the distance, a white city pierced the clouds, carved out of the ice, the entrances to tunnels little more than black periods on a page at this distance.

Across the plain, a line of figures in white moved to and fro from the city. I made out the squamous, glimmering backs of shoggoths, huge gelatinous creatures that were a holdover from the days of the Great Old Ones, and the tall, many-jointed limbs of some kind of life-form I didn't recognize, another creation of the Old Ones.

"Beautiful, isn't it?"

I whirled around, recognizing the voice before I took in the robe, the lank black hair and the skin whiter than the glacier behind us.

Crow was the only dark spot on this landscape, which was fitting. He was in darkness always, trapped in the world created by humans' dreams. If dreams ceased, so did he.

"Where are we?" I said. The last time I'd seen Crow, he was where he'd been since the beginning of his existence, in a small glass bulb at the center of all the Lands, a space outside the laws of physics or time.

"We are at a place out of space, out of time and distance," Crow said. "This was once your world, Aoife. It's the only safe place where we can speak."

"I don't understand," I said. "One minute I was . . . well . . . trapped in another sort of dream, and now I'm here?"

Had I woken up? Or was this something worse, some other layer of Nylarthotep's game?

"You're not dreaming," Crow said. "What he's done to you is a perversion of a dream, using your own happiness and desire to forge prison bars."

"I got that much," I said. "But I left. I passed his test."

Crow sighed. "No, Aoife," he said. "You didn't."

I felt the void again, and I was plummeting through it, guts-first. It was the same sinking feeling I'd gotten when I'd realized Tremaine had tricked me, and again when I'd realized that the cost of setting right what I'd wrought would be freeing the Old Ones.

"He tricked me," I said matter-of-factly.

"More like sidelined you," Crow said. He reached for me and drew me into his robe, which was a welcome relief from the cold.

"He trapped you here to study you, to exploit your weakness. When you return he will present you with the only choice you can make: allow him his freedom from the Deadlands in exchange for your life, Dean's life and the lives of everyone else in the Lands. He'll try to scare you—"

"He *does* scare me," I snapped, pulling away from Crow. "He *made* the Deadlands to amuse himself by damning souls. He's evil, Crow. He's the root of all evil."

"I don't disagree," Crow said. "But he cannot be allowed to leave that unholy playground he's created. You cannot accept his bargain, because if you do, the Old Ones' coming will be the least of your worries. Nylarthotep is more than a creature of evil. He is a force of nature. He is the end of all things."

"The one who waits," I murmured.

"Who waits for the end of the world," Crow said, "and for his chance to dance on the ashes."

I looked back at the city. I still felt nauseated, but unlike the last time Crow and I had met, I didn't scream and cry and try to wrap myself in denial as thick as his robes. I just sighed. "What do you need me to do?"

"The Old Ones trapped Nylarthotep the first time with the same power that turns the Gates," Crow said. "The

238

same power that flows in your veins. They created the opposite of a Gate, a lock so strong not even the first evil could break it."

He pressed an aged piece of paper into my hands. "It's called an Elder Sign—a representation of the Old Ones themselves, or at least their light half. The good they can bring to a world, the flip side of the devastation. The same minds that built this city here, this first place where living things crawled from the mud to begin what would become humans and Fae and even me, they created the Elder Sign. But the Old Ones have lost their way, and the knowledge has faded. Not even I can locate it."

"What's this?" I asked. I didn't open the paper. I felt beaten-down and hopeless. I should have known that an impossible bargain with Nylarthotep was still too good to be true. That it wasn't a bargain at all but a setup to permanently rid himself of the one person who could harm him, a person who would only be released when she was compliant and desperate, ready to free him instead.

"It's the only clue to the Elder Sign I've been able to locate," Crow said. "It was written down in the twelve hundreds by an Arabic scholar. He went mad, but he was the last to directly communicate with the Old Ones."

"Probably why he went mad, then," I said. Crow allowed himself a small smile.

"Likely. Good luck, Aoife."

"Because I've had so much of that so far," I muttered.

"Listen," Crow said. "There's nothing wrong with wanting to bring back your dead friend. There's nothing wrong with loving someone so much that you would cross oceans and distances and over from life itself to look into his eyes again. You did what you had to do for Dean."

He took my face in his hands. They were warm, surprisingly so, and they stilled the horrible emptiness inside me, filled me with something that wasn't hope, but wasn't the sucking hopelessness of a moment ago, either. I felt myself stop shaking for the first time.

"Now do what you have to do for the legacy in your blood. For the world, and for everyone in it," Crow whispered.

I shut my eyes, feeling a tear freeze on my face, and when I opened them I was back in the awful hallway, lying on my side with tears still wetting my cheeks.

Nylarthotep sat a few feet away, watching me intently. "So how did you enjoy my test?" he asked, that pure white-bone smile slicing from under his cowl.

"I've had better days," I said, pulling myself to my feet.

"Don't be snippy," he said. "And don't pretend you wouldn't give it all up for even ten more seconds with that Dean boy."

Here it was. I'd ask for Dean back. He'd threaten me. And I'd . . . what?

Dutifully, I said, "I did what you asked. Let Dean and me go."

Nylarthotep laughed, and he kept laughing. "My, you humans are simple creatures. Every time I think evolution might have finally made a jump, you do something that convinces me all over again just how wide-eyed and stupid you all are."

I tried to put a convincing tremble in my voice, at the

same time praying he wouldn't see I'd known this was coming. "But you promised . . ."

Nylarthotep stood to his full height, looming above me. I didn't have to fake the trembles then. "Little girl, I made this world. What makes you think my promises need have any weight? I'm in control. Of you, of Dean's soul, of every ounce of this place."

"Yes," I whispered, not able to look into the terrible blackness beyond his cowl. "You're in control."

"And I've been watching you, and I know that you're weak. So you're going to find me a way out of here, and I'm going back to a world of smoke and bone and blood, a world I can taste and touch. And if you do this, I might spare your life and Dean's soul. Do you doubt me?"

I forced myself to look up, to face him. "No," I said. My voice was small and raspy, like I'd been inhaling toxic smoke. "No, I believe you."

"Good," Nylarthotep said. He held out his hand, and I took it. The shock was like that of touching something long dead that had lingered underwater, grown spongy and rotten. Something that would corrupt you through your skin.

I drew back, wrapping my arms around myself. "I told you, I can't go back to the Iron Land on my own. My soul is alive, sure, but I can't put it back in my body like some stage-magic trick. The only way is if they wake me up."

"Hmm." Nylarthotep paced in a slow circle and then faced me. "Then I suppose we'll just have to talk to them, won't we?"

The thought of him getting his hooks into Conrad or Cal

241

spurred me. "Show me that Dean will be safe," I said, "and I'll do it."

Nylarthotep cocked his head. "But you just said you couldn't."

"I'm a liar too," I said. There was no untruth in that. I was an excellent liar, better than anyone in my family, besides my father, could ever hope to be. "I've had a way out of here since I came to you."

In my waistband, Crow's paper crackled. It warmed to the same temperature as my skin, and I showed no reaction. It was my only weapon against Nylarthotep.

"Clever little thing," Nylarthotep said. "I knew you'd been holding out on me."

"I'll release you from the Old Ones' hold," I said. "But you're going to give me Dean." I straightened my spine and put force behind my next words. "Or you might as well kill me right here."

Nylarthotep stared at me for a moment and then shook his head, as if he couldn't believe my audaciousness. "Very well. Take the boy's soul, take his body as it was when he lived. What lies in his grave will be returned to wherever his soul ends up, and it will be restored. Just take it all and bring it back to the living world. His remaining thread is yours." His teeth showed. "There will be many more where he came from when I slip these bonds."

"I'll need space to work," I said. "Constructing a Gate here is very complicated. I'll need real materials."

Nylarthotep caused another one of the iron doors to open, and inside I saw a complete inventor's workshop, the best any engineer could ever hope for. "Take anything I can create for you, little girl. I look forward to our partnership."

"There's one more thing," I said as he started to sweep away. I had to seem defiant and angry, as if I were doing this under duress.

"What?" Nylarthotep demanded. "What is it now?"

"My name," I said, glaring at him. "It's not 'little girl.' It's Aoife."

The Elder Sign

A s SOON AS Nylarthotep left, I pulled out the paper and unfolded it. The paper was stained with rust-colored marks that I suspected were blood. There was a single word on it, and I felt as if it might have originally been in a language I couldn't read, but the ink shifted under my eyes, a small enchantment I'd seen before. My father used it to encrypt his diaries. He'd been going to teach me someday.

The ink spelled out a single word.

BLEED

There was a small symbol below the word that looked like an ampersand turned on its side. With every blink of my eyes it twisted into something new.

"Oh yes, Crow," I muttered. "You're so helpful and direct. Never cryptic. Everything's spelled right out."

I looked around the workshop, though I knew there was nothing useful there. That had been pure distraction for the Yellow King so it would seem like I was puzzling over the most difficult sort of problem, one that required solitude and concentration. Either he'd believe me and leave me alone, or he'd figure out what I was really doing and he'd kill me.

Then I'd be trapped here forever. Perhaps I'd even be turned into one of the Faceless.

That alone was enough to keep me staring at the page until pinpoints of light swam in front of my eyes.

Bleed. Hadn't I done nothing but bleed ever since I'd come here? Bleed from the wound Dean had left in my soul, bleed for all the sleepless nights without him? How could I possibly bleed more?

I considered, watching that symbol turn and turn under the enchanted ink, until I knew I was out of time. After a number of minutes, a pattern began to emerge. It was of five symbols relentlessly flashing under my eyes.

Was the Elder Sign one of them? None of them? Some kind of optical illusion or trick?

I swatted the paper aside and then threw the rest of the materials on the table at the wall for good measure. A glass beaker shattered in my grasp and the shards went deep into my palm. I cursed and wrapped my hand in the hem of my shirt, but the blood was flowing freely.

Everywhere it hit the ground, I saw the image of the room Nylarthotep had constructed begin to melt away, like someone had applied heat to the celluloid film wound in a lantern reel.

Bleed. It was so simple I hardly believed it possible, but the evidence was before me.

I picked up the paper again and folded it so the enchanted images were superimposed over one another. They made a pleasing pattern, and I wondered if the mad scholar hadn't been trying to tell whoever found his diary something, without being too obvious about it.

Crow had trusted me to do this. He'd trusted me to be smart enough to figure it out. I couldn't let him down.

I put the paper down and brushed my fingers along the broken glass. I was going to need a lot more blood.

It could have been minutes or hours until Nylarthotep came back—the time passed in a blur, and I finished dizzy and cold, sitting in the middle of the floor.

He regarded me and finally laid aside his cowl. His face was narrow and white, like a skull with a hide stretched over it rather than the face of a living thing. His skin, if you could call it that, was white, and long white hair trailed from the back of his head, gathered into a braid at the nape of his neck. His mouth was full of terrible, sharp teeth, and I saw stars and planets and galaxies whirling behind his black eyes, as if Nylarthotep had created worlds even within himself.

"What do you have for me?" he asked.

I'd cobbled together an utterly fake frame of pipes and wood, and pointed at it. "I need a . . . matrix for the Gate to work within," I said. "We should be all set."

Nylarthotep approached, and before he could realize the trickery I'd wrought, I shut the door of the workshop behind him and moved away from the fake Gate, where my feet had been covering the blood symbols.

Nylarthotep reacted as if I'd thrown boiling water on him. He whipped back and actually hissed, like a cat who'd seen a wild animal.

"You think this will stop me?" he howled. "You think *you* can stop me?"

I felt my Weird unfold and I pushed it into the symbols, allowing the ancient power to flow through them. They began to glow and rise from the floor, and then to combine, to vibrate before my eyes with the power of the cosmos.

"No!" Nylarthotep raged. He turned on me as the symbols began to engulf him, wrap around him, the blood they were made of running over his face, his bare skull, those terrifying eyes.

"Do you really think you've fixed anything?" Nylarthotep smiled. "Do you really think you've stopped anything set in motion by me aeons before you were born?"

"I don't know," I said. Nylarthotep's images began to burn away all around us as the Elder Sign covered more and more of him. "But I do know that everyone dies eventually." I took another step. "Even you."

When I turned to run, I didn't look back. The Deadlands were burning around me and I knew I didn't have much time.

As I fled, the chaos caused by my proximity to Nylarthotep lessened, and I had another bout of vertigo and pain. Who knew how long Conrad and Cal had been trying to wake me up?

I had only a little time to do what I had in mind before

they yanked me back into the land of the living, and so I ran faster.

The first thing I saw was the great plain of the screaming sands again, rippling and rushing along the road of bones, snaking back and forth, seeking prey.

I saw the bodies, too, black robes and skulls emblazoned with the Yellow Sign. The Faceless hadn't lasted long once their master wasn't around to protect them.

The road stretched just as long as before, and I wanted to let out a howl of hopelessness. I didn't have that kind of time, not to mention a way to get back to the Catacombs, where Dean's soul resided. Nor any way to stop the encroachment of the Old Ones. I was right back where I'd started.

I sank to my knees on the bones of those who had come before me, and I wept. The Klaxons still wailed in the city, in a metallic imitation of my own sobbing, and on the horizon I saw a line of smoke billowing into the sky, which was now the color of a days-old bruise, yellow and green and sickly.

I saw the Moaning Marsh to my left, the mud bubbling and steaming. In daytime the lost souls were sad scraps of things, and they clustered at the edge of the marsh, staring at me.

"Don't cry." A pair of pointed men's shoes, covered in the dust of the bone road, came into my field of view. I couldn't see clearly at first through the blur of tears, but I swiped at my eyes and regarded Tesla for the second time.

"And why not?" I demanded. "Now seems as good a time as any."

"You did something I could never do," Tesla said. "You kept this place alive, and you kept the Yellow King at bay."

"But this place is his creation," I said, trying not to start sobbing again. "I've doomed all of you."

"No," Tesla said softly, placing his hand on the top of my head. "No. As long as he's trapped here, he won't destroy this place. If he does, he'll be floating in a void with nothing. And he's too vain to be alone."

"But what about Dean? What about all the other souls who'll still be trapped here?" I said. I sucked in air for the first time since I'd landed in the Deadlands. It hit my empty lungs like a hammer, and I tried not to flinch.

"I have a feeling that with his power so diminished, this place won't be the torment it was," Tesla said. He gestured toward the city, where the green smog was starting to blow away in long wisps, like streaks of gangrene in the sky. "It might even be the sort of place one would want to visit after death. But as for Dean . . . you'd better take him and go," Tesla said, looking truly grim for the first time. "Go right now, while Nylarthotep is still battered and confused, because that's going to be your only chance to escape." Tesla gripped my arms and stared into my eyes. His were pale and set far apart, but they were among the most intense I'd ever seen. Whatever life lent us the Weird, it burned behind his eyes like a living fire.

"Run for your life," Tesla stated. "And forget this place. Never come back until the day you die."

I looked toward the columns of smoke and wanted to sob all over again. "It's too far. . . ."

Tesla shook his head and stepped away from me, into the center of the road. "Stand back," he warned. "It's been a while since I've done this."

I watched in a mixture of wonder and horror as the air shimmered around us. White bone dust, fine and sparkling, rose in a whirlwind around Tesla's body, and then pain spiked through my head as a clap of displaced air rolled across the landscape, and a black, swirling void in the landscape, surrounded by a mist of dust and cosmic flotsam, stood before us. I couldn't see what was on the other side, could only hear the scream of air as the portal sucked it in.

"I may be dead and without my Weird," Tesla said, "but I still have my skills." He stepped aside and gestured me in. "This Gate will take you where you need to go, but you need to go quickly. Take Dean, take your reprieve, and go back to the land of the living."

I started to step through the Gate, feeling its power pulse against my Weird, then stopped and turned back to Tesla. I wanted to look at him once more, and there was a question I needed to ask—really, the only question I'd wanted an answer to since the moment I'd discovered I could manipulate the Gates. The moment I'd discovered that Tremaine betrayed me, and the moment I'd discovered that to save my family, I might have doomed the world.

The question that lurked beneath the iron madness and the nightmares and the bad memories.

"How did you live with it?" I asked him. "Starting the Storm? Changing the world forever? How did you ever close your eyes again?"

Tesla gave me a sad smile, his fingers brushing my temple as our hair whipped around our faces in the wind. "I didn't," he said. "It haunted me for the rest of my life, Aoife. You don't ever stop wondering if things could have been different if you'd just turned your face away from the shadows, away from the unseen, and pretended the world is just as it appears in daylight."

I caught his hand, feeling the pull of the Gate but needing a few moments longer. "And what did you do instead?" I whispered, somehow knowing he could hear me even over the roar of the space-bending Gate.

Tesla stared into the heart of the Gate for a moment, before he switched his gaze back to me. "I found a way to endure," he said. "I got up and I tried to fight against the evil I had unknowingly wrought. I made it my mission to protect my world from those who would seek to destroy it, and to help my world find those who would better it and bring it forward into a new age of the supernatural being entirely normal."

He gave me a gentle push toward the Gate, and I was powerless to resist any longer. "Endure, Aoife," he said. "Keep your head up, even when it feels like you can't. You survive because you must. Because your gift can break the world, but it can also save it."

Traveling through the Gate was merely a blink of an eye, but in that blink I could feel myself spread across a vast distance, every atom of me separate and distinct. Then, just as quickly, I was gasping on the wet floor of the Catacombs as the roof shook above and the restless spirits drifted around me, mouths wide open and screaming.

Tesla had said it would pass. That Nylarthotep could never be alone, would never destroy his world. I thought he was probably right—the Yellow King reveled far too much in his subjects' misery to ever destroy this place.

Still, it wasn't right, or natural. The dead didn't belong to Nylarthotep. They didn't belong to anyone. Someday, when I was stronger, when I was the Gateminder I was meant to be, I'd disregard Tesla's advice and I'd come back here and make sure the Deadlands were as they should be—different for each soul, none in torment except those who brought it on themselves.

I knew it for a certainty as I made my way to Dean's cell and shoved the bolt back on the door. "Dean?"

He came toward me at once, and wrapped his arms around me. "You can't be here," he said. "You have to leave, now."

"You're coming with me," I said.

"No," Dean murmured against my hair. He drew back and looked me in the eye. This was Dean, really him, and seeing his face I realized how pale the imitation that Nylarthotep had cooked up had been.

"There's no arguing," I said. "I came here to get you, more than anything, and I'm at least going to do that."

"No," Dean insisted. "I have to stay here, Aoife, and you have to get back."

The Catacombs vibrated around us again, and a rush of souls flowed past the door like a flash flood.

"It's not your choice," I told Dean, and gripped his hands.

252

I felt my Weird tug at me and realized that the shaking was not Nylarthotep but the thin tether that held me to the living world via the séance machine. Chang had said spending too much time in the Deadlands would make me harder to bring back, decay my living soul until it died, and I could feel it happening even as I wrapped my arms around Dean, even as he struggled, protested, tried to save me.

"It's not your turn to save me!" I shouted as the cell collapsed around us with a great roar and blinding white light seared my vision into nothingness. "I have to save you!"

Awake

AT FIRST I thought I was in the void of nothing, the same place that contained the Old Ones. I saw flashes of their great eyes and limpid bodies, drifting between galaxies, between supernovas, on and on, until one turned to look at me and I thought if I could just hold its gaze, I would know all the secrets of the stars. But I couldn't, and meeting the great eye burned me like staring into the surface of the sun.

I screamed, and the burning coalesced into the center of my chest, until I thrashed with pain and fell onto a hard floor.

"She's back," Chang said. He put away two small paddles hooked up to a battery run off the Tesla coil.

I rolled to the side, feeling my throat and guts constrict, and vomited.

"You're all right," another voice said, and I felt Conrad's hand rub my back. "She's all right, isn't she?"

254

"We'll have to see," Chang said. "She was under for much longer than I've ever seen anyone survive."

"She's tough," Cal's voice broke in. My head was throbbing, and in that moment, prostrate on a cold floor and covered in my own sick, I felt miles away from tough.

"Good thing, because we have to move," Conrad said. "Those boys outside aren't going to wait much longer."

Over the drone of the Tesla coil and my own blood humming in my ears, I heard a voice echo off the front of the building. "We know you're in there, Miss Grayson! Come out with your hands up!"

Chang, Cal and Conrad jumped, but all I could do was take a deep breath and let it out. It hurt, like somebody had taken a bat and smacked me across the chest, but it was the best pain I'd ever felt. I could feel the blood moving through my veins again, my heart thrumming, electricity shooting through my nerves just like it hummed through the Tesla coil.

Tesla. He'd told me I had to endure. I had no choice now, because here I was, right back in the grasp of the Iron Land.

"Who's out there?" I rasped. My voice sounded as if I'd scraped it across gravel, and speaking sent hot fire down my throat.

"Who do you think?"

This voice was the one I'd been dreaming about. The one that had the power to set me sobbing or inspire joy. It was for this that I'd endured all the pain and nightmares.

I sat up and looked into his eyes. "Dean?"

"Hey, princess." He crouched next to me, brushing sweaty hair out of my eyes with his rough, sure fingers.

255

He looked pale and sick too, but he was holding it together much better than I was. "You sure are a sight for sore eyes, you know that?"

I said nothing; I just grabbed him and wrapped him in my arms and pressed my face into his neck, smelling his sweat and his skin and feeling him warm and alive against me.

In that moment, everything was perfect, every bit of suffering had been worth it, and nothing, not even the encroachment of the Old Ones, could render me completely hopeless.

And just as quickly, it all shattered again.

"Miss Grayson!" Pounding started up on the door, and Chang shot a nervous glance toward it.

"The Brotherhood?" I guessed, looking to Cal and Conrad for confirmation.

"They showed up a few minutes ago," Cal said. "Guess they got tired of watching the door. That's why Chang had to shock you."

Conrad was still staring at Dean. "How are you here? I thought you were dead, and you just—pop up here. What the hell is going on?" His brow furrowed. "You *were* dead. I saw your body."

Dean gave Conrad a grim smile. "Dead as a doornail, man. And by the way, it's great to see you, too."

"I hate to interrupt this tender reunion," I said, clambering to my feet. Even though I felt sick and my heart was throbbing, part of me was elated. My mother hadn't been completely crazy after all. Dean was here, and he was holding my arm when I started to sway, and he had his time back—all of the thread that he should have had, the thread that had been cut because of me, repaired. I used him to hold myself steady. He was here, body and spirit. Here with me. "But we have a decision to make."

"What's the decision?" Cal said. "We're out the back and we disappear into Chinatown. And let's do it now, before they bust the front door down."

"They'll have agents at the back," Conrad said. "Trust me, I've spent months with these people. They're organized, and they're not stupid."

"This place have a basement?" Cal asked Chang, but Chang shook his head.

"No basement," he said. "Too close to the bay."

Everyone erupted into arguing and shouting, but I took a step toward the front door, and then another.

Dean caught my hand, and I turned back to him and shook my head. "Don't try to stop me," I told him. "You know this is the only way we all get out of here alive."

"Wouldn't dream of trying to stop you," he said, squeezing my hand. "Just trying to make sure you stay out of trouble."

I put my hand on the rough wood of the door and tried to smile at Dean. "If I hadn't just thrown up, I'd kiss you right now."

He winked at me. "Rain check, princess. When all this is said and done."

Conrad realized what I was about to do, and he came bolting through the front of the store, but it was too late. I'd grabbed the doorknob and twisted, throwing the door open into a welter of raindrops, sodium lights and shock pistols pointed at my face.

Did I think it was the right decision? I thought it was

stupid. I was sure I was being foolish. But I also knew it was the only way to keep my brother, Cal, Dean and myself alive. Not to mention Chang and anyone else who crossed the Brotherhood's path.

I stepped onto the front stoop and held up my hands. Dean did the same.

"Don't move!" someone bellowed from behind the spotlight. It hissed as the raindrops burned up against its blinding brilliance, and steam drifted around us, obscuring the rest of the street. I was in my own world, just Dean and me—and the Brotherhood, even now advancing to clap iron shackles around my wrists.

"You don't have to do that," I told them. "I'll come peacefully."

"Orders, Miss Grayson," the man said. He didn't sound much older than me, his face obscured by a fedora and his coat collar turned up. "I'm sorry. I know about your abilities."

Another agent, a woman, handcuffed Dean, and when I looked back into the house, it was empty. My brother, Chang and Cal had gone. I trusted that Conrad would be smart enough to keep the rest of them out of harm's way, especially Cal.

They put us into separate jitneys, and the last I saw of Dean before the door closed was his reassuring smile.

I sighed as I watched the lights of Chinatown recede behind the jitney's treads. I wished I shared Dean's confidence that everything was going to be all right.

*   *   *

The Brotherhood took us to a house high up on Haight Street, near Golden Gate Park. It was sandwiched between two other, identical houses and painted bright blue. It was such an incongruous spot for an outfit like the Brotherhood that I could barely worry when they separated Dean and me again in the hall and took me upstairs, to a study in the turret that looked down Haight Street to the Port Authority, its white spire gleaming with raindrops against the streetlights.

The young Brotherhood agent shackled me to my chair and left. I waited, watching the rain on the glass, listening to the hiss of the aether lamps and trying to do calculus in my head to keep the iron from getting to me.

Iron madness could come on slowly, over years, or all at once, depending on how much you were exposed to. The background hum of a city was one thing, but iron against my skin was another thing entirely. I probably had only a matter of hours before I started hallucinating, a day or two before I was completely mad.

I focused on the raindrops. They weren't just raindrops, I reminded myself, but tiny prisms, each containing fractals of infinite design and possibilities. The math inside a raindrop could keep my mind from breaking down for months.

Fortunately, I didn't need to wait that long. After barely an hour by the clock hanging above the vast chestnut desk in front of me, the door opened and a single figure came in.

"Hello, Aoife," he said. "Didn't think I'd be seeing you again so soon."

I had last seen him covered in mud, running like a scared dog with his tail between his legs. I stared, unable to believe what I was actually seeing. "No," I said. "There's no way they'd let you . . ."

"The Brotherhood makes deals with a lot of unsavory folks, Aoife," Grey Draven said. "Fae, Erlkin. I had an agreement with Crosley that if I ran across your father I'd turn him over. We both had a vested interest in keeping the Fae off our territory. Of course, they're filthy heretics, but that doesn't mean we don't have the same end goal."

"Trust a snake to find a warm nest," I grumbled, and Draven clapped me on the shoulder.

"Aoife, I'm hurt. I thought you'd be much happier to see a familiar face."

"Then I guess we're both disappointed," I said. "Now, even though I know it's your favorite hobby, why don't you cut out the pointless blather and tell me what you want?"

Draven sat on the edge of the desk and removed a cigarette from a gold box. He lit it, inhaled and watched as the smoke curled in the bluish light of the aether lamps. "You're wrong, Aoife. It's the threats that come after the talking that I actually enjoy the most." He favored me with one of his razor-thin smiles. "I spent some time in Proctor custody after I dropped back into the Iron Land, you know. It's not a pleasant place to be."

I sighed and looked directly at him. After what I'd seen in the past few . . . hours? days? who knew how long I'd been under? . . . he didn't frighten me in the least. "It's not my problem if you don't like the taste of your own medicine. If you're going to kill or torture me, would you please just do it? I'm getting bored sitting here listening to your rambling stories."

"Kill you!" He barked a laugh, before he stubbed his cigarette out in a dish that looked like it was carved from a ram's horn. "Dear girl, I would no sooner kill you than I would kill Nikola Tesla himself returned from the after-life."

"You might get a shot at that sooner than you think," I muttered, but I don't think he even heard me. Dr. Draven was certainly a man impressed with the sound of his own voice.

"You have a purpose in life, Aoife, though you may not realize it yet. And that purpose is to serve the Brother-hood. You are a young girl, I realize, and that is why I don't hold you responsible for your selfish actions."

He got up and pulled a ring of keys from his vest, sorting through them until he found one that fit my shackles.

"I hold them to your father far more closely, these respon-sibilities. There are things you should have been indoctri-nated in from birth that you never so much as considered."

I watched as he unlocked my shackles, and felt the im-mense weight of the iron against my skin lift. I calculated the distance to the door. If I was fast, I'd decided while I'd been waiting, I could reach the street before anyone could stop me, and then I could start screaming if I had to. It wasn't like the Brotherhood could gun me down in a public street. That privilege was reserved for the Proctors.

"Such as?" I said, shooting him a glare. "What exactly should I consider? That you manipulate people and cut deals with the very creatures that should be your sworn en-emies? I know all about Crosley making accords with the Fae, giving them leeway in exchange for information about

261

the Thorn Land. I know that when my father objected, you cut him out and threatened his life."

"Harold Crosley threatened his life," Draven said, perfectly calm. "And that had more to do with Archie's predilection for running off with people's daughters than his objections about our methods."

"That's a load of crap and you know it," I shot back, borrowing one of Dean's indelicate phrases.

Draven twitched an eyebrow. "I see you're about as personable as Archie, even if he didn't teach you anything you need to know to be a proper Gateminder."

I sighed. "I know you're going to threaten me or make me an offer. So why don't we get on with it?"

Draven gave me a thin smile. "And you're direct like him too. I miss the days when young women were taught manners."

"I miss the days when I wasn't being harassed by the likes of the Brotherhood," I grumbled.

Draven laced his fingers over his knee. He looked for all the world like a headmaster relishing the scolding he was about to give. "I'm going to be frank with you, Miss Grayson—you don't have a choice any longer. You've denied the Brotherhood, but your birthright is working for us, to keep the darkness of the Fae and magic and the Old Ones at bay. Why would you deny that?"

"My *birthright* is to create and control the Gates as I see fit," I snapped. "There wouldn't be a Brotherhood if it weren't for people like me, so why don't you try another tack? This one's not working." I glared at him harder than I'd ever dared glare at any teacher of mine. Draven was getting on my nerves, and I wasn't in the mood for any more of the Brotherhood's mind games cloaked in manners.

"You know," Draven said, getting up and going to the window. He watched the bob and sway of the lamps atop the Golden Gate Bridge for a moment before turning back to me. "It would be a shame if anything happened to that boy Dean. Especially after you've worked so hard to be reunited."

Just like that, all the fight went out of me. I hated that the Brotherhood could find my weakness so easily. Hated that they had something to hold over me, even now.

"What do you want?" I sighed.

Draven spread his hands. "For you to do your duty, of course. To come back to the fold of the Brotherhood and give up these foolish dreams of putting things back exactly as they were before." He leaned forward into my face, so close that I could smell garlic and whiskey on his breath.

"There is no changing what you've done, Aoife. There is only forestalling the inevitable." He looked out at the sky, and at the growing dark spot, the blot on light. "And from the looks of things, that won't be much longer."

"You don't want any sort of forestalling," I said in disgust. "You just want leverage against things like the Fae."

"Of course I do," Draven said with a shrug. "In the scheme of things, humans are relatively powerless. Only one of us can create and use Gates, as opposed to any Fae who thinks to raise their head from the mud long enough to step into a *hexenring*. That will not stand. Not when humans are superior."

"Nice as it is to get a dose of xenophobia along with

263

paranoid ramblings," I said, "why don't you just tell me what I'm going to have to do to keep you from hurting Dean?" I raised my chin. I might not have had any leverage left, but I did have my dignity. I wasn't going to cry or beg. I'd done enough of that in the Deadlands.

"You're going to do exactly as we say," Draven told me, "until we have no use for you any longer. And you're going to cease all contact with Dean and your family. Except for that mother of yours. She could be useful. Her feelings for you make her vulnerable."

I almost choked on my laughter. "You think I have any influence over Nerissa? You're even dumber than you look."

"A mother cares for her daughter. A mother who would stay in a city overrun by ghouls to reunite with that daughter cares more than most." Draven tsked. "I don't think you give your mother enough credit, Aoife."

"And I think you give her entirely too much," I grumbled.

Draven sighed and then grabbed me by the arm. "Come with me, Aoife."

He pulled me along, down a set of spiral stairs so tightly curled my shoulders could barely pass between the walls, and into a kitchen lit by a single bare bulb. Most of the cabinets had been ripped out, and a chair was bolted to the tile floor. I recognized it as the sort used in madhouses to keep patients restrained.

My stomach lurched as I saw that the chair's occupant was Dean, hands and ankles bound with leather straps, and blood running from a split lip. One of his eyes was blacked and there was a cut on his cheek. A Brotherhood thug stood to one side, flexing his hand.

"Tough nut, boss," the thug said. "Won't say nothing except to tell us to screw off. Trying to tenderize him a little bit."

"That's fine, Hobson," said Draven. "Why don't you leave us for a moment? We have something to discuss."

I ran to Dean and smoothed the hair back from his forehead. It was thick with blood and sweat, and I tried not to show my anger as Draven watched us, his arms folded. "I'm so sorry," I whispered as I cradled Dean's head, pressing my lips to his forehead. "I tried, I really did. I thought this was the right thing to do."

"It was," Dean muttered. "You know they would have pasted all four of us, princess. You made the right choice."

"Do you have any doubt, Miss Grayson, that I am willing and able to follow through on my threat?" Draven asked.

I kept holding on to Dean, and shook my head. "I know what you're capable of. Now and before."

Draven nodded. "Then you'll do as we ask. There won't be any need for more melodrama."

He went to the door and pulled it open. I saw a plain hallway beyond. Strange, to think that all around this torture chamber there was an ordinary house on an ordinary street, surrounded by people who knew nothing of the Brotherhood. Nothing of the Fae, nothing of people like me or the creatures that stalked through their nightmares.

"No," I said quietly. Dean looked up at me.

"Princess," he said urgently, "what are you—"

"Just trust me," I muttered.

Draven turned. He looked angrier than a bank of thunderheads, but I forced myself not to fall back into fear.

Draven couldn't scare me.

He couldn't even come close.

"What do you mean by that no, Miss Grayson?" he snapped, his mouth twisting. I recognized the look. It was the look that all powerful men got when you told them what they didn't want to hear.

"Do you want me to repeat myself?" I said softly. "Because I will. As many times as it takes."

Of course I knew this might be a stupid decision. I knew that I might be sealing my and Dean's fate. But I couldn't bring myself, after all I'd seen—the vast stars, the Old Ones, the face of the Yellow King—to believe it would be the worst thing that ever happened to me.

"Think very, *very* carefully about the next thing you say, Aoife," Draven told me. "Because I would hate to have to do something unpleasant to you. Or to your little man-friend here."

"It's funny," I said. "I've heard a lot of threats since I found my Weird, you know that? More than I ever did when I was just some poor girl who was a city ward. But you know what else?" I stepped away from Dean and faced Draven. "You're not going to follow through on them. You're not going to raise one finger to me. Because you *need* me. Without my Weird, you're just scared little men, cowering in the dark and watching the last of your fire go out. You're playthings for the Fae if they feel like visiting the Iron Land for their amusement. Without me, you're nothing." I curled my lip at Draven. "You're *human*."

"I don't need to do anything to *you*, stupid girl," he snarled. "Dean—"

"If you harm one hair on Dean's head I swear I'll never help you again," I said. "You might as well just kill me, because you won't get the benefit of my gift. You can do your worst to me, but face it—it will never be enough. I've seen what lies beyond it all, Iron and Thorn. I've seen the worst things in the universe. What on earth makes you think I'd be afraid of *you*?"

Draven said nothing, just stood there, chest heaving impotently and face growing crimson. I felt intense satisfaction at being on the other side of that outrage for once, to be the cause rather than buffeted by the consequences.

"We're leaving," I said. "And if I feel like helping you unwind all of Crosley's sneaky little bargains with the Fae, I will. And if I don't, and I see another one of your little trench-coat brigade anywhere near me"—I narrowed my eyes—"I'm going to make you regret the day you looked into the shadows. You're going to wish with every fiber of your being you knew nothing of this world."

I expected bluster and shouting, the things Draven was so good at. I expected threats and recriminations. I didn't expect Draven to give a primal snarl and yank a shock pistol from under his tweed jacket, closing the distance between us and shoving it against Dean's temple.

"What?" he shouted as I recoiled, my hands flying up in a gesture of placation. "No clever rejoinders, Aoife?" His face twitched in a crazed man's imitation of a smile. "Maybe you're not quite as smart as you think you are, little girl."

"Aoife," Dean choked out. He tried to pull away from the barrel of the pistol, but he couldn't move under the restraints. I watched the muscles in his jaw twitch in panic and my stomach roiled in response.

I wanted to kill Draven. I wanted to leap on him and beat him with my bare fists until he realized the error of his ways, but I didn't move. That was the anger, the rage that I'd kept down for so long begging to be let free. It wouldn't help me, and it certainly wouldn't help Dean.

"It'll be all right," I told Dean.

Draven grimaced and jabbed Dean's temple again with the gun. "Will it?" he snarled. "Or have we beaten you again, just like we did in the Arctic?"

"Beat me?" I started to laugh. It was better than screaming, or crying. "You didn't *beat* me, Draven. I used you to get what I wanted. I needed you and the Brotherhood to get my mother back. You let yourselves be manipulated by a little girl, someone you think is beneath you. No wonder you're so angry now."

Dean stared at me, his eyes wide and unblinking, and I looked back. I didn't *think* Draven would kill him, not when he had my allegiance on the line, but I couldn't be sure.

The thought of backing down felt like a leaden weight settling in my chest in place of my heart. But it wasn't about my feelings for Draven. I wasn't the only person in play here.

I had to think of Dean. Had I brought him back only to lose him again?

"There's no more talking," Draven said. "There's you doing as I say, or his brains on the wall. Am I making myself clear?"

Dean still looked at me, and then, impossibly, he winked. "You're better than all of this, Aoife," he said. "I love you."

I felt a small smile touch my mouth. All at once, the doomsday scenario I'd been playing out in my head vanished. Dean understood. He loved me, even if I'd screwed everything up and brought us here.

Dean trusted me, and his look told me now I had to trust myself.

"I love you too," I said, and then turned my eyes to Draven. There was strength in the admission—I'd known ever since the first time we kissed that I loved Dean, but to say it out loud made it real, inevitable and final.

I loved him. I always had.

"I don't care what you do," I told Draven. "You might kill him. You're a bad man. You have no morals and a soul that's rotten to the core. But I'm not that person. I know what I have to do to close my eyes at night, and working for your corrupt little gang isn't it." I took a deep breath and put my eyes back on Dean. "Do whatever you're going to do. My answer won't change."

Draven tightened his grip on the trigger of the shock pistol, and I felt a cry rise in my throat. I'd hoped it wouldn't come to this, but I knew I couldn't give in to him, couldn't agree to become the Brotherhood's weapon without dire consequences for this already shredded world of iron.

Before Draven could do more than inhale, the door banged open, nearly smacking him off his feet.

"That's enough," a voice said.

I let out a breath I hadn't realized I was holding when I saw my father standing in the doorway, and a small cry escaped. Just a ghost of the scream I would have given if the shock ray had pierced Dean's skull.

Dean slumped in relief. "Never thought I'd be glad to see you, Mr. Grayson," he muttered.

"Likewise," my father said, and came over to me, wrapping his arms so tightly around me I could barely speak.

"Y-you're all r-right . . . ," I stammered.

"I am," he agreed. "A few days ago I came to. I'd been having the strangest dreams, Aoife, but suddenly they receded, and I was back to my old self. Conrad had left word where he'd gone, so I came here with Bethina. Conrad's been bringing us up to speed on . . . everything."

"That's all well and good," Draven said, "but I think you'll find that I'm in charge here, Grayson, and you're a traitor." He raised the pistol again. "It's amazing what people will do when they're desperate and in need of a strong leader. It was ridiculously simple to take over from Crosley and get everyone loyal to me."

My father turned on him, and the expression on his face was the coldest I'd ever seen. His mouth was a thin line and his eyes could have cut glass. "Maybe this cell of the Brotherhood, yes. But not all."

He advanced on Draven, who backed away, pistol wavering. "You think Crosley is the only one who escaped the Bone Sepulchre? He wasn't. The others remember what you did to them, and the friends you threw into your Proctor prison. They want nothing to do with your little freak show. They're loyal to me."

"No," Draven said. "You're a traitor, Grayson. You left the Brotherhood when they most needed you, left them vulnerable to the machinations of the Fae. Hell, you reproduced with one of those silver-blooded monsters. Nobody trusts you or your offspring."

"Better to leave than to be a part of this sideshow," my father said. "But I'm here now, and the Brotherhood is going to start doing some things differently."

He snatched the shock pistol from Draven's grip with an economical move. "And if you *ever* threaten my daughter again . . ."

I saw Draven's hand flash down while my father's anger had him distracted. I saw it grasp a small black handle in his waistband and the flash of the blade as he pulled it free. I saw all this in slow motion as my blood roared through my ears like a crashing zeppelin, propelling me across the room and into Draven with my whole weight. We staggered together, caught in a rough dance, until his foot tangled in the rung of Dean's chair and he stumbled.

The knife blade lowered a fraction and I took the opening. I slammed my fist into his nose with all my strength. Broken noses hurt, and it was no less than he deserved. So much less than he deserved. But it would have to do for now.

Archie kicked the knife out of Draven's reach and I rushed to Dean. I unbuckled the cruel leather straps and massaged his wrists, and he let his forehead fall against mine. "You have a hell of a left hook, princess," he said. "Remind me never to get you mad."

I pressed my lips against his, tasted blood and sweat, and felt relief swell in me when I did. He was alive. He was bleeding, and alive, and I hadn't lost him again.

Archie cleared his throat, and we pulled apart. I felt my cheeks flush slightly, and then really focused on my father for the first time. He still didn't look very well—he was thinner and pale, and stubble coated the bottom half of his face.

"Thank you," I said. He smiled at me.

"No need to thank me, Aoife. I'm just doing my job as head of the Brotherhood." He took a step, all he needed with his long arms, and enfolded me in an embrace. "And as your father."

I looked up at him, tears pricking the corners of my eyes. "Are you really in charge?"

"Valentina is, technically," he said. "Crosley was her father, and most of those simpleminded sheep are just happy somebody else is making all the hard choices for them. But she'll do what's right. She won't make backdoor deals with the Fae, and she'll teach them to really fight in the face of what's coming."

I pulled away from him and looked down. "I'm sorry. For my part in everything. I'm sorry I ran away and I'm sorry I let Crow release the Old Ones. I was just trying to fix things."

"You can't fix the world, Aoife," my father said softly. "The world was broken long before you got here. And the harder you try, the faster it turns to dust in your hands."

I did start to cry then, long, heaving sobs that were humiliating. I wished I could stop, but it all became too much.

Dean came to me and held me, but that did nothing to stop my tears. "Will you look at what you did?" he snapped at my father. "She's hysterical."

"She's tired and angry and she feels guilty," my father said. "Just let her cry it out."

He was right—I was guilty. And I knew from his last

words that he blamed me. "I'm sorry," I choked. "I let you down. . . ."

"I didn't mean that," Archie said sternly. "You made a mistake, Aoife. We all make them. But the Old Ones were going to break through whether or not you made that mistake. Even if you'd turned your back on them in the dream realm, they'd have found a way through. The barriers between their world and ours are too weak to hold them any longer."

He sighed and ran a hand through his hair. "I think that's why you were born, Aoife. Because unlike Tesla, you have no doors to open, only doors to guard. The world needed your Weird to fight off the influence of these things, and that's what you're going to have to do."

I swiped at my tears, and as I did, my father turned me from Dean and looked into my eyes. It wasn't his usual vaguely irritated look that said I was an annoyance he was trying to shape into something useful. It was a dead-serious look, one I'd only seen him give other adults.

"You are our protector, Aoife," my father said. "You are the one who balanced the spheres, and you are the one who can keep the darkness at bay. It's not fair to ask such a thing of you, but I must. I'm your father, and I love you, and I will stand by you, but from now on, this is your calling. Tell me now—can you do it?"

I returned his look, this new one that said I wasn't a disappointment, his renegade daughter who was nothing like he'd expected her to be. He was regarding me as an equal for the first time, and in some ways that thought was more terrifying than the idea that I would have to take up the mantle of Gateminder once and for all, to stand alone against the forces, out there among the stars and here on earth, that crawled out of the mud and the mist and my dreams themselves to bedevil the human world.

I had come this far, I thought. I hadn't destroyed the Iron Land. I had fought back against Nylarthotep. I had conquered the nightmare clock.

I was Aoife Grayson, and I was no longer just a scared little girl from Lovecraft. No longer a changeling who didn't have a place in any of the Lands. I was myself. I was the Gates, and the Gates were me. How it should have always been.

I nodded at my father. "I can do it," I said. "I can be what I was always meant to be."

My father gave me a slow nod and smile. "Of course you can," he said. "You're my daughter, after all."

At Home in Arkham

THE JOURNEY HOME was almost comically uneventful. We picked up Conrad and Cal in Chinatown and flew back across the Rockies under the cover of a river of stars wide and broad as the Mississippi. My father's personal aircraft, the *Munin*, was much smaller and faster than the zeppelin Cal and I had crossed on, which was made of wood rather than metal, so the trip took a matter of a day.

When we got home, however, the good mood had largely ceased. Arkham was still under quarantine, but there was no one manning the walls to make sure citizens stayed out. I hadn't seen one Proctor since we touched down, and my days largely went back to what they'd been when I first arrived—read, sleep, eat and do it all over again.

Bethina flung herself on Cal and barely left his side as soon as she saw him in San Francisco, and home was no different. Conrad and I were getting along as well as we ever had. Valentina, when she returned to Graystone shortly after us, was the only one still chilly toward me.

She knew what I'd done, how my releasing the Old Ones had nearly killed my father, and only by a lucky chance had they been distracted by Nylarthotep from casting their net of dreams over the world.

My mother was on my mind a great deal, but I had to wait until everyone else in the house was asleep or otherwise occupied to act on my anxious, ever-running thoughts.

Archie and Valentina were in charge of the Brotherhood now, but that was only half of my problems solved. There was still my mother, and everything she represented.

I set my chronometer to wake me when it was just light, the first streaks of milky sunlight catching the granite cliffs around Arkham, setting them to glittering as if they were alive.

A bowl of fog still rested in the garden and the orchards around Graystone, and danced across the waters of the pond like it was a spirit seeking a place to rest.

I bypassed the garden, the pond, the hedge maze and the barn, and walked on to the apple orchard.

I remembered the first time I'd come here, how scared I'd been to walk through these grounds. I could sense the malevolent force lurking.

This time, when I came upon the small ring of mushrooms in the center of the apple trees, I stepped in without hesitation.

My Weird flared, and I got the sense that the twisted, ancient hulks of the apple trees had taken an interest in my presence, that if I watched long enough, I'd see the gnarled branches uncurl and beckon to me.

Instead, I focused on the energies swirling around me. The *hexenring* was different from a man-made Gate, but it worked on the same principles.

I shut my eyes and reached for that place inside that connected me to the universe, to the places beyond the stars that only the Weird could touch. I felt the tug, the pain in my head, and when I opened my eyes I was in the Thorn Land.

My accuracy was getting better—I'd come through within sight of the Winter Court, inside a *hexenring* by the side of a crumbling farmhouse. When I reached the gates of the court, the Fae moving around the courtyard stopped what they were doing and stared at me.

I stared back, suddenly no longer as nervous. *They're afraid of me*, I realized. That was a new feeling, and I let the surge of power ripple up and down my spine.

"Don't just stand there," I said when the closest Fae held my gaze a bit too long. "One of you go find Tremaine."

He scurried away, and I stayed where I was. The courtyard had eternally falling snow that blanketed the ground beneath the silver branches of dead trees. Ripe red fruit still hung from them, in spite of their desiccated state, and crystals dangled, suspended above my head. Occasionally they collided and chimed, giving the ever-blowing wind a voice.

Tremaine appeared from the archway that led deeper into the palace, a blot on this ethereal space. His waistcoat was a deep blue, the color of the night sky, and contrasted with a silk shirt in the gradient red of an angry sunset. His crystal buttons and black cravat were impeccable, but his face was a mess of anger and uncontrolled rage.

My mother came in on his heels, starting to say something to placate him, but I held up my hand.

"What I have to say is important, so you better shut that shark mouth of yours and listen," I told Tremaine.

He shot me one of his infuriating grins, so smug I was sure he had to practice it in front of the mirror to get it so perfectly right. "Come back to threaten me? I wouldn't think I was in such a position, were I you."

I glanced from side to side and saw the guards of the Winter Court moving in. My mother took a step forward. "Stop! You stop this at once. That's my daughter!"

The guards drew back, lowering the short gladii they carried as weapons. I returned Tremaine's smug look. "I guess the sister of the Winter Queen has a little more pull than some sneaky regent that nobody actually likes."

I heard snickers go around the courtyard. There was nothing the Fae enjoyed more than a good show—the bloodier, the better—and I intended to give them just that.

Tremaine's cheeks grew two blooms, crimson fire-flowers of rage that told me I'd managed to throw him off balance. "How dare you come back here and hurl insults at me after what you did!"

"I'm not staying long," I told him. I saw my mother flinch, but I could deal with that after I'd said what I'd come to say.

"I'm not Fae," I told Tremaine, raising my voice so everyone gaping at us could hear.

Tremaine's mouth curled cruel and sharp as a fishhook. "Tell me something I don't know, Aoife."

"I'm not afraid of you," I shot back. "I know that you want me on your side so much you can taste it. I know that with a power like mine, you could destroy the Summer Court and get what you've always wanted—the favor of your queen. Real power. That's what I have, and it's what you want so badly it burns in your blood."

There was only silence now, except for the wailing of the wind. The entire Winter Court was waiting. On a high balcony, I saw a flutter of white and red as the queen appeared, staring down at us. A bright-eyed cardinal sat on her shoulder, also staring. I wasn't silly enough to think she'd missed a word of what Tremaine and I had said. Octavia didn't get to be Winter Queen by being un-observant.

"I'm also not human," I pressed on. "Thorn is in my blood as much as Iron. I can't live in the Iron Land or I'll go mad. Nor can I live in Thorn, because I'm not one of you. I can't live the life of a Fae. I'll grow old while you all stay exactly the same."

"I assume you have a point," Tremaine snarled. "Make it, why don't you?"

"I propose a truce," I pressed on. "I will be a citizen of both lands, ruled by neither. I'll do favors for you, Tremaine—*when I feel like it*—and in return, you stop. Stop trying to trick me, stop grasping for power, stop trying to manipulate Octavia and my mother."

He surprised me by not immediately shouting. A calculating look stole across his face and one hand tapped his velvet-clad leg. Then, as quickly as the wind whipped fallen leaves across the courtyard, he stepped within arm's length of me and extended his hand. "You have a bargain."

This was it, then. A Fae bargain was serious business, and he'd made it in front of everyone, even Octavia.

I took a step of my own and gripped his hand. It was cold and smooth, like snakeskin, and I could feel the incalculable strength behind his grasp and see the flash of the silver blade he kept spring-loaded in his sleeve. I wasn't naive—I knew if we hadn't had an audience, that blade would have found a new home in my still-beating heart.

"You're not as stupid as you look," Tremaine muttered. "You better hold to what you say. I will be calling in your so-called favor."

"I'm not the one who has a problem with lies," I said. I pulled him close, so close that we could have felt each other's heart beating. "And if you *ever* get up to your old tricks," I whispered in Tremaine's pointed shell of an ear, "if you ever try to deceive me or use me or use someone I love to harm me, I will show you things so much more ancient and hungry than you are that your mind cannot contain them. And they will devour you. And the last thing you hear will be my victorious laughter. Are we clear?"

Tremaine pulled back and regarded me, not with a sneer but with a degree of circumspection I'd never witnessed before. "Now, that," he said, a smile forming, "that was the tongue of a Fae speaking."

He dropped my hand and threw me a lazy salute. "Well played, Aoife. Enjoy wallowing in the mud with your humans."

"Oh," I told him, "you know I always do."

As Tremaine stalked back into the palace, my mother

came to me and threw her arms around me. "Don't stay away too long," she mumbled into my hair. "I've only just gotten to know you."

I squeezed her just as hard, feeling how small and frail she was under my grasp. But it was misleading—she wasn't frail. She was the strongest survivor I knew. She had weathered the years of iron madness and the machinations of Tremaine. She'd be alive long after Archie and Dean and probably even Lovecraft itself were gone.

Often, when I was young, I'd try to see something of myself in my mother—nose, eyes, hair, voice. I'd never seen anything, until this moment. The strong will that drove us was the same. I might get my stubborn nature and inquisitive mind, my green eyes and my insane hair from Archie, but the will to live, to survive at all costs, came from Nerissa. Her Fae blood was her gift to me, and I carried it in my veins no matter what was on the surface.

"I love you, Aoife," Nerissa said softly, and then stepped back. Her eyes glimmered, but the tears didn't fall to crystallize on the snow. "Run along, now. I imagine your brother's waiting."

"I'll be back," I told Nerissa. "I won't leave you."

Nerissa didn't say anything. She simply swiped at her eyes and then turned away, the pain clearly too much.

As I walked out of the courtyard, I raised my eyes to Octavia on her balcony. The cardinal took flight, a bloodred blot on the white sky, and as the Winter Queen watched it, she gave me a terrible and predatory parting smile.

*   *   *

I stepped out of the *hexenring* in the orchard disoriented and with my head pounding, as usual, and looked for a stump or a rock to sit on for a moment to collect myself.

"Having fun with your little Fae friends?"

I screamed and nearly jumped out of my skin. "Dammit, Conrad! What's wrong with you?"

"You've been skulking around all week looking like you were ready to take off," he grumped. "I followed you to see if you were running away."

I sat down on one of the massive stones that had at one point composed the foundation of the cider house and massaged my forehead. I couldn't have another dustup with my brother. Not now, not while I was still shaking from the memory of the Winter Queen's smile.

"And would you have stopped me if I was?"

Conrad shrugged. "I don't want you gone, Aoife. I just don't understand why you do the things you do."

"I can't ever explain it," I said. If I told Conrad the truth, I'd lose his trust forever. Still, the urge was almost overwhelming. "I just . . ." I sighed and rubbed my forehead. "I have a lot to make up for."

"You don't owe me a thing, Aoife," he said. "If anything, I owe you. I tried to kill you. I hurt you, and you're the only one who's ever stuck by me."

"Don't take that weight," I said, almost too quickly. "Don't blame yourself for that, Conrad."

"I don't," he said, giving me a wan smile. "I just don't want you to think you're the bad guy, Aoife. No matter what you do, I'll still be your brother." He sat next to me and pulled out a letter on good paper that smelled of woodsmoke and rich ink. "Now that we've cleared that up, any chance my little sister will celebrate with me?" He handed the envelope over and watched as my eyes danced across the letterhead. *Miskatonic University Office of Admissions.*

Dear Mr. Grayson,
  We are pleased to offer you admission to our undergraduate class starting in the fall term of 1956. . . .

"How did this happen?" I said, feeling a curious mixture of sadness and surprise bubble in my chest. I was happy for him, but he hadn't even hinted that he was thinking of leaving. "You didn't apply anywhere," I said. "You didn't graduate from the Academy. . . ."

"Archie pulled some strings and made sure my transcript was filled out by private tutors," he said. "I imagine next year he'll do the same thing for you."

"But a *university?*" I said. "Back among all those people yammering about Rationalists and heretics? People who think we should be burned alive for what's in our blood?"

"Miskatonic isn't like that," Conrad said. "Archie went there. It's a place where they value real science and real reason, not that frightened screeching that comes from the Bureau of Proctors. Besides," he added, "the Bureau might be on the way out, if the past few weeks are any indication. There's all kinds of hearings, high-ranking types are being arrested. . . . The world's changing. I want to be part of that."

"I can't believe you're leaving us," I said softly. What

would I do without Conrad? We might fight all the time, but I needed him. He was the stable one, the rock. Without him, I would be anchorless.

"Look, Aoife," Conrad said. "I'm not you. I don't have the ability that you and Archie do, and I never will. I don't understand what makes either of you tick. This is my chance to fit in, to finally make something of myself that's not just being the third wheel dragging the rest of my family down."

He put his hand over mine. "You don't need me. Your destiny is this big thing, big as the stars, and mine is here, weighted down by iron. That's all. That's all I was ever trying to say."

He shoved the letter into his pants pocket and got up, starting back across the orchard. I watched him go, feeling as if someone had ripped out some essential organ and cast it away. Then I jumped up. "Conrad!"

I ran and caught up with him when he stopped. "I need you, stupid," I said, giving him a shove on the shoulder. "You're my *brother*, for crying out loud. My *family*." The tears started, and I let them come. "The only family I had, for a really long time. You're the one who protected me, even when you went mad. You're the one who wrote me that letter, Conrad. You saved me from myself. I can't . . ."

I was going to say more, how I couldn't ever thank him enough for that, even if he was stubborn and curt and sometimes mistrustful, but he grabbed me and pulled me into a bear hug. "Stop crying," he muttered. "You can be such a girl sometimes."

"Easy for you to say," I said. "Big college man."

He gave a small laugh. "Going to try, anyway. I figure if I stay on campus and come back here, I can stave off the iron madness." He started walking again, and I fell into step beside him.

"Did you ever think you'd be destined for a quiet life?" I asked.

"Did you ever think you'd have anything but?" he asked me with a grin.

"Good point," I told him, and we shared a silence that was unstrained for the first time in months as we walked back toward home.

Cal and Bethina were sitting around the aethervox when I entered the kitchen. I cleaned the mud off my shoes and hung up my jumper, and they still hadn't moved.

"What's all this about?" I said.

Bethina shushed me with a wave, so I joined them at the table and bent my head close. The reception was terrible, every third word a burst of static.

"Repeat: Congress has called for an emergency shutdown of the Bureau of Proctors after evidence revealed that its former director, Grey Draven, was caught . . . using Bureau funds . . . prison for his political enemies . . . many prisoners found not to be viral . . . suspected of consorting with terrorist organization known as the Brotherhood of Iron. President McCarthy has denounced Draven as a traitor, though there are some members of the House also calling for the president's impeachment, as the full scope of his knowledge of this conspiracy is not yet known."

I felt my mouth open, and looked up to see that Cal and Bethina shared my look. Bethina shook her head. Her curls, which had gotten longer and more unruly, bounced like a copper waterfall.

"Always knew that man was crooked as a coat hanger," she said. "My mother said politicians are all crooked at both ends and bent in the middle."

"They're actually talking about disbanding the Proctors," Cal said. "Can you imagine?"

"Might give poor folks some peace for once," Bethina said. "Always thought virals were the worst thing imaginable, but after everything I've seen with the two of you, I feel downright sorry for some. Locked up and tortured. You wouldn't even do that to a dog."

She got up and bustled out of the kitchen, throwing Cal a wide, gleaming smile over her shoulder as she left.

He returned it and then looked at me. I raised one eyebrow. Cal had been putting this off for far too long; it was time someone got firm with him.

"You and I are best friends, right?" I said. Cal nodded, brow already wrinkling anxiously. To look at him, you'd never know he wasn't human. I had that thought at least a hundred times since I'd found out what he really was.

"We are," he agreed. "And I know what you're going to say, but I can't—"

"Cal," I said, "she's a smart girl. If she loves you, she'll understand."

I started to get up and leave, but his next words stopped me. "I'm scared, Aoife."

I looked back at him. "You think I'm not, Cal? Every day? I'm scared all the time. The trick is not to show it."

I sat back down and looked him in the eye. Cal was the one person who'd never questioned me, never left my side, and the last thing I wanted was to hurt him. "You're my best friend," I said. "You're the only person I was able to trust for a long time, and I know that you'll always be there for me." I sucked in a breath and chewed on my lip for a moment before continuing. "But you have to be yourself, Cal. I know you want to be human, but Bethina deserves the truth. And if she leaves, she wasn't right for you anyway."

Cal looked at the scarred tabletop. Decades of Graysons eating and cooking had made it satin-smooth, full of deep grooves and notches. "I don't want to be alone, Aoife. Even in my nest, I was always the odd one. I can look like this, and the rest of them can only be ghouls. They don't trust me." He sucked in a shuddering breath. "I just don't want to be alone anymore."

"You'll never be alone!" I exclaimed. I couldn't believe Cal would think I'd just drop him suddenly, when I hadn't even after he'd showed me what he truly was. Then again, he hadn't shied away from me either, when he'd found out that not only human blood was in my veins. "You'll always have me," I said. "We're supposed to be friends, Cal. Because of who we are, and what we are, and because I know I can trust you." I pointed to the door Bethina had gone through. "And trust me when I say that you need to go tell her the truth. Will you do that for me?"

Cal sighed, but then he nodded and pushed back from the table. Moving with the greatest of reluctance, he stepped through the door. "Bethina, wait up. I need to talk to you."

He looked back at me before he walked on, and I gave him a reassuring smile. Cal was lucky. He had someone who loved him, and I hoped it would be unconditional. Not too long before, I would have been jealous of what he had, but now . . . I got up myself and went upstairs to find Dean.

The small door to the roof-deck was open, cool air drifting through. I climbed the ladder and found Dean leaning on the railing, smoking and looking out over the valley and the village of Arkham. A few people moved on the narrow streets, the first residents to return after the Proctors had abandoned the quarantine.

"You want some company?" I asked. Dean turned and gave me one of the slow, lazy smiles that started a warm feeling in my stomach and spread it everywhere, from the top of my head to the tips of my toes.

"From you, princess?" he said. "Always."

I went to him and wrapped my arms around him inside his coat, placing my head on his chest and listening to his heart beat. "I'm so glad you're here, Dean. Just stay here, all right?"

His breath hitched and I looked up. Dean's expression was pained. I let go of him, already fearing the worst. "What is it?"

"Aoife," he said, and I knew it was bad. Usually I was "princess" or "darlin'."

"Please," I said. "If I did something, just tell me and I'll try to make it better. Please don't just dump me."

"No." Dean held up his hands. "It's not you, Aoife. I could never be ticked about anything you did. You saved me from that place where I was dead. And even before that, you got me out of the Rustworks. I was going nowhere fast, and you gave me something I needed and didn't even realize it."

"But?" I said, feeling the word on the tip of his tongue.

"You made a sacrifice for your ma, and I understand that," he said. "My mother and I don't see eye to eye, but she's still my mother. But you made an even bigger sacrifice for me, Aoife, and I can't have that. I won't have you putting yourself in danger for me like that ever again. I'm not worth it."

He put his hand against my cheek. "You're destined for greatness, princess, and I'm just going to get in the way. So I'm going to get out of it and head home. I'll head back to the Mists, maybe finally do what my mom always wanted and serve the Erlkin on Windhaven for a while." He leaned forward and pressed a kiss against my forehead, even as I felt myself beginning to shake. "I'll never forget you, princess. But for your own good, I can't stay with you."

I pushed his hand away, my heart throbbing so hard it was like the great pistons that powered the Engine. "Dean Harrison," I bit out, "you're an idiot."

He blinked and looked down at me. "I don't—"

"I *love* you," I said, feeling myself start to cry. I kept talking, not caring that hot tears were pouring forth to cool against my cheeks in the cold spring wind. "I crossed life and death to be with you, Dean." I swiped furiously at my eyes, trying to clear away the blur of tears. "Guess what? It's not *up* to you to decide whether or not I want to be with you. It's *my* choice, and I choose you. Only you, Dean. Forever."

Dean pulled back, and pushed a hand through his hair. "I had no idea you felt that way, darlin'," he said.

"Do you love me?" I demanded. The initial shock had worn off now, and I was focused only on keeping him by my side. I needed Dean. I'd learned that much. Without him there was a void that nothing could fill, a void as deep and black as the universe.

"Of course," he said softly. "You're the best thing that ever happened to me, princess. I love you so much sometimes I can't think of anything else. I love you so much it makes it easy to get up in the morning. When I was dead, I remembered that I loved you and it agonized me that we'd never be together again." He dropped his gaze from mine. "Some spirits tried to forget, tried to get deliberately torn apart so they wouldn't think of their lives anymore, and it hurt so much down there that sometimes I wanted that. But every time I got close, I'd think of you and how you'd want me to keep fighting, and it was you that kept me going in that place." He squeezed my hand. "So yeah, I love you."

"Then there's nothing else to talk about," I said. "We belong together, Dean. I can't imagine my life without you. I want to see what's coming with you."

He shivered inside his jacket, putting his arm around me and pulling me close. I molded myself to his side, sharing his warmth. "Storm's what's coming, princess," Dean said as we watched the clouds roll across Arkham Valley, the mist covering everything, hiding the monsters and the people alike.

"I know," I said. "And I'm going to need you, Dean. The only way we're going to survive it is together."

Dean turned me toward him and kissed me gently. "I'm not worried about the future, princess. Not as long as you're by my side."

I smiled at him, the first genuine smile I'd felt in some time. "Then neither am I."

The Vastness of Stars

THAT NIGHT I slept the first real, deep sleep since I'd lost Dean, but when I woke I found myself standing and staring down at the same gray spires, the same terrible configuration of an ancient city that I'd visited far too recently.

"It's a terrible sight," Crow said, as if he'd been summoned by the wind to stand next to me. One moment he wasn't there and the next he was, his robe swirling around both of us like errant smoke.

"It looks just the same to me," I said. "And I really wish you'd stop showing up in my dreams. I didn't give you permission to invade my sleep whenever you want."

"This is no dream," Crow told me. "Look again."

I sighed but looked back at the unfamiliar city. I saw that the tall spires were crumbling, that many of the odd angles of glass had shattered, leaving jagged mouths where windows used to be. Shoggoths and nightjars crept among the ruins, and strange, many-winged birds flapped from place to place.

Again we were in the cold, and I felt it in my bones. Crow took off his robe and put it around me. "It's a cold place, the bottom of the world."

"Outer space is colder," I said.

Crow sighed and looked up at the darkening spot in the sky. "They want to speak with you, Aoife."

I also followed the spot, which had grown a bloodred corona as it got larger and larger, the Old Ones boring through space and time to reach the Iron Land.

"I did what they asked," I said. "I used the Elder Sign to take Nylarthotep. I'm not doing them any more free favors."

"They gave you safe passage when you left the Deadlands," said Crow, "and they must be repaid."

I glared at him, even though his face was as guileless as a child's. "Is this coming from you or them?"

"I'm merely their voice," Crow said. "I'm the aethervox for things so old they were created before voices."

"I didn't ask for your help," I told Crow, even though I was really speaking to the Old Ones. "I released you because I was desperate. I never *asked* you for anything."

"We require the way prepared," Crow said, his eyes going blank and rolling back in his head. "We require a Gateminder to resurrect our ruined city, to make us whole again and give us a place to dwell while we bless the mud-crawling humans with our presence."

I took a deep breath. This time, I wasn't backed into a corner. This time, the lives of people I loved weren't hanging over my head. There was only my own fear, my own feeling of helplessness in the face of something so vast.

For the first time, I knew I had to fight that feeling with everything I had.

"No," I said, raising my chin. "I've done enough to help you come back. More than I ever wanted to. From here on out, you make your own way."

"We are old and vast beyond imagination," Crow croaked. "We will return, and we will gift the humans with our knowledge and humble them with our incomprehensible power. We ruled once, and we will rule again, Gateminder. Do not test us."

"I'm not much for being ruled," I said. "And neither are the rest of the humans. This world isn't yours. You may have laid the foundation, but humans built it up. They made the world. Tesla discovered the Gates. Not you."

I straightened my spine and looked into Crow's vacant eyes, raising my voice so it echoed back from the terrible spires that rose like skeletonized fingers from the city of the Old Ones. "Go back to the stars," I said. "I released you because I had no choice, but I will *not* stand by and let you conquer my homeland."

Crow started, his face composing itself into its usual lines. "Oh, Aoife," he sighed. "Do you have any idea what you've done?"

I looked up at the spot in the sky and felt a curious vibration through my body, as if something were reaching across the aether, tapping the frequency directly into my mind. I looked back at Crow as the sensation grew and grew, building to a shriek inside my skull. "Yes," I said. "I do. And I'm not afraid."

We will not be swayed, the Old Ones' voice rumbled inside my head. It was a voice before there were voices, the sound of an eldritch thing born of star fragments and the vacuum of space, of a place beyond space, beyond dreams, beyond all matter and reason. I knew such a voice should break me, turn me into nothing but a gibbering shell of flesh racked with madness, but I stood firm. I would not be bowed, not this time. Not threatened. *I* was the Gateminder, the protector of the ways between the worlds, and not even the oldest power in the universe could move me.

We will come, the Old Ones shrieked. *We will come and we will have your world. We will come and you will tremble at the sight of us. We will live again.*

"Someday I'm sure you will," I said. "But this isn't your time. It's ours. Go back to the stars until the humans have vanished and the earth is yours again."

It will not be so, the Old Ones whispered, a sound a thousand times worse than their screaming. *It will be in your lifetime, Gateminder, and we will make sure you meet us face to face.*

I looked at the sky, which burned out as I watched, atmosphere going up in flames to reveal the vastness of the universe—not empty, but full of a million stars, a million worlds circling, a million other places that only I could visit.

"Come, then," I told the Old Ones as I watched them unfurl their bodies and blot out those stars one by one. "I'm ready."

ABOUT THE AUTHOR

Caitlin Kittredge is a history and horror movie enthusiast who writes novels wherein bad things usually happen to perfectly nice characters. But that's all right—the ones who aren't so nice have always been her favorites. Caitlin lives in western Massachusetts in a crumbling Victorian mansion with her two cats, her cameras, and several miles of books. When not writing, she spends her time taking photos, concocting alternate histories, and trying new and alarming colors of hair dye. Caitlin is the author of two bestselling series for adults, Nocturne City and the Black London adventures. *The Mirrored Shard* is her third book for teens, and the final book in the Iron Codex trilogy. Look for book one, *The Iron Thorn*, and book two, *The Nightmare Garden*, both available from Delacorte Press. You can visit Caitlin at caitlinkittredge.com.